233Page

7/2020

A FULL COLD MOON

Recent titles by Lissa Marie Redmond

Cold Case Investigations

A COLD DAY IN HELL
THE MURDER BOOK
A MEANS TO AN END
A FULL COLD MOON *

* *available from Severn House*

A FULL COLD MOON

Lissa Marie Redmond

This first world edition published 2020
in Great Britain and the USA by
SEVERN HOUSE PUBLISHERS LTD of
Eardley House, 4 Uxbridge Street, London W8 7SY.
Trade paperback edition first published
in Great Britain and the USA 2020 by
SEVERN HOUSE PUBLISHERS LTD.

British Library Cataloguing in Publication Data
A CIP catalogue record for this title is available from the British Library.

ISBN-13: 978-0-7278-8987-4 (cased)
ISBN-13: 978-1-78029-683-8 (trade paper)
ISBN-13: 978-1-4483-0387-8 (e-book)

All Severn House titles are printed on acid-free paper.

Severn House Publishers support the Forest Stewardship Council™ [FSC™],
the leading international forest certification organisation.
All our titles that are printed on FSC certified paper carry the FSC logo.

MIX
Paper from
responsible sources
FSC
www.fsc.org   FSC® C013056

Typeset by Palimpsest Book Production Ltd.,
Falkirk, Stirlingshire, Scotland.
Printed and bound in Great Britain by
TJ International, Padstow, Cornwall.

For Peggy Redmond Hayes

ONE

'I thought everyone in Iceland was blond.'

Buffalo Police Detective Lauren Riley raised her eyebrow at her temporary partner as she crouched over the body, but said nothing.

A young man with dark hair was lying face down in the alley that ran between the Sussex Hotel and the Fordham Center Bank. He'd almost made it to the light at the mouth of the alley, but had gone down less than a foot from where someone on the street might have seen him. Might have saved him. The attack had started halfway down the alley. His leather messenger bag lay intact on the ground thirty feet from the body. A black glove was next, fifteen feet away; its twin still on the victim's hand, the leather marred as he had tried to defend himself. The victim's knit hat had come off in the struggle – a vicious struggle – and was lying next to his outstretched arm. The dark stains on his knees and elbows showed Detective Riley he had desperately tried to crawl away, even as his attacker had been pounding his head in.

The sheer will of this man to survive had been as fierce and ferocious as his attacker's intent to destroy him. The killer had overwhelmed him after pulling him back again and again, raining vicious blows to his head and face, finally wearing him down. The nails on his exposed hand were bloody and jagged. A knot clenched in Lauren's gut as she realized this man had been literally inches from safety when he finally succumbed.

'Did you find some ID?' she asked, done with her initial notes. She flipped her notebook shut, tucking it in her front coat pocket, keeping it close. She'd need it again soon enough.

'It says he's Gunnar Jonsson from Reykjavik, Iceland.' Sheehan was holding a bagged Icelandic passport, opened through the plastic, reading off the information to Lauren.

'The customs stamp says he arrived in Toronto seven days ago. Crossed into the United States on the same date.' Doug Sheehan was sixty-one years old and waiting for his birthday so he could collect Social Security and his pension at the same time. They'd been paired up only until Reese, her real partner, got back from his medical leave for an on-duty injury, but it was hard for someone like her to work with Doug. Clearly the mandated sensitivity training had been a waste of time. As far as Lauren was concerned, the sooner he blew out the candles on his cake the better.

Hell, she'd bake the cake herself. And blow out the candles.

Lauren brushed a strand of her short brown hair out of her eyes. The knit hat she'd worn against the December wind couldn't even keep her shaggy bangs in line, let alone keep her ears warm. Her self-proclaimed stylist, also known as her neighbor, Dayla, had told her to try something new. So she had cut her long blond hair off and let it grow in naturally darker. *I should have gone out for Thai food instead*, she thought as she shoved another strand back under her hat. *But at least now I don't look so much like the pictures that ran in the paper.*

'We'll have to check the Peace Bridge, Lewiston-Queenston and Rainbow Bridge records,' she said, now snapping some quick photos with her work phone. Nothing beat the police photographer's pictures, but in the beginning stages of an investigation she hated to wait.

The bridges were the three main crossover points between Toronto and Buffalo. Less than one hundred miles from each other, Toronto was the closest major international airport to Buffalo and its residents flew out of there quite often. While Buffalo Niagara was an international airport, it was only a mid-sized one and had very few direct flights out of the country. Lauren had taken many flights from Toronto that would have been a two-stop layover had she flown from Buffalo Niagara. She made a mental note to call her friend Brendan, who worked customs at the Peace Bridge. Maybe he could help get this man's crossing records.

Sheehan had his other hand stuffed way down into his pants pocket, making his jacket ride up, exposing his beer gut. He brought the passport back up to his nose to take another look – he forgot his glasses in his desk back at the office. At least it wasn't his gun this time. He had walked around a shooting scene two days before with an empty holster on his hip the entire time. When Lauren pointed it out, he got so red in the face she thought he was going to have a heart attack right there next to the crime scene tape.

'Gunnar was hit from behind.' Lauren pointed a gloved finger at the deep laceration that cut through the back of his head, tracing its path as it parted his jet-black hair in a wide bloody grin.

'No signs of a robbery.' Now Sheehan was crouched next to the body, still clutching the passport the evidence techs had taken out of the messenger bag. Sheehan motioned to the gold watch on the victim's wrist. Gunnar's wallet had been untouched as well, with three hundred in cash and an ATM receipt still tucked inside. The address on the ATM slip was just on the other side of the alley, and the time on it put his withdrawal within minutes of his murder. Hell, it *was* still within minutes of his murder. Not quite an hour had passed since Gunnar had taken the cash from the machine.

Lauren stood up, hands on her hips, stretching out her back. It sucked being over forty. Seemed like hitting that milestone meant overnight everything was either stiff or aching. Looking down at the young man's body before her she immediately felt guilty. Aches and pains were definitely better than the alternative. She moved out of the way of the Buffalo Police photographer, Andy Knowles, as he adjusted his lens to get a long angle on the body from the mouth of the alley.

The victim was wearing jeans and a green sweater under his brown parka, which was soaked in blood. He'd been repeatedly struck in the head and face with a blunt object. Patrol officers had recovered a bloody brick two streets away and were now standing guard over it until evidence could come and collect it. Lauren could picture two young cops standing in the cold staring down at a blood-and-hair-encrusted brick that had probably been plucked from one of the numerous construction projects going on all over downtown. There seemed to be more scaffolding some days than skyline.

Lauren silently regarded the body before her. The skull looked crushed. The face practically erased. That was a lot of rage.

His clothes were intact. His heavy black boots were still laced and tied on his feet. This Icelandic man had been surprised and struck repeatedly, fought for his life, and left for dead. For nothing.

It didn't make sense.

The wind was blowing sideways off Lake Erie. An hour earlier it had been a calm, clear bright night. The weather changed by the minute in Buffalo. The alley was perfectly sheltered from the snow blowing across the sidewalk just a few feet away. Lauren scanned the narrow passage. It was more of a walkway between the two multistory buildings than a typical city alley. There were no dumpsters, no garbage bags, no homeless stretched out over grates. During the day, business people would use it to cut through to the eateries and dry cleaners and office supply stores on the next street. At night, the only illumination was from windows high up on either side. She looked for cameras mounted above the few exit doors that opened into the alley but didn't see any. She would double check with the building managers. Sometimes they got lucky.

The pavement was icy, and devoid of any usable shoe prints. Had a delivery driver not needed to take a piss in a hurry, Gunnar's body could have laid there for hours unnoticed. After six in the evening on a Thursday in December this part of downtown Buffalo grew pretty desolate.

'He has a key card to the Sussex Hotel,' Lauren said to her partner. The new medical examiner and her assistant had arrived, and were waiting off to the side for her and Sheehan to give the OK to move the body. 'We'll stop at the front desk once the ME is finished.'

'Are you done with the initial scene?' Sheehan asked the photographer as he motioned toward the medical examiner and her assistant with the evidence bag. 'I want them to turn the body over.'

The fifty-ish, curly-haired police photographer raised his monster of a camera, so unusual in this age of the cellphone picture, and snapped a couple quick photos. 'All set, detective,' he told Sheehan, backing up to make room and avoiding the large pool of blood outlining the upper body.

'You're good to go, doctor,' Sheehan called, giving a thumbs up in case the howl of the wind outside the alley drowned out his words.

The ME walked over and gave Lauren a firm handshake, which was not all that easy to do with gloves on, then pulled latex gloves over the top of leather ones. Most people shed one for the other, but Doctor Heartly did things her own way. She was the third medical examiner Erie County had had in three years. The job, obviously, wasn't that attractive. 'How are you, Lauren?'

'I'd be better if I had the bastard that did this in cuffs,' she replied, eyes returning to the dead man's body. Snow had started to accumulate on the back of his coat and in his hair. Older than Lauren's daughters but younger than her, this man had been snuffed out and left in the alley like trash.

'Detective Lauren Riley: avenging angel.' That was as close to making a joke as Dr Heartly got.

Inwardly cringing at the nickname the media had bestowed upon her less than a year ago, Lauren told her, 'That's one part of my past I'd like to forget.'

'I think I may have said that same thing once or twice.' The medical examiner gave her a knowing half-smile, which Lauren managed to return. Lauren had been national news for a few months, hence the new hair. People knew her as a tall, long-haired blond, not a bespectacled, short-haired brunette.

But people see what they want to see, Lauren thought as she watched the doctor become all business. Heartly's face settled into a neutral mask, ready for the task at hand.

Doctor Brenda Heartly drifted forward in that strange way she had of walking, a sort of glide combined with a limp. Headquarters speculation was that she was in a car accident when she was younger, but no one knew for sure, and no one knew her well enough to ask. She'd only been with Erie County for the last six months. Lauren felt bad for her on cold nights like this one because the limp definitely became more pronounced.

'Help me, Kent,' she told her assistant, and together they

gently rolled Gunnar onto his side. Kent held the victim in place so that the medical examiner could do her thing. Heartly regarded the body for a moment, then pulled a digital recorder from her heavy wool coat's pocket. She clicked it on and spoke into it. 'Doctor Brenda Heartly, Erie County Medical Examiner. It is Thursday, December twelve; approximately' – she glanced at the digital watch on her wrist – '8:03 p.m. The temperature is currently twenty-nine degrees Fahrenheit.'

Lauren retrieved her notebook and scribbled the details so she could write up the scene later. The doctor continued with her examination. 'Cursory on-scene impressions: the victim is a white male, approximately thirty years of age. Visual inspection notes numerous blunt force trauma wounds to the head and face. Livor mortis is not yet apparent in the extremities.' She leaned forward over Gunnar as Kent steadied the body, trying to take in as much as possible before they took him back to the morgue. 'Note that there is at least one wound to the victim's skull where bone is exposed.' She stood up and waved the ambulance crew in, as the photographer snapped a few pictures with the victim's face visible.

'Are you all set?' Lauren asked the medical examiner.

She nodded. 'I won't be able to determine anything else until I can get him undressed and on the table. I'll see you first thing in the morning at the post, Detectives.'

'You'll see one of us,' Lauren told her. She hoped Sheehan would volunteer for the post. The post-mortems, or autopsies for the lay person, were always done at six in the morning. Lauren knew Sheehan was trying to build up his pension with overtime and he'd sacrifice a good night's sleep for the extra money. The medical examiners worked on a straight salary, but Lauren doubted Dr Heartly ever got more than two or three hours of sleep a night. It seemed she always answered her cell on the first ring, no matter what time it was.

'One detective is all I need,' Dr Heartly responded and moved out of the way.

Kent helped the two ambulance attendants place the body on a stretcher. *He looks so small*, Lauren thought as they loaded the victim up. *So small and broken*.

Lauren hovered nearby as they prepared to wheel the body

away. *Gunnar, with his Viking name, came all the way here to Buffalo from Iceland to get run down in an alley and bludgeoned to death. Welcome to America.*

'You ready to go talk to the hotel manager?' Sheehan's nasally voice cut through Lauren's thoughts.

'Yeah.' She watched as they trundled the body to the waiting ambulance at the end of the alley. The lights were off, the siren silent. There was no rush to get this poor man to the morgue – dead is dead.

Three patrol cars were parked on the street blocking the front of the alley. Behind them the ambulance attendants prepared to leave. Now that the city had gone to one-man cars, you got three patrol vehicles showing up to a scene instead of just one with two people in it. How that saved money Lauren wasn't sure, but that was why she'd turned down supervisor jobs in the past. She didn't want to be in charge of anyone but herself.

Thankfully, detectives still worked in pairs, but Lauren was known for going off on investigations on her own. It had gotten her in a lot of trouble and had almost cost both her and her partner, Reese, their lives this past year. She'd vowed to do better, try to work well with others, with mixed results so far.

The street cops nodded to the detectives as they ducked under the crime scene tape. A news van was illegally parked on the other side of Delaware Avenue facing south, its camera crew set up in front of it, angling to get the front of the Sussex Hotel, the ambulance and the police cars all in the same shot. *Very cinematic,* Lauren thought. *Let's make this crime scene Christmas card worthy.*

'Where are Anthony and Garcia?' Sheehan asked. He looked a little disheveled, his thin gray hair mussed from the wind. He'd been relaxing in the men's room for quite a while when Lauren had pounded on the outer door to alert him of the call out.

'There was a shooting on Grape Street in the Fruit Belt. Doesn't look like the guy's going to make it,' she told him. They paused to watch the ambulance pull away from the curb. 'Lema and Avilla are over there too. That's why we're short-handed. They've got two crime scenes. We're going to have to make do.'

'We always got more cops than detectives,' Sheehan said, trying to smooth his rumpled hair down. 'Good for the overtime, bad for the follow-up.'

Lauren silently agreed with him wholeheartedly.

They ignored the news crew and hooked around the sidewalk to the valet parking area of the hotel. Four red-coated valets were standing on the curb watching the police cars with a knot of blue-suited managerial types. A short lady with a sharp steel-gray bob haircut broke off as Lauren and Sheehan approached the double door to enter the hotel.

'I'm Theresa Hatten, the night manager. Can I help you?'

'I'm Detective Riley, this is my partner Detective Sheehan. I think you might be able to,' Lauren said, as Sheehan held the door open for both of them. 'Is there some place we can go and speak to you in private?'

'In my office,' she said, eyebrows pulling together in a concerned V. 'Follow me. We can talk in there.'

The manager led them through the brightly lit lobby. In the far corner a massive evergreen was decorated with red and gold bulbs. It was December twelfth and the holiday season was in full swing. Piped in Christmas music came at them from hidden speakers on all sides, adding to the festive mood. Everything looked perfect, except for the reflection of the blue-and-white police lights from the patrol cars bouncing off every surface.

While Lauren could pass for a disgruntled hotel guest, with her choppy brown hair and dark wool coat over black pants and winter boots, there was no mistaking Doug Sheehan for anything other than what he was. He oozed cop from every pore, another reason Lauren hated working with him. It was easier getting information from people if they didn't feel like they were in a 1940s-style police interrogation. He even wore a stupid fedora when the weather was nicer. Every time he put that thing on the top of his head she wanted to slap it off.

The manager's office was behind the front desk, a plain door discreet off to the side. *Probably so the managers can monitor the front desk activity better*, Lauren thought, as Hatten pulled out a swipe card and opened the door. The Sussex wasn't the most exclusive hotel in Buffalo, but it was up there. It was one of those places that billed itself as a 'boutique hotel' and charged an extra hundred a night because they left a chocolate on your pillow. Lauren had never spent the night there. She was too cheap and single and she could fetch her own chocolates.

Crammed into Hatten's tiny office was a desk and two chairs, a file cabinet and a printer. There wasn't much room for anything else. It didn't even have a window. She was neat, though. Color-coded folders sat stacked in perfect piles on her desk, unlike the papers on Lauren's desk that looked like they'd been dumped there by a cyclone.

'The valets are saying he was a guest here.' Hatten maneuvered around the desk to her chair and took a seat. Now she was looking up at them with her round face and equally round glasses, hopeful that they would say no, he was not a guest of the hotel. 'Do you have a name?'

Sheehan pulled his notebook out of his jacket pocket and flipped it open. 'Gunnar Jonsson,' he said.

'Yes.' She snapped her fingers in recognition. 'I remember one of our staff saying we had a guest from Iceland booked here for a week.' She swiveled to the computer monitor on her desk and started pecking away at the keyboard. 'Just give me a second to pull up the details.'

'Is that unusual?' Lauren asked as the manager scrolled through some documents on her screen.

'Someone coming from Iceland to Buffalo in the winter months?' She shook her head. 'I can't remember a single booking like that, and I've been with this hotel for two years. We don't get a lot of business travelers. Our clientele usually favors short visits for some personal reason: a family function, a wedding, wanting to scratch Niagara Falls off their bucket list. Those sorts of things.'

Lauren nodded along. 'He was here on business?' she asked.

'I don't know for sure. Just an educated guess. It is between the two big holiday weeks – you know, Thanksgiving and Christmas. Those are big for family travel. Maybe one of our cleaning staff who was assigned to his room could help more with that.' Hatten squinted at the screen. 'There are charges on his bill from the business center, where he made some copies, and for room service. Here's the reservation.'

'Can we take a peek?' Lauren asked.

Ms Hatten swiveled the monitor around so they could see it. 'I can let you look at it, but company policy says we need a subpoena for his records and a search warrant for the room.'

'You've done this before,' Sheehan said, bending over to peer at the screen.

She nodded. 'Unfortunately, yes. And I'll have our corporate security make copies of the hall and front door camera footage for today. That's stored offsite, but we can usually get it from the server within forty-eight hours. But we'll need a subpoena for that as well.'

'I'll go get the search warrant typed up.' Sheehan turned to Lauren and asked, 'You want to sit on the room? Make sure no one goes in or out?'

Lauren scanned the reservation. He'd extended his stay just the day before from seven to twelve nights. Something was keeping him in Buffalo. 'Sure. I'll just grab a cup of coffee.'

'I'll have the kitchen staff bring you a pot,' Hatten told her. 'And a chair. His room was on the third floor, 317.'

'You have done this before,' Lauren remarked, marveling at her efficiency in the face of a brutal murder.

'I worked for a major chain in Las Vegas for twelve years.' She righted her computer and sighed. 'I thought when I took this job in Buffalo it'd be a nice change of pace. But it seems like hotels are magnets for crime.'

'Anywhere human beings congregate are magnets for crime,' Lauren assured her. 'Thank you for all your help.'

'Don't thank me. Unfortunately, I know the more I cooperate the sooner you'll be gone and I can get back to convincing my guests everything is fine.'

Smart lady, Lauren thought.

TWO

Waiting outside a hotel room while her slow-as-molasses temporary partner typed up a search warrant was pure torture for Lauren. The manager had given her a spare key card and she was literally one swipe away from getting into Gunnar's room. She kept fingering the smooth plastic rectangle in her coat pocket. A lot of cops would have just gone in, knowing the search warrant was coming. She couldn't say that she wasn't tempted, not because she was in a hurry, but because she hoped there might be something in that room that helped explain what happened to Gunnar in that alleyway.

Lauren looked at the round black bubble in the corner near the ceiling. The hotel camera watched her as she sat in the folding chair a maintenance man had provided. Even if she was tempted, she wouldn't risk getting everything thrown out in court because she was in a hurry. *I'll say one thing about constant video surveillance,* she thought, crossing her arms against her chest, *it keeps you honest.*

Lauren checked the time on her cellphone. She had gone through almost the entire pot of coffee one of the girls who worked in the kitchen had brought her. A few curious guests had side-eyed her as they passed to go to their rooms, but not one asked who she was or what she was doing sitting alone in the hotel hallway. Maybe they assumed she was a cop because of the television crews outside, but maybe everyone had moved on by then to another tragedy striking somewhere else in the city that needed immediate live coverage.

As of this week, she'd been working in regular Homicide for five months, ever since Shane Reese got shot and fractured his skull when he went down. Reese was still off, recovering. The doctors predicted he should be back to work in the spring but, in the meantime, Lauren had gone to Homicide from Cold Case to have a more flexible schedule to help with his care.

Reese and his dog, a West Highland terrier named Watson, had taken up residence in the guest room at her house. Nurses and physical therapists were constantly in and out, but they didn't want Reese living on his own until he was in better shape. Thankfully, both of her girls were away at college, although they'd be home for winter break in a matter of days. They'd be a great help taking care of the Prince, as she'd taken to referring to him. She couldn't complain though; she was the reason he had gotten shot in the first place.

She missed working the cold cases.

She'd seen a lot of dead bodies. People murdered in every way imaginable, and some you wouldn't want to imagine, but this one? Gunnar's murder was different somehow. In Cold Case, there was a distance between you and the murder and the victim. Now that she was working regular homicides, that buffer was removed. In the few months she'd been there she'd seen robberies gone bad, random attacks on women by predators, gang-related drive-bys. But Gunnar's murder seemed especially personal, purposeful, and cruel. He'd fought back hard, almost escaping, but his assailant persisted until he was dead. And then some. The extent of the wounds was overkill. Lauren was sure the autopsy would show some were post-mortem, that the killer had kept pounding away after he was already dead.

Gunnar's passport showed no other trips to the United States in the six years since he'd gotten it. Lauren studied the photo she had taken of it with her phone. The information was a little hard to read because it had been in the clear plastic evidence bag, causing a glare, but she could see Gunnar's picture just fine. His longish dark hair had been swept off his face and he was smiling right into the camera with even white teeth. A handsome man. Not tall, on the short side by American standards, especially if he really was five foot five like his passport said. A small, slightly built man. Lauren was almost four inches taller than him.

Lauren racked her brain trying to figure out a connection to Western New York. Maybe he'd been here before, using an older, now expired, passport. Maybe he worked for a company that did business in the States. Maybe he'd been an exchange student in college. Maybe he had an ex-girlfriend living in Buffalo. Lauren needed to look at the paperwork in his room.

And Sheehan was pissing her off.

She kept checking the time on her phone. The squad had templates for search warrants right in their city-issued iPads. Some things you always needed a warrant for: a hotel room, a computer, a house. You just pulled up the template you needed and plugged in the relevant facts of the particular case, sent it to an ADA to look over and approve, then printed it up and took it to the on-call judge to sign. For something like this, the entire process should have taken less than two hours.

It was ten minutes after midnight when Sheehan came strolling off the elevator. She'd been waiting there for over three hours.

'What the hell took you so long?' Lauren asked, standing up. Both of her knees popped. Another surprise gift of turning forty that year.

He stopped in front of the door and stood next to Lauren. It must have started snowing again because there were flakes caught in his scarf and melted droplets dotting what was left of his hair. 'Sorry, Lauren. I was starving so I stopped at that all-night sub shop and grabbed a sandwich.'

'I've been sitting here with my thumb up my ass while you were eating a turkey hoagie?'

His cheeks burned crimson. 'I got you a ham sub, toasted roll, just like you like it; it's down in the car.'

She shook her head and motioned to the door. 'Please just tell me you got the warrant.'

He reached inside his wool coat and pulled out a jumble of papers. 'I left one with the manager. This is our copy and the return.'

He wanted her to take the paperwork from him, but as long as she knew they were signed and on scene, he could keep his papers.

'Careful,' Sheehan cautioned in a whisper. 'I got your back.'

It was her front she was worried about. Lauren didn't think the killer would be inside Gunnar's room. *But with my luck*, Lauren thought as she approached the door, blading herself to the left side, out of view of the peep hole, *the killer's been sitting on the bed this whole time, knowing the police were waiting outside and wasn't going down without a fight.* Another fight.

Sliding her Glock out of its holster, she extracted the key card from her coat pocket and stuck it in the lock without a word. It blinked green with an audible click. She put her shoulder into the heavy hotel door and it swung inward. The room was dark. Still blading herself, she reached around, feeling the side of the wall for the light switch. She brought her gun up before she flicked on the light, covering the immediate darkness in front of her. They'd lost the element of surprise but she was still going to be tactical.

She flipped the switch and the room lit up. It was empty. The bathroom door was open to her left and it was unoccupied as well – only Lauren's reflection in the mirror greeted her.

She let out the breath she'd been holding, which she shouldn't have been doing, and entered the room. Her dad had been a deer hunter and used to chastise her for holding her breath when they would go target shooting together. It was a bad habit she was still trying to break, almost twenty years into the job.

The hotel room itself was typical, if a little nicer than most. It definitely wasn't so grand Lauren would drop the extra money to stay there over one of the big chains she had a rewards card for. The main difference was that it seemed a lot bigger than a regular hotel room, without being a suite.

A king-sized bed that would have eaten up the space in a normal hotel room was made up, complete with a yellow rose in the center of the middle pillow. The room had a green, yellow and gold color scheme; very upscale and tasteful. Lauren walked in with Sheehan at her back, letting the door fall shut behind them.

'Well, that was anticlimactic,' Sheehan observed, looking around.

'Really?' Lauren stopped and stared back at him.

'No bad guy.' He shrugged his shoulders and Lauren noticed a piece of lettuce on his tie, near the bulge of his gut. 'I'm just saying.'

'You take the closet,' she told Sheehan as she pulled two

latex gloves out of her back pocket and proceeded to snap them on. Every good homicide detective has gloves in one pocket and evidence bags in another. 'I'll go through the drawers and suitcase.'

'Got it, Lauren.' On the plus side for partnering with him, unlike a lot of guys on the job who hated taking orders from a woman, Doug Sheehan was glad to give up any and all responsibility whenever possible.

I have to get my real partner back to work, Lauren thought, watching Sheehan pull his own gloves on, *for my sake and Sheehan's.*

Standing upright in the far corner of the room was a large moss green suitcase. Lauren walked over to it as Sheehan dutifully began to go through every piece of clothing hanging in the closet. She had to give it to him, he wasn't ambitious but he was thorough.

Thankfully, there was no lock on the suitcase. Lauren turned it on its back and unzipped it. Like she'd suspected from the amount of clothes hanging in the closet, it was mostly empty. It looked like once Gunnar had worn something and thought it was dirty, he returned it, neatly folded, to the suitcase. After Lauren had inspected every inner and outside pocket, she zipped it back up and went over to the chest of drawers facing the bed.

Pulling open the top drawer, she struck gold immediately. Inside was a trove of papers, some of them in a foreign language she couldn't identify, some in English. She immediately pulled out her cellphone and snapped some pictures before she touched anything.

'I think I got something over here,' Lauren called over to Sheehan.

'I found a few dollars and some change in a couple of the pockets,' he said, walking over. 'Some receipts for Uber rides. He must have printed them out down in the business center.'

'You grab those?'

'Got 'em.' He held up an evidence bag with a gloved hand, shaking it in front of her face.

Lauren didn't bother to try to look at them right then, she was more interested in the neat stacks of paper in her drawer. Slipping her readers out of the inner pocket of her jacket, she

perched them on her nose. She recognized the logo on one of
the top papers right away. It was a printout of a DNA report
from one of those genealogy sites that were all the rage. It
was written in that same language she didn't recognize. Picking
up the stack, Lauren leafed through the pages, stopping on
one with the pie chart on it.

Last year her sister had bought Lauren one of those kits for
Christmas as a lark. They'd all laughed around the dinner table
that maybe they'd find out they were royalty, or distantly
related to one of the presidents of the United States. Lauren
had sent in her sample, and six weeks later got the same, exact
pie chart in an email. She was Polish and Irish just like she'd
always been told, and not one of her relatives had come to
the states before 1900. No surprises. She was exactly what
both sets of her grandparents had told her she was.

Her chart had been neatly divided into three pieces: 60
percent Polish, 34 percent Irish and 6 percent random ethnici-
ties. Lauren had read somewhere that Icelandic people could
trace their roots all the way back to the Vikings, so she
was a little surprised to see Gunnar's – and she knew it was
Gunnar's because his name was at the top – was split in half.
He was 48 percent Scandinavian and then a whole mess of
other nationalities: Italian, British, Native American, Spanish,
sub-Saharan African.

'What is all that?' Sheehan asked as Lauren snapped another
picture of the page with her cellphone.

'It's one of those DNA reports. You know? Like the ones
they advertise on TV where they trace your ancestors for you.'

'Why does our victim have all that with him in here?'

Lauren flipped through to the next page. It showed a list, just
like she had gotten, of possible relatives who had also used the
site and how close a relative they thought you were. Right at
the top of the list was a man's username and location and, under
it, a word in that same foreign language. Lauren scrolled through
her cell phone to the translator app and typed in '*Bróðir.*'

The result popped up immediately.

She switched back to the camera app and snapped a picture
of the information.

'Because he has a half-brother here in Buffalo.'

THREE

They called Evidence and Photography back and had them come up to Gunnar's room and collect the paperwork they'd found. But not before Lauren had snapped a picture of every piece of paper in that DNA report. She and Sheehan then headed back to the Homicide office to start filling in all the paperwork.

It was late, almost four thirty a.m., and headquarters was dark and practically deserted. A few cleaners wandered the floors trying to stay ahead of the slobby cops who worked in the building, Lauren included. The other crew who'd caught the beating earlier had long gone home.

'Listen,' Sheehan said as Lauren was about to settle into her desk, 'I'll stick around and finish the paperwork and then head to the post. It's all overtime, right? Just cover me in the morning so I can get a couple hours sleep before I come in, OK?'

A typical cop barter. And Lauren was exhausted. As it was, she had to be back in the office at eight a.m. for her regular shift. He'd get to go to the post at six, be done with that at eight and be able to put in a twelve-hour overtime slip. Mentally, Lauren forgave him for stopping to eat and leaving her sitting in the hallway. 'You got it, Doug,' she told him, grabbing her duffel bag from under her desk. 'I'll see you later this morning.'

'Good deal.' He sat down and immediately started their activity report. Lauren took that as her cue and headed out the door.

The entire ride back to her house near Delaware Park, she thought of the victim. She needed to examine the pictures of the documents more closely, but it was a good guess that Gunnar was in Buffalo on family business. Lauren knew she'd have a lot to do when she got back to the Homicide office in the morning. She had no idea who you called when a foreign citizen was murdered. The state department? The FBI? In all the years she'd worked in Cold Case, and now Homicide, she'd never handled a non-citizen's death. Not even a Canadian's. Seemed like Americans were good at only killing each other in the city of Buffalo.

Lauren's mind kept replaying the scene in the alley, going over the details in her head like it was stuck on a loop. She parked her car then trudged to her front door with keys in gloved hand. As cold as it was downtown, it felt even colder at that early hour. It took her a moment to fumble her key in the lock and get the door open. Slipping inside, the heat hitting Lauren's face felt like slice of heaven.

Reese and his dog, Watson, were asleep on top of each other on the sofa, where Watson was not allowed. They must have tired each other out because neither even lifted their head when Lauren came in. She paused in the doorway of the living room and stood looking at them for a moment, overcome by that strange feeling she'd been having lately when she caught a glance of Reese and he was unaware.

She was too tired to move them to the spare guest room where Reese was staying, so she just shuffled past and up the stairs, shedding layers of clothes as she went. She dropped her coat on the top landing. Wet tracks followed her. She should have kicked her boots off by the front door but she was too exhausted to wrestle them off. It wouldn't be the first time Lauren fell into bed with her shoes still on.

The house was so quiet, all she heard was the faint howl of the wind outside coming across the lake and Watson's occasional sleepy grunts. She lived in the city because she couldn't stand silence. Even though her upscale neighborhood was considered serene by city standards, its sounds were all around her. She needed noise: sirens, horns, people walking by, the rustle of the leaves in the trees, icicles breaking from the gutter and smashing to the ground. The racket calmed her brain.

But her mind was still on auto-play as she walked into her bedroom that night.

Someone chased down and brutally murdered a man who, as far as she could tell, had never even been to Buffalo before.

It definitely could have been a street robbery gone bad. Buffalo certainly had more than their share of those in the downtown area. Tourists made easy targets, so hanging out by a hotel would give a predator plenty of victims. The perpetrator could have gotten spooked by something and overreacted. Unless they had a psychopath on their hands and Gunnar was just the beginning. That was a scenario Lauren didn't even want to consider.

Peeling back the comforter, she smoothed out the cool white case covering her pillow. Lauren always made her bed before she left for work so it was nice and inviting after a night like tonight. Reese used to say it was one of the best things about Lauren – her neatness compulsion – until he started living with her and she tried to put an end to his slobbery.

When Reese had been grazed by a bullet back in March and fell forward, fracturing his skull, he took a turn for the worse and no one was certain he was going to pull through. It was during this time that she'd had a conversation with his mother, who had intimated that maybe, possibly, Reese had feelings for her. She'd spent the last nine months nursing him back to health and trying to decipher how she felt about that, if it were true. Reese had never confirmed it. As far as she knew, he wasn't even aware the conversation had taken place. The longer Lauren mulled it over the more she had convinced herself that maybe Reese's mom just *wanted* there to be something between the two of them. All those TV shows made it seem like police partners fell into bed with each other all the time. It was ridiculous to think that there was anything other than a mutual respect and deep friendship, grounded in insults and put downs, between them.

And yet, and yet . . .

She'd gone back and forth about asking Reese what his mother meant. Each time she ended up asking herself, what would it change? She didn't know the truth about her own feelings. Every single relationship she'd had with a man ended badly. Putting him on the spot could end what they already had: a steady, stable friendship that she cherished. Wasn't that more important than a love affair that could poison everything?

Fairy tale romances only happened in books and movies. What she had right now with Reese was real, and it was good. She'd messed up a lot of things in her life, she wasn't about to screw that up.

But she couldn't stop thinking about that conversation. She couldn't stop thinking about the way their lives had become so intertwined since they'd known each other.

As difficult as living with him while he was recovering with all these questions was, Lauren couldn't dispute the fact that she was the reason he had multiple scars on his head. She'd made a terrible mistake and Reese had almost paid for it with his life. She had to push her wants and needs aside for once and put him first. She'd do whatever it took to get him back on his feet.

No matter what.

FOUR

'So who *do* you call when a foreign citizen gets killed in the United States?' Lauren asked her sergeant bright and early the next morning as she leaned against the doorframe of his office.

Sergeant Brad Connolly was always at the Homicide office at least a half hour before their shift started. They worked days, from eight to six, but the afternoon shift had been short on manpower the day before, so Doug Sheehan and Lauren had both stayed on overtime and that was how she caught Gunnar's murder. Lauren was surprising herself by referring to the victim in her own head as Gunnar. Stuff like that made cases seem personal, which was a bad thing. Homicide detectives have enough going on in their own lives without taking their murder cases personally. But sometimes they do because they're still mostly human. Those parts of them that the job hadn't managed to poison, anyway.

Lauren got to the Homicide squad at ten to eight that morning, and the sarge was waiting for her. She and the sarge had gone to the police academy together a lifetime ago. He was almost ten years older than her, having spent eight years as a corrections officer before changing lanes and becoming a Buffalo cop. He had decided to take the supervisory route once he got on the job, whereas Lauren was happy to be a mere detective.

Connolly had thinning blond hair so light it you could see his scalp, pockmarked cheeks and a gravelly ex-smoker's voice. 'Doug Sheehan called my cell,' he said. 'He's finishing up the post – won't be in for a while.' He motioned for Lauren to sit in the extra chair across from his desk. A steaming cup of black coffee was already waiting. He knew if he wanted her to produce, she had to have loads of fresh coffee.

She wrapped her fingers around the white ceramic to warm them up. She was always cold. Even in the middle of summer, her hands and feet were like ice. Being perpetually cold made living through a Buffalo winter that much harder. But maybe not, if hot flashes were coming her way. At forty, she was a little young for menopause, but it was definitely on the horizon.

'I almost came in last night when dispatch notified me about the body. Then I called the on-call assistant district attorney and asked him. He didn't know. So I called the chief of detectives and he didn't know. Then I called Reggie Major, who's been in Homicide longer than anyone and *he* didn't know. He said they had a murder suspect from Borneo once and they had to get the US Marshals involved, but that was after they got a warrant for his arrest. He couldn't even remember a case with a Canadian citizen getting murdered in Buffalo, not in the twenty-something years he's been a detective up here in Homicide.' He slurped his coffee, made a face, and put the mug down. 'Careful. It's hot, like molten lava hot.'

Lauren blew the steam across the top of the cup but didn't take a sip. 'So what do we do?'

He slouched back in his seat. He wasn't a tall guy, but he was wide, like a linebacker and had enormous lumberjack hands. Lauren imagined getting slapped by him would be akin to getting hit by a Mack truck. 'I was just about to call my brother-in-law who works for the State Attorney General's office when Ansel Carey called me back.' Ansel was their new chief of detectives and his *modus operandi* was to delegate every bit of authority he could to someone else, whenever he had the chance. 'He had a three-way call with the commissioner and the district attorney. They agreed he should call Samuel Papineau, the special agent in charge of the FBI's Buffalo branch, so he did and they're sending us an agent to help assist with the case.'

'Wait. What?' The last thing they needed was to bring the Feds in on a simple homicide investigation. Historically, the two agencies didn't play well together.

'They have the resources to reach out to the family in Iceland – to be able to translate the information in his phone,' he spread his big paddle-like hands out, 'to be able to actually get into his damn phone. For once, I have to agree with Antsy.

We need their help.' Antsy was what the squad called Ansel behind his back. Antsy-and-Agitated, to be exact, which is exactly what he was 90 percent of the time.

'Who are they sending over?' She braved taking a sip and promptly burned her tongue.

'A new guy. He's on their computer task force, so he should be somewhat useful.'

'Computer power is what we need.' Pulling her phone out of her back pocket, she thumbed it open and slid it across the table to Connolly. 'I want you to take a look at these. See that chart? That family tree?'

'It's written in Klingon,' he said, pinching the screen to try to zoom in on the picture of the paperwork.

'It's written in Icelandic,' Lauren corrected. 'That family tree says he has a father, a brother, a sister and fifteen cousins here in Buffalo. I bet that was who he was here to see.'

'What the hell is all this?' He turned her phone upside down, squinted at it, and flipped it around again.

'It's one of those genealogy reports; you know, the ones that are always advertised on TV? That's how they break down your lineage: in a pie chart and family trees.'

'How do you take a test for fun in Iceland and come up with a match in America? I don't understand that crap.'

'The site he used is international. I took a DNA test from the same company and had a couple of cousins pop up in Poland.'

'Did you contact your new-found kin?'

'No,' Lauren admitted. 'They were listed as third and fourth cousins and I thought it would be weird. I just wanted to find out where I was from, not find long-lost family members. To be fair, none of them tried to contact me either.'

The sarge took a second to digest that information before he asked, 'But Gunnar Jonsson's family is here in Buffalo? What about his relatives in Iceland?'

'Ah, now, that's the tricky part,' Lauren reached over and took her phone back from his huge paw. 'Gunnar Jonsson's profile is set on private, so no one can see his Icelandic relatives, but his half-brother's profile was set on public, so his family tree is out there for the world to view. Says here his father is John

Hudson and his siblings are Brooklyn and Ryan, both much younger than him.'

'All locals?'

'I'm about to find out. I'm going to run all three. Get as much information as I can. I want to do the death notification before the noon news. As of right now, he's still a John Doe as far as the press is concerned. They're going to have a field day when they find out he's an Icelandic citizen.'

'If his father is American, he could have dual citizenship. Maybe it's not as big a deal as we're thinking it is.' He reached up with his enormous free hand and scratched absently behind his ear.

'The plane ticket we recovered says he flew into Toronto seven days ago – sorry, eight days ago now,' Lauren corrected herself. 'He had a customs form from the Peace Bridge dated the same day. He must have flown in and drove down across the border. His rental car was in the hotel's valet lot. It didn't look like anything was inside, but we had it towed to our impound lot anyway. The manager at the hotel said he had extended his stay for five more days. He must have had some pressing business here in Buffalo. That hotel is not cheap.'

'Airline tickets?' The sarge asked. 'Do we know when he was due to return home?'

'I found them in his hotel dresser. He came into Toronto on a redeye flight. Looks like he had a flight back for today but changed his airline ticket as well.'

'Find out what was keeping him here.'

'I was going to call my buddy over at customs on the bridge—'

The sarge cut her off. 'We'll leave all that to our new federal friend when he gets here.' A loud click echoed through the hallway signaling someone was coming into the Homicide wing. Lauren leaned back in her chair to see who was coming in. Craig Garcia's annoying laugh was followed by the noise of Vatasha Anthony's footsteps tracking down the hallway past Marilyn's desk. Lauren looked away without saying hello. Garcia and Anthony weren't her favorite people on the job.

'Sounds like the troops are filing in.' The sarge knew there was bad blood between Lauren and those two. 'Get to work on grabbing the father's address so you can do the notification. I'll brief the FBI guy when he shows up and handle Antsy.'

Pushing away from his desk, Lauren stood up. 'OK, Sarge. I'm on it.'

'Take that coffee with you. It doesn't grow on trees you know.'

'Actually, Sarge, the Arabica plant is a pretty large bush—'

'Zip it, smart ass.' Connolly pointed to the door as she grabbed her coffee mug, sloshing a little over the rim and searing the back of her hand. His voice was a bark, but he was wearing a lopsided smile. 'Get to work. Don't embarrass me. The Feds are watching.'

'Aye, aye, boss.' Giving him a mock salute, Lauren retreated out into the main hall and down to her crew's office. When they'd been at 74 Franklin Street the Homicide squad had been housed in two huge open rooms, pieced into workspaces by desks, filing cabinets, and tables. Now that they'd moved to the old federal courthouse, each homicide crew had its own separate office off a long corridor, with the sergeant's office at the top, next to the homicide report technician's desk. It was so fancy their offices even had leaded glass doors. This made it easy for Lauren to shut out Craig Garcia and Vatasha Anthony.

Lauren, Garcia and Anthony had notoriously bad blood between them. Garcia had cheerfully watched as Carl Church, the district attorney, had put Lauren in front of a grand jury three months earlier for a manslaughter charge. Anthony had actually taken the stand to testify against her.

Lauren had been involved for over a year in a deadly cat-and-mouse game with a sociopath named David Spencer. After he'd shot Reese in the head she'd managed to corner Spencer in an abandoned warehouse. Or he had cornered her, which turned out to be the more likely case, and she had ended up killing him. When the grand jury returned a 'no bill' and refused to indict her, the police commissioner declared that David Spencer's death at Lauren's hands had been an act of self-defense. Lauren had come off of administrative leave and gone back to work in the regular Homicide squad. That surprising turn of events made Garcia and Anthony lose their swagger, and the bad mouthing they had been doing about Lauren and Reese had ceased. Garcia had always been a petty bully, but he was deathly afraid of Reese. Even though Garcia and Anthony were on a separate crew, they still had to see her around the office every day, and Lauren never missed a chance to rub both of their noses in it.

Walking past their crew's closed door, Lauren took another sip of her coffee, now drinkable, and wished Reese was back to work. As she walked into her own crew's office, she realized how short they were on manpower. Their crew consisted of Doug Sheehan, Hector Avilla and Mario Aquino. She was filling in for Reggie Major, who was off on a medical leave, and would go back to Cold Case once he was cleared for duty. But with Aquino on vacation until after the first of the year, the entire squad was desperately understaffed. Hence, she and Doug had had to take the night crew's homicide.

She fired up her desktop and got to work. With every minute she wasted, Gunnar Jonsson's murder got colder.

FIVE

'Hey Lauren, I heard you caught a real nasty one last night.' Hector Avilla pulled a chair up next to her as she sat at her computer. His black hair was gelled up in front, away from his pockmarked face, which already showed a hint of five o'clock shadow.

'Yeah, Hec. Poor young guy run down in an alley,' Lauren said as she began scrolling through the public records. Now that everyone's life is on display on the internet, people don't realize how much information detectives have to wade through just to find a simple address. Just narrowing down on a common name could take hours. There were a lot of John Hudsons in Buffalo. 'But it was wrong. Something was off about the whole thing, you know what I mean?'

'Robbery gone bad?'

'Could be,' she conceded, then added, 'but it just doesn't feel right.'

Hector's dark brown eyes ran over the page she was looking at. 'Is this the possible suspect?'

Lauren shook her head. 'I'm trying to find his next of kin. He had some paperwork on him that said he had family in Buffalo.'

'Good luck with that. The chief just told me I'm doing the video canvas for you because he's bringing in someone from the FBI to help you.'

Good news traveled fast in the department. 'Sorry about that. The chief is here already?'

'He stopped me on the way in. It's no problem. I'm going to grab Scott from Photography. He's a whiz at that stuff. We'll be done before you know it. And maybe we'll have something for you.'

Lauren gave an exaggerated sigh. 'A nice clear shot of the assailant's face would be nice.'

'Yeah, that'd be something.' He smiled. 'Too bad that never happens.'

'Only on TV.'

Hec slapped her shoulder as he got up. 'I'm going to make some coffee. Want some more?'

Lauren looked down into her half-filled cup. 'I'm good for now,' she called as he made his way through the open door and toward the coffee maker at the end of the main corridor.

She turned her attention back to the most likely candidate on the screen: John Robert Hudson, age fifty-two, with an address out in a swanky new subdivision in the town of Orchard Park.

John Robert Hudson. Lauren knew that name from somewhere.

She hit the print icon and heard the copier rumble to life out in the hallway as it spit out the information. All around her the homicide squad was waking up for the day. The new space they had given them, when they moved police head-quarters from Franklin Street to the old federal building on Niagara Square, seemed less than ideal at first, but cops will complain about anything. It took a couple of months for the lot of them to realize just how crappy and dilapidated their old building really had been. It was nice to walk into a building where you didn't have to fight cockroaches for your desk chair.

'Can you grab those for me?' she called out to Marilyn. The homicide report technician, a fancy way of saying office manager, was the department's unofficial den mother. Or more like a referee, which was what she was most of the time. With the door open, Lauren could lean back in her chair and the two of them would go back and forth chatting all day. She'd miss that when she had to go back to the Cold Case office, which was further down the hall and out of sight.

'You got it.' Marilyn scooped them up and brought them over to Lauren, her navy slacks *swoosh, swoosh, swooshing* as she came. Lauren would have gotten up herself, but Marilyn insisted on retrieving paperwork, getting coffee refills, and bringing her squad members whatever office supplies they needed. She said it was her only exercise, but Lauren knew she loved mothering the group of detectives.

'Thanks,' Lauren said, shuffling them around, trying to put them in some kind of order.

'You still seeing that dreamy UPS driver?' she asked. Marilyn was in her early sixties and was married to her high school sweetheart. She took a great interest in Lauren's love life, or lack thereof.

'Nope,' Lauren told her. 'He was nice to look it, but the elevator didn't go all the way to the top floor.'

'As long as he can deliver the package, does it matter?' Marilyn laughed.

'Trust me, it never even got close to that,' Lauren assured her. They had a total of six dates, including her taking him to the Homicide office holiday party the first day of December. It was four dates too long and the party was the last time she had seen him in person. Lauren was still ignoring his texts and phone calls, not quite ready to totally block him, but definitely done with dating him.

'You're so tough on the poor guys you go out with.'

Lauren puckered her lips in a smirk. 'I can't help it if they can't keep up with me. I have to cut them loose quick or they get too attached.' Which was true. Before she'd met her first husband she'd spend hours getting ready trying to meet someone. Now she'd go to the grocery store in sweatpants and keep right on wearing them out to dinner. *Middle age is a wonderfully freeing time*, Lauren thought, *because now I just don't give a shit.*

Marilyn walked back to her desk where the phone line never stopped blinking and sat down. The huge calendar the police union put out every year framed her head. Lauren looked over at her to ask something and found herself staring at the month of December. Something caught her eye.

Marilyn noticed her staring. 'What?'

Lauren got up and approached Marilyn's very organized desk, bypassing the inbox and going straight for the wall. In the right-hand corner of certain dates on the calendar were the phases of the moon. Lauren had looked at the Buffalo Police Union's calendars almost every day since she had gotten the job, and never really cared about the phases of the moon. Now she leaned in and took a good look.

'What in the hell are you doing?' Marilyn asked, leaning back so she could see what Lauren was squinting at.

'Last night was December twelfth – a full moon,' Lauren told her, stepping back, knocking over a Mason jar full of pens and pencils.

Marilyn scrambled to gather up all the writing utensils Lauren had just displaced across her desk. 'Yeah? And we caught a couple homicides, so what? All the crazies come out during the full moon, you know that. And today is Friday the thirteenth, if you're superstitious.'

'Sorry about that,' Lauren said as she tried to stuff as many pens as she could back into the glass jar. She grabbed a few more, trying to get them in, but a couple went point side down, which was not allowed on Marilyn's desk.

Marilyn quickly plucked them back out and righted them.

'It's not a problem but I want you to go sit down,' Marilyn said, shooing Lauren with her hands as she looked up at her. She worried in her mom-like way that Lauren was not 100 percent recovered from getting stabbed the year before. 'You're as white as a ghost.'

Lauren could feel her brow furrowing as she went back to her paperwork. She googled the lunar calendar on her phone. She'd been right. Last night had been a full moon and since it was December, that made it a full cold moon. A chill ran down her spine.

Gunnar Jonsson had been killed under a full cold moon.

She had another case, a very old case, that had happened during a full cold moon. She'd been working on it since she first got to the Cold Case squad. She'd worked it with every resource she had, chasing every old lead, putting more man-hours into it than any other case.

And she hadn't solved it yet.

SIX

Lauren was not a superstitious person. Not at all. But her dad had been a hunter. The kind that actually ate what he killed and was respectful of conservation. The kind of hunter that had learned from his dad and grandfather. He took it very seriously, even if she didn't totally understand why he had loved it so much. He'd take a trip south of the city to his cousin's land at the start of the season, spend a few days in the woods, maybe get a deer, maybe not, but always came back happy. Then with a clear head, he'd put on his work clothes and go back to the Ford plant.

One of the things Lauren Riley's dad really believed in was the cycles of the moon. He used to tell her that October was the hunter's moon and just like the tides, the moon had an effect on the wildlife in the forest. Sometimes the December moon was called the long nights moon or the Yule moon, for obvious reasons. Around Buffalo, in December, when you woke up it was dark; and when you got home from work it was dark. It wasn't a bad thing, or a scary thing, just the natural order of things. For her, that December moon would always be the full cold moon, because that was what Billy Munzert's dad had called it.

On her first day in the Cold Case squad one of the old timers about to retire had put a thick file on her desk. 'I caught this case decades ago. Good family. All heartbroken. I don't know what you can do with it, but try, OK?'

She'd looked at the faded cover of the file, then back to the detective who would end up dying later that year of a heart attack before he got his pension. 'OK,' she'd said, and meant it. Because when you first get to Homicide you haven't had your heart broken over and over yet, and you were willing to take on the hard cases.

Lauren hadn't been a new detective, she'd transferred over from the Special Victims Unit, and before that she'd spent years on patrol. So she thought she was ready. She believed she was immune to emotional attachment at that point. She thought this would be a good first case to get her feet wet in Cold Case.

Lauren dug into the file as soon as he walked away from her desk. In 1978 a twelve-year-old boy from the Kaisertown neighborhood had gone to the milk machine on the corner for his mom. It was past dinnertime, around seven p.m., and his mother had wanted to make sure her kids had milk for cereal the next morning. She had forgotten to grab a carton at the now closed grocery store earlier that day.

The quarters his mother had given him were found scattered on the ground in front of the machine. Three days later his bike was discovered caught on some branches on the banks of the Buffalo River. His body was never recovered.

Billy Munzert had been in sixth grade, loved playing army guys with his friends, and couldn't wait for *Star Wars* to come to his local movie theater because his parents didn't own a car and he could walk there.

Lauren had stayed at the office until almost midnight reading the file. She took an entire yellow legal pad of notes. She flipped through the interviews and photos of the boy's bike caught up in the bare branches of a low-hanging tree along the river. She kept going back to the school picture his mother had provided: a red-headed, toothy-smiled, freckle-faced boy grinning right at her in his cowboy-styled shirt.

She went to see his mother the next day.

The mom was distraught and grateful and mad and hopeful, even all those years later. She'd heard rumors about a local pervert that lived near the corner where the milk machine had been. Her husband and some neighborhood guys roughed him up before the detectives got to him, but he had an alibi. An alibi the detectives couldn't shake. Those rumors and that alibi had been checked and rechecked by the original detectives two and three times over. They got nowhere. The pervert moved from the neighborhood shortly after he'd been officially cleared.

The streetlight above the machine had been out, Mrs Munzert explained as her husband hung in the doorway of their living room with sad, mournful eyes. Haunted eyes. 'I should have gone myself,' he muttered, passing an old-fashioned tobacco pipe over and over between his hands. 'I should have gone when I got home from the plant. I still had my work clothes on. I could have walked. But Billy wanted to go. I thought it was light enough, with the full cold moon out. I thought he was old enough . . .'

Lauren hadn't heard that phrase since she was a kid herself, from her own father.

The only light on the corner that evening had been from the moon, Billy's father told her, a full cold moon. As big around as a dinner platter and as bright as a bare light bulb in an empty room. The milk machine was only two blocks away. It hadn't snowed so the sidewalks were clear, which was why Billy had ridden his bike. Though kids in Buffalo rode their bikes in blizzards if they had to. Everyone in the neighborhood should have seen him riding by, but no one had. Not one person.

As Mrs Munzert sat in her living room on the blue-and-green afghan she'd probably knitted herself, she begged Lauren to finally find her son. Her husband's watery eyes joined in with her desperate pleas. They were both in their seventies by then, beat down by the circumstances surrounding the loss of their child.

'I don't want to die without knowing what happened to my son,' she said as she clutched a framed school picture of him to her chest. 'It's the not knowing. It eats away at you. My other children don't even talk about Billy. It's too hard. Too hard.' Her head drooping down over the photograph and she whispered, 'Please. Please find him.'

And Lauren made the biggest mistake a new homicide detective could possibly make: she promised she would.

She promised Billy's parents she would find their son.

Lauren had tirelessly worked and reworked every lead for the last five years. She had talked to the mother weekly, then monthly, until their oldest daughter had asked Lauren to call her instead with any updates; the stress on her parents was too much. And when Reese had come to the Cold Case squad, Lauren had dragged him into Billy's case as well.

But no matter how hard they tried, they just could not catch a break. They couldn't develop a suspect, or even a new lead. They re-canvased the neighborhood, looking for older residents who'd lived there when Billy went missing. They checked the national databases on missing children and unidentified bodies. She uploaded his dental records and swabbed his siblings for DNA for familial comparison. They had all the old evidence tested with the newest technology and came up with nothing.

And still the promise remained unkept.

A full cold moon. If Lauren hadn't wanted to make it personal with Gunnar Jonsson, circumstances possibly just made it so.

SEVEN

L auren stuck her head into the sarge's office. 'I think I got a good address for John Hudson, the victim's father. It's over in Orchard Park. Want to take a ride?'

He shook his head. Unlike Marilyn's tidy desk, his was wild with papers and files and notepads. 'They're sending the FBI guy over now. I have to wait and brief him.'

She looked at the time on her phone. 'I really have to make this notification. Tell him or her I'm sorry I couldn't wait.'

'Just handle it. Hopefully Hector will come up with something on the video canvas.'

'Hopefully. I'll be on the air if you need me.' Lauren touched the portable police radio sticking out of her coat pocket.

'Hey' – he scooped up a set of car keys and tossed them to her. She snatched them easily out of the air – 'if you're heading to Orchard Park, take my Explorer. I heard they got four inches last night. I don't want you getting stuck out at the Bills stadium in one of our shitty motor pool cars.'

'Because I'm irreplaceable, right, Sarge?'

'Because you're the least pain in my ass. For the moment. Now go and bring my truck back in one piece before I rethink this.'

She held the keys up, jingling them for effect. 'Thank you.' Getting the sarge's truck was an honor akin to getting knighted by the Queen. The motor pool cars were so notoriously bad that detectives would steal the car keys to the better ones right off of your desk if you left them out. Lauren figured she'd stop at a Tim Hortons on the way back and bring him a coffee and blueberry muffin. She'd known the sarge for a lot of years, but it was always good practice to butter up your superiors whenever the opportunity arose.

She walked past the holiday decorations clustered together against the back wall: a plastic Christmas tree with blue-and-white ornaments, a pretty metal menorah, a Kwanzaa Kinara with seven candles, and a pole someone had leaned up against the wall to symbolize Festivus. Technically, they were a government building and shouldn't have had anything displayed at all, but the unsaid rule of the office was to put up whatever you wanted to celebrate, and everybody else would respect it. It was actually one of the best things they did together as a squad all year long.

Tugging her knit hat on and tucking her scarf down the front of her jacket, Lauren double checked that her fingerless gloves were in her front pocket. She always pulled those on last. Mentally, she took stock of everything she had on her: Glock, handcuffs, radio, zip-up folio with her paperwork in it, a good pen in her inside pocket. She was ready to do the death notification and get some background on Gunnar. Maybe his dad would be able to shed some light on who might have wanted to hurt him.

It was always a delicate dance, getting information after telling someone their loved one had just been murdered. Lauren knew how to tread lightly.

She checked the address with the GPS on her phone: 251 East Glass Lake Road. She had pulled up a picture of the house on Google Maps. Gunnar Jonsson's father had a house worth almost a million dollars in one of the priciest suburbs just outside of the city. One of the siblings, Brooklyn, had the same address. Another son lived just a few miles away in a somewhat less expensive, but very exclusive, neighborhood.

The ride out of the city was a nice change of pace for Lauren. Snow coated the trees, settled in the bare branches and sat on top of bushes like dollops of whip cream. A fallacy about Buffalo is that it's always sub-zero, temperature-wise. The truth is that they did get a lot of snow, but the temperature rarely dipped below zero degrees, even with the wind chill factor. Lauren didn't love winter. She was not a skier or a snowmobiler or an ice fisherman, but she loved the look of Buffalo in the winter. It was like the whole region was frosted in a clean, white glaze. And once that melted away, everything would be new again.

John Hudson's house was located in Orchard Park's newest subdivision. So new, some streets only had ornate black lampposts marking where the houses would be built in the spring. Lauren carefully ticked off the numbers as she cruised down East Glass Lake Road. Glass Lake, the manmade body of water the mansions backed to, was frozen over in a veil of ice.

The enormous blue-sided colonial had an attached four-car garage. Smoke poured from a brick chimney on the side of the house. If anyone was home, there was no sign of it from the outside, except for that smoke. Even when she pulled into the driveway behind a cherry-red, snow-covered Mustang, not a curtain was parted. The snow on the front walk and stairs leading to the front door was undisturbed. Where were Hudson and his daughter – away? It hadn't snowed since late the night before. Surely someone would have left some tracks on their way to work in the morning.

Her city-issue boats crunched all the way to the front door. A festive wreath decorated with a huge gold ribbon adorned the massive red door. Lauren took a deep breath and hit the bell.

She could hear a faint bonging echoing through the house. Then it was just the sound of her breathing. She watched the clouds of steam escape from her mouth for almost a minute. Waiting is something you become excellent at when you worked in Homicide. She was just about to hit the bell one last time before she left a notice to call the office when Lauren heard someone approaching.

The door swung inward, revealing a tall, slim black woman in blue hospital scrubs with an open black cardigan over the shirt. Tight curls framed her oval face. 'Can I help you?'

She pulled her coat open to reveal the gold badge on her hip. 'I'm Detective Lauren Riley with the Buffalo Police Department. Is this the Hudson residence?'

The woman's eyes narrowed ever so slightly. 'What did Brooklyn do now?'

Lauren was thrown off script for a second. 'Brooklyn? No, I'm looking for Mr John Hudson? Gunnar Jonsson's father?'

Now she was met with straight up suspicion. 'Can I see your credentials please? Who did you say you worked for again?'

Lauren fished the wallet that contained her official identification out of her back pocket. The woman cracked the glass
storm door and took it from her. Lauren watched her study it
carefully before passing it back. She tried again. 'I'm Detective
Riley with the Buffalo Police Department. I'd like to speak
with John Hudson, please.'

'I'm Mr Hudson's nurse.' She crossed her arms in front of
her. 'He's not taking visitors now. I'd be happy to pass along
any message you might have. Or a business card, if you have
one.'

It was time to stop dicking around. 'Ma'am, I need to speak
with Mr Hudson immediately.'

From somewhere in the house a nasally voice yelled out:
'Erna? Who's at the door? Is it for me? I'm waiting for a
package.'

The nurse half turned and yelled behind her, 'No one for
you, Brooklyn. Mind your business.' Turning back to Lauren
she mumbled, 'Can't be bothered to come up for breakfast.
Now she sticks her head out of the basement like a gopher.'

'Ma'am,' Lauren said bluntly, 'I'm with the Homicide
Unit.'

Erna's brown eyes went wide for a second, then she opened
the door. Lauren tried not to let on exactly what squad she was
with until she had the immediate family present, but she could
tell she was going to meet further resistance getting into the
residence. Nurse Erna obviously took her job of taking care of
Mr Hudson very seriously. Stepping aside so Lauren could
come in, she held the door open for her.

'Mr Hudson is in the media room. Follow me, please.'

The interior of the house made it seem like it was unoccupied. Everything was brand new, everything matched
perfectly, and nothing was out of place. It could have been a
model home on display. Or a funeral home before a wake.

'The house is lovely,' Lauren commented as they passed a
huge unlived in living room.

'Mr Hudson had it custom built two years ago when he got
his settlement. He's very proud of the way it turned out.' Erna
talked over her shoulder as she led Lauren deeper into the
home. 'He has two maids to do the housekeeping, a landscaper,

and a handyman. He came from humble beginnings and he's determined to keep what he's built in fine order.'

'I can see that,' Lauren marveled as they passed floor-to-ceiling windows in a dining area. The view of Glass Lake would be spectacular in the warmer months.

'Erna!' The same disembodied voice echoed through the house. 'Who the hell is here?'

This time she didn't bother to answer, let alone turn around. 'That's Mr Hudson's daughter, Brooklyn,' she said as she pushed open a set of double doors.

'I might need to speak with her as well.'

'I'm sure she has no plans to leave her basement hideaway any time soon.' She stopped and motioned to another door in front of them. 'Mr Hudson is in a wheelchair. He was in a terrible accident some years ago and is in need of constant medical attention. Would you mind just waiting here for a moment before I let you in? I'd like to lessen the stress on him, if I could.'

Not possible, Lauren thought, but said, 'Yes, of course.'

Erna cracked the door. 'I'll only be a moment,' she told her as she slipped into the other room.

Clasping her hands in front of her, Lauren studied an abstract painting done in greens and browns hanging to her right. It looked like someone had framed some moldy moss snot and hung it on the wall. From inside the media room, she could hear the faint murmur of conversation. After thirty seconds or so Erna stuck her head out. 'Mr Hudson will see you now.'

Lauren didn't know what she had expected; maybe a stately older man in silk pajamas with a cashmere throw over his lap, gray hair combed back off of his high regal forehead. What she got was a shaggy salt-and-pepper haired man, not much older than her, in red, white and blue sweatpants and a stained Buffalo Sabres T-shirt. Nasty scars crisscrossed the left side of his weather-worn face, trailing down his neck. He sat in an expensive-looking motorized wheelchair, framed by the huge flat screen TV that covered most of the wall behind him. A projector from somewhere behind Lauren cast a dizzying display of sportsmanship against it. She had interrupted the hockey game he'd been watching.

There were no windows in the room and the walls were lined with sports memorabilia in shadow boxes, and framed posters of famous football teams. Dark and claustrophobic, it was more like an underground cave than a media room.

The man smiled, or at least did his best to with the only working side of his mouth, as Lauren came into the room.

'Mr Hudson?' Lauren asked.

'Yes. Would you like to have a seat?' He motioned with his right hand to the leather couches positioned in front of the big screen. His left hand rested immobile on the arm of his wheelchair. Lauren wondered if he was able to move it at all. Erna silently walked behind him and hit the mute button on a black remote sitting on a glass coffee table. A frenzy of passing continued in the background as he talked. 'Something to drink?'

'No, thank you.'

'Erna says you're with the police and want to talk to me?' His speech was slurred and jagged, like he had to gulp for air after every syllable.

'Are you John Hudson,' Lauren asked, for confirmation, 'father of Gunnar Jonsson?'

'I am,' he said with obvious pride. The way his sunken chest puffed up at the mere mention of the young man's name made her stomach twist a little.

'My name is Lauren Riley and I'm with the Buffalo Police Homicide Squad.' She paused for half a second before she rattled off the ugly truth of her visit. 'I'm truly sorry to have to inform you that Gunnar died last night.'

His chest deflated in that instant. Confusion flashed across his broken face. 'He what?'

'Gunnar was found dead last night near his hotel. I'm very sorry.' Lauren braced herself for what was coming next.

His head swung back and forth in denial. 'No. There's been a mistake. He was here all day yesterday. He didn't leave until almost six o'clock.' His eyes darted to his nurse. 'Tell her, Erna. Tell her Gunnar was here all day.'

Before Erna could speak, Lauren pulled her work phone out of her pocket. She already had Gunnar's passport picture pulled up. Walking over to Mr Hudson, Lauren handed him her cell. 'Is this your son, sir?'

He grasped the phone with his good hand and stared down at it. Behind him, out of his line of sight, Erna made the sign of the cross. His voice lowered to almost a whisper. 'How?'

'He was murdered.'

The phone slipped from Hudson's fingers and clattered against the polished hardwood floors. 'How?' he demanded again as Erna circled around his chair and draped a protective arm across his thin shoulder.

Lauren bent over and picked up her cell, stowing it away as she spoke: 'He was bludgeoned to death, in an alley next to his hotel. Sir, I know this is shocking and difficult, but I'm going to have to ask you some questions.'

Hudson's chin dipped down and he shaded his eyes with his good hand as he took a staggering breath. When he got some control over himself, he stretched his arm back out and looked up at Lauren. She watched as he gripped and ungripped the arm of his chair with his good hand. 'Did you make an arrest? Do you have the guy?'

Lauren shook her head. 'No, sir. That's why it's really important I get this information from you now. It could help the investigation.'

'Bludgeoned? Are you sure it's Gunnar?'

Actually, until his prints or dental records came back, Lauren was relying on his identification of Gunnar's photo for the positive ID. She hated to say the next lines: 'If you want to view the body before we turn it over to your funeral home director, that can be arranged. Does he have a spouse or other next of kin that needs to be notified?'

Mr Hudson broke into a spasm of coughing, causing Erna to quickly grab a box of tissues from a table next to her. She pulled two out and put them in his hand.

'He has a half-brother in Reykjavik. Apparently, his mother is dead. Gunnar wasn't married,' Erna filled in as Mr Hudson tried to catch his breath. 'That's why he was so happy to find his birth father after all these years.'

'Go get Brooklyn,' Mr Hudson finally said, turning his good eye to his nurse. 'Get her in here now. And call Ryan.'

Nurse Erna gave his shoulder one last comforting squeeze and hurried from the room. Lauren waited a moment and continued. She pulled her notebook out of her inside jacket pocket and poised her pen over it to jot down notes. Usually one detective asked the questions and the other writes down the answers, but Lauren was solo and she didn't want to risk losing any information or having to come back by not writing things down.

'Do you have a contact number for the brother in Iceland?'

Hudson shook his head. 'No.'

'Was Gunnar in a relationship with anyone?'

'I don't know.'

'Do you know anyone who would want to harm Gunnar?'

'You don't understand.' The words came out slightly garbled and he took a second to compose himself. 'I have no idea who'd want to hurt him. I never met Gunnar until he knocked on my door six days ago.' He turned his broken face up to Lauren's, and she couldn't help but think how similar his eyes were to those of Billy Munzert's father. 'I didn't even know he existed.'

EIGHT

'I was in the Air Force. Stationed right here, out of the Niagara Falls Air Force Base. It was the early 1990s. I was eighteen, green as hell, and they deployed us over to Iceland for six months. There used to be an Air Force base there, the Naval Air Station Keflavik. It's closed now. Right before I left to come back home, I had a one-night stand with Gunnar's mother, Katrin. That's all I knew about her – her first name.' He gave a bitter laugh. 'It was the only one-night stand I ever had in my life. I came home and met my future wife. I haven't given a thought about that night in years. Until Gunnar knocked on my door a week ago with those papers in his hand.'

Lauren was dumbfounded. 'And you have no doubt that you are his father?'

'He's the spitting image of my mother – got her nose, her eyes, same chin. Gunnar's mom in Iceland was as pale as a calla lily and just as delicate. As soon as Erna brought him to this room, well, I thought I was seeing a ghost. In a way, he even sounded like my mother. Then he pulled out those papers and showed me that my son Ryan was his brother.

'Gunnar did one of those DNA genealogy tests. When he said that, I remembered Ryan telling me ages ago he was going to take one. I'm such a mutt, I had no idea what it was going to say. Ryan phoned me and told me the initial results. He was still living out west then. It all seemed like a lot of nonsense to me. I never dreamed it would come back after all this time and say that I had another son.' His voice caught again on that last word.

'You had no clue Gunnar was coming to visit you?'

'None. But I was so happy. I've been on cloud nine since he showed up. I have a son and daughter. And two grandsons. I thought that was my whole family. And he was so wonderful. Gunnar had my mom's smile, her laugh. He was even built like she was, on the small side, but wiry.'

'I couldn't believe I was so blessed. I spent every day with him after that meeting, and paid for him to extend his stay here in Buffalo. I didn't want him to leave. He told me he'd just go home long enough to take care of some business and come back. He was an assistant to the CEO of a big shipping firm.' His words cracked in his throat. 'Do you have children?'

Lauren swallowed hard. 'Yes, two daughters.'

'Then you can imagine what it felt like.' Tears welled in his eyes but refused to spill over. 'It was a miracle. His existing and coming into my life, especially now. He was a gift from God.' He made another of those choking sounds. 'All because he and my son Ryan took a stupid DNA test. And now he's gone.'

There was something Lauren didn't understand. 'Your son didn't tell you about possibly having a brother when he got his results?'

Just as he was about to answer a tall, thin woman about twenty-one years old came bursting through the door with Erna in tow. 'Why is a cop here?' she demanded, walking up to her father wearing flannel pajama pants. 'Queen Erna won't tell me a goddamn thing!'

'Where were you last night?' Mr Hudson asked, his voice lowering an octave.

'Wait, what?' She took a step back and almost ran into Lauren.

'I asked where you were last night?'

Lauren absorbed the reality of what was happening. Mr Hudson was actually suspicious that his daughter had killed Gunnar.

Brooklyn Hudson's forehead creased in anger. 'I was at Lenny's. All night. I swear. We were playing *Fortnite*. You can ask him. What's going on?'

'Your brother Gunnar was murdered last night,' Mr Hudson told her.

Lauren didn't know what she had expected, but she absolutely hadn't imagined Brooklyn snorting with laughter as she said, 'Well, that's another gold-digging-relative problem solved, right?'

'Brooklyn!' Erna exclaimed, her hand covering her mouth.

'What? It's the truth.' She crossed her stick-like arms against her sunken chest. 'He shows up here saying he's my brother. And everyone just believes him. Why'd he wait until now? Why didn't he show up when you were just a garbage man, Dad?'

'Why didn't you?' Erna countered. 'You were living in Las Vegas with your mother until he finally got his settlement. You and your brother.'

Brooklyn opened her mouth to reply but Mr Hudson cut her off. 'Enough. I want you to give this detective all of Lenny's information, right now.'

She threw her hands in the air. 'What? No way. No way is Lenny going to talk to cops—'

There was steel in Mr Hudson's voice now. 'Then I will get into my van and take the detective there myself if I have to. And if I have to, you'd better be gone when I get back.'

Brooklyn's shoulders slumped in her retro Van Halen T-shirt as she repeated an address Lauren knew quite well on the east side of the city. The apartments had been known to house drug dealers for years. When she was briefly in Narcotics, they'd hit one apartment and the dealers would set up shop the next day in the apartment upstairs. Lauren wrote it down, noticing the tremor in Brooklyn's hands and the track marks on the inside of her elbow. Erna must have caught her off guard. Most junkies at least tried to cover up for the sake of appearances.

'Ryan and Kristin are on the way over,' Erna said, as Lauren finished jotting her notes on Brooklyn.

'Did you tell them?' Mr Hudson asked his nurse.

'I did. I hope that's all right, Detective?'

Not ideal, but what was done was done. 'Not a problem.'

'You better ask *them* where they were last night.' Brooklyn turned her venom on Lauren now, pointing a boney finger at Lauren's notepad as she flipped it shut. 'You better get their alibis because they had just as much to lose as I did.'

'Lose?' Lauren asked, a look of confusion flitting across her face.

'Do you really think this is the time, Brooklyn?' Erna was back at Mr Hudson's side, practically propping him up as he slumped against her.

'And you too,' she spat at the nurse. 'I'm sure you've managed to get yourself into my dad's will.'

'Brooklyn, you can go now.' Mr Hudson's face was red and blotchy. 'Unless you have more questions for her, Detective?'

Lauren shook her head. 'I will, but we can do that in my office later.'

'Good. Go downstairs, Brooklyn. Now.'

She didn't argue but Brooklyn Hudson's thin face twisted up in a look of sheer hatred as she stomped out of the room. Her father visibly relaxed when she left, sitting up straighter against his wheelchair, as if a great weight had just been lifted off him. *Does he have to go through hell with this kid every day?* Lauren wondered.

'What settlement were you speaking of?' she asked Hudson.

'I used to work for Garden Valley's sanitation department. Ten years ago, my coworker backed over me. The driver was the town supervisor's nephew and a drunk. He'd been out partying the night before and was still hammered when he came to work. I told my boss I wouldn't get on the rig with him driving and he threatened to fire me. Then I almost died. It took seven years and twelve surgeries, but I got a $17 million settlement.'

The light bulb flipped on in Lauren's head. It had been a high-profile case when it went down, and that's why his name had been so familiar to her. Gross negligence, his attorneys had argued, coupled with an attempt to cover up the extent of knowledge of the driver's drinking problem by the town's elected officials. A few people lost their jobs. Very sensational stuff. John Hudson was now a very vocal local advocate for better workplace safety laws.

'As you can see, I'm not in the best health,' he went on. 'My kidney was crushed. Now my other one is failing. I'm on dialysis three times a week. There's so much scar tissue and damage I'm not a candidate for a transplant. My days are numbered and those numbers are running out.'

'I'm so sorry to hear that.'

He waved off any sympathy with a shaky hand. 'It's nothing. Nothing compared to what happened to my son. I can't believe this. I can't believe he's dead.'

'I'm so sorry for your loss,' Lauren repeated, and she was. Discovering you have a child just to lose them was beyond heartbreaking.

'Did Gunnar know anyone else here in Buffalo?' She gently pressed on with her questions. 'Anyone at all?'

'No one. He only came to meet me. Meet his family. And now he's gone.' His uneven lip quivered a little. 'I followed Gunnar to the door last night. He hugged me before he got in his car and left. I watched him go. It was already dark outside but the moon was so bright. I called to him from the doorway to be careful and he just waved and smiled. I should have told him to stay here. I shouldn't have let him stay in a hotel . . .' The tears came freely and he made no move to wipe them away. Lauren heard the echoes of Billy Munzert's father saying he should have gone for the milk himself, the blame and regret and pain.

Lauren could see him starting to unravel, so she suggested: 'Why don't we take a break?' It was as much for her as him. She had to put Billy Munzert out of her head and concentrate on Gunnar Jonsson. 'Erna, can you make me some coffee while we wait for Ryan and his wife?'

'I think that's a good idea.' She bent down and adjusted the blanket over Hudson's lap and checked to see if he had enough water in his cup on the table. 'I'll only be gone a few minutes. If you need anything, call. OK?'

Grasping the joystick on his wheelchair, he nodded and silently turned away from them, facing the hockey game. Erna motioned toward the door and they left Mr Hudson alone.

'The kitchen is this way,' she said.

Following her through the house, Lauren kept her eyes peeled for Brooklyn, who apparently took her father's command to go back in the basement to heart.

The kitchen was done in classic black and white, including a checkered floor and dark-stained island with matching bar stools set around it. Lauren pictured a little Italian lady cooking Mr Hudson's meals at the huge modern black stove.

'Please, have a seat.' Erna said, motioning to one of the chairs, then immediately started fussing with the coffee machine.

'I'm so sorry to have to tell you this terrible news,' Lauren reiterated as she sat down.

'It's been an unbelievable week,' Erna replied, opening a cabinet and extracting two coffee mugs. 'First, Gunnar shows up out of the blue. Then both the kids went ballistic. They wanted to hire a private investigator, you know, to find out what he was about. They were afraid for their inheritance,' she said as she waited for the coffee to drip down into the carafe. 'Neither one of them had anything to do with their father until he got his settlement. Then they both hopped on the first plane from Nevada, where they'd been living with Mr Hudson's ex-wife, to be here. Ryan took that test before Mr Hudson got his settlement, while he was still in Las Vegas. He was probably hoping to find a rich uncle he could leech off of.' She gave a bitter laugh. 'He never would have taken that test nowadays. No way he'd risk finding more heirs.'

Lauren asked, 'Have you been with Mr Hudson long?'

'I've been Mr Hudson's nurse from the beginning. I was assigned to him from a temp agency two weeks after he was released from the hospital, when he was living in a one-bedroom apartment over a dry cleaner. He couldn't leave because there was no wheelchair ramp. When he had a doctor's appointment I had to call one of my sons to come over and carry him down the stairs until the state put a cheap-ass lift in for him. Where were the kids then? Nowhere to be found.' Erna shook her head in disdain as she poured the coffee. 'And now all they do is leech off of him. Cream? Sugar?'

'Black is fine.' Lauren's phone vibrated in her pocket, but she let it go to voicemail.

Erna gathered up the mugs and came over to the island. A glass sugar bowl and a little pitcher of cream were already sitting on a serving platter next to Lauren. 'Mr Hudson likes his coffee as soon as he wakes up,' she explained, sitting on the stool across from Lauren. Erna carefully scooped some sugar from the bowl into her cup. 'Although I suspect he waits until eight in the morning to ring me, because I know he doesn't sleep much anymore. And now this.' She propped an elbow on the island and leaned her head into her hand. 'This could really set him back.'

'You live here with him?' Lauren asked, even though it was obvious.

'I do now. When he had this place built, he insisted. I have three rooms on the second floor. A separate staircase leads to the outside from the back of the house. He has been so generous to me. It breaks my heart what his children put him through.'

Lauren sipped her coffee. 'Even the one who's on his way here?'

Her brown eyes narrowed. 'Especially him. Miss Riley, I don't pretend to know a thing about doing your job, but watch out for Ryan. Brooklyn is a needy, unstable addict, but what you see is what you get. Ryan is a whole other animal.'

'Meaning?'

She put her mug down and looked Lauren straight in the eye. 'Don't trust him. Don't you believe a thing that man says.'

NINE

Ryan Hudson was nothing like his emaciated, strung-out little sister. He and his wife, Kristin, came strolling in looking like a pair of Manhattan socialites. Reese liked to call people like that 'Beverly Hills by way of Buffalo,' a saying to describe those people who stumbled upon their money in one way or another and tried to mask their humble beginnings by being the most insufferable snobs possible, as if that gave them some sort of status. That was the first thing that popped into Lauren's head when Ryan offered her his hand and said, 'Ryan Hudson, how do you do?'

She wanted to say, *I just saw your brother with his head caved in, does that concern you in the least?* but replied with a tame, 'Fine, thank you. I'm very sorry for your loss.'

'This is unbelievable,' the wife said, opening the cabinet to grab two coffee mugs. Erna and Lauren were on their second cup when the couple had let themselves in and finally appeared in the doorway. Apparently, they felt there was no rush to talk about their murdered relative.

'Mr and Mrs Hudson, maybe you could answer a few questions for me before you go back to talk to your father?'

'I don't know what we'll be able to add. We only saw the man once when my father called us over here a week ago.' Ryan took the hot coffee his wife was holding out to him but neither of them made a move to sit with Erna and Lauren. Instead they both leaned up against the marble countertop, shoulder to shoulder. 'We spent an hour with him and went home.'

'And called our attorney,' the wife added, with the husband nodding slightly as he sipped his coffee.

'And you made no effort to see him again? He was your brother. I'd think you'd be interested in getting to know him.'

'Just because he had a piece of paper in his hand that said we were related doesn't mean he was my brother.' Color rose to Ryan's unnaturally tanned cheeks. He and his wife had either just gotten back from somewhere sunny or they were both hitting the tanning booth hard. 'Who knows whether he was a scam artist? Maybe he read about my dad's settlement and came up with this crazy scheme. I took that DNA test years ago. How do we even know he was from Iceland? He spoke damn good English for someone from another country.'

'I thought the same thing,' his wife said, her brown hair bobbing along in agreement. 'It was too good to be true.'

'Well, ma'am, I understand they teach Icelandic, Danish, and English to children in Iceland.' Lauren was not that smart; she had googled Iceland before she'd left for work that morning. 'And with the proliferation of genealogy sites, a great many people are now being united with relatives they never knew they had. According to the paperwork we found he only took his test recently and it matched to yours.'

'It all seemed very convenient to me,' Ryan said.

'Very,' his wife concurred. Lauren wondered if she always threw in a word or two of solidarity along with every statement he made. 'I read about the women and men from Eastern Europe who run these scams on unsuspecting people here in the States. If the Russians can hack our social media, they can hack one of those websites. Who knows? Maybe he goes from city to city pulling the long-lost-son scam.'

'That seems like a very elaborate scam – finding someone who visited Iceland thirty years ago, who's just come into some money,' Lauren said. Erna sat silently, clutching her coffee, mouth set in a hard line.

'When there's millions of dollars at stake, I'm sure it would seem worth it,' the wife replied. Lauren noticed Ryan gave his wife a quick shot to the ribs with his elbow. She stared straight ahead at Lauren and didn't even flinch.

Lauren's phone vibrated in her pocket again. She slipped it out, saw the call was from Doug and let it go to voice mail. She then seized the opportunity to open her photos to look at the date of Gunnar's copy of the DNA report. 'So that was the first you knew of Gunnar Jonsson? When you met him here in Buffalo?'

Ryan hesitated, just long enough to debate whether he should lie or not. 'I took that test years ago. I got the kit as a birthday gift from my future mother-in-law. All I've gotten in the last three years have been distant cousins. The website sends you a notification when there's a match. All of a sudden, two months ago I get a DNA report back saying I have a half-brother, but his profile was set to private, so I didn't know who he was or where he was from. I sent him a message but he never responded.'

'Is that why you didn't tell your father?'

'What could I say?' he shrugged. '"Hey, Dad, you have a son out there somewhere, but I don't know who or where he is." That wouldn't have been great for his health.'

Lauren wasn't buying it, but the Hudson family kitchen was no place to have that conversation. 'I hate to have to do this,' she told him, 'but I'm going to have to ask both you and your sister to come down to headquarters and give me a statement. Preferably later today.'

'A statement about what? I just told you every single thing I know about that man.' The red on his face was becoming more pronounced. A vein started to bulge in his forehead.

'It's standard procedure. I just need to document what you told me and also get your whereabouts last night on paper.'

'My whereabouts? I was with my wife and two small kids, at my home.'

'He was,' Kristin Hudson tossed in, 'home with us all night.'

Lauren stood up. 'Once again. It's standard procedure. I need your sister to come in as well. Maybe you could arrange to come down together? That way we can get it over with and I can get down to business finding out what happened to Gunnar.'

'This is ridiculous,' Ryan's wife said.

'I need to talk to you too,' Lauren told her, buttoning up her coat.

'Me? Why?'

Lauren wanted to say because she was Ryan's alibi, but once again held her tongue. 'I'll need statements from all of you, including Erna. But I'll wait on that until Mr Hudson has had time to absorb the shock a little.'

Ryan and his wife exchanged glances and then he said, 'I'll work it out with Brooklyn. Do you have a business card?'

'I was just about to ask you the same question,' Lauren countered, producing hers like magic from her coat pocket.

'I manage my father's investments,' he replied, taking the card from Lauren's fingers and looking down at it. 'I don't have a business card.'

'I can give you both his and Brooklyn's information on the way out,' Erna said. She rose from her stool, gathered up their cups and deposited them in the sink.

'Always the helper, aren't you?' Ryan said to her as she passed by him.

'That I am,' she called over her shoulder. Lauren saw the look he gave Erna when she followed her out of the kitchen. There was no love lost between those two.

Lauren jotted down both Ryan's and Brooklyn's cell numbers as Erna led the way back to the front door.

'I'm no private eye, but you know what I noticed, Detective Riley?' she asked as she held the door open for Lauren. 'Neither one of those kids ever asked how Gunnar was murdered.'

'You caught that too, huh?' Lauren asked as she made her way down the icy steps.

Smart lady.

TEN

Lauren's phone vibrated in her pocket again as she drove away in the sergeant's SUV. Someone was trying like hell to get ahold of her. She didn't have her power cord to plug into the truck's system, and she didn't want to get on her phone while she was driving on a sheet of ice. She'd be back at headquarters soon enough. She could see and hear the calls being put out by the dispatcher over the radio and scrolling down the computer mounted to the dash, so she knew it wasn't a police emergency or another body. But she wondered if she should pull over and look. She needed to be reachable in case Reese needed something.

The roads were pretty empty, it being the middle of a workday, but Lauren took it slow anyway. The plows had gotten to the streets in the subdivision and to most of the main roads, but a tricky layer of ice had formed since the snow stopped falling. Driving during the winter in Buffalo is almost an art form: knowing when to turn into the skid, rock the car when you got stuck, use your momentum to push yourself over a snowbank. In North Carolina, her cousin's kids' school closed when there was two inches of snow. In Buffalo, two feet wasn't even enough for a half day off.

Lauren thought about how the notification went the whole way back to headquarters, dissecting it in her brain. She had one obviously distraught father on her hands, two selfish kids more worried about their cut of the inheritance than the murder of their brother, and a caregiver who was trying her best to shield her boss from his offspring. And it wasn't even noon yet.

Lauren parked in the sarge's underground spot once she inched her way into headquarters, and dug her phone out of her pocket as she headed for the stairs. Nothing from Reese. Four missed calls from Doug Sheehan. Two from the sergeant. Two texts, one from each of them saying the same thing: Call the office ASAP.

She made it to the Homicide wing as fast as she could, realizing on the way up she had turned off her portable radio to do the notification. She'd made every rookie mistake possible, except leave her gun at the Hudson household. Lauren double-checked to make sure it was still on her hip, just to be on the safe side.

'Sergeant Connolly wants to see you,' Marilyn told her as soon as she walked in. 'He's in his office.'

'Got it,' Lauren called back, making a beeline to his door. He liked Lauren, but he was not the kind of guy who does you a favor and then appreciates you going radio silent on him in the middle of a murder investigation. She fully expected him to chew her out as soon as she walked into his office.

Rapping on the leaded glass with her knuckles, Lauren eased the door open a little and stuck her head in. 'Hey, Sarge,' she said, pushing herself the rest of the way in the room. 'Sorry I didn't call you back. I was in the middle of the notification. Wait until you hear this one.'

'Lauren Riley, I'd like you to meet Special Agent Matthew Lawton.'

She'd been so focused on groveling her apology and telling her big news that Lauren had totally ignored the kid sitting in the room with the sergeant. He looked so young she thought he must be one of the eager new vendors that were always coming around trying to sell the squad paper or office supplies, not knowing you had to go through a whole bidding process with the city.

Lauren extended her hand and he stood up and shook it. Not too tall, and athletically built, he had neatly cut dark hair and a nose that looked like it had been broken at least once. 'It's nice to meet you,' he said. 'Looks like we're going to be working together on this.'

'Nice to meet you, too.' His hand was warm and his voice was deeper than she expected. 'Did the sergeant bring you up to speed on the case?'

'He did. And I can request those records for the bridge right away.'

'That'd be great,' she said as they awkwardly faced each other. He couldn't have been more than twenty-seven or twenty-eight, but that was just a guess based on him being an FBI agent. He looked closer to twenty or twenty-one, but Lauren knew the requirements of getting in the Bureau meant he had to be at least twenty-five. With a shiny gold wedding ring on his left hand, he looked like the type of Boy Scout who would marry his high school sweetheart, all clean cut and straight-laced. 'Excuse me,' Lauren told him as she turned away from his earnest brown eyes and addressed her boss. 'Sarge, I found out some very interesting things during the notification.'

Lauren rehashed the entire visit to the Hudson household to both of them. When she was done, the sarge leaned back from his desk, eyebrows knit together, hands now folded in his lap. 'You're telling me the dad had no idea he had a son in Iceland.'

'But the siblings did, at least the older one. And neither of them were very concerned that he'd been brutally murdered last night.'

The sergeant's forehead crinkled the way it did when something concerned him. 'You're bringing them both in, right?'

Lauren nodded. 'I told them I want them in here this afternoon. They weren't too thrilled about that either, but I want to lock them into their statements as soon as possible.'

'Make it happen.' The sarge straightened up, rearranging the stapler and tape dispenser on his desk. His big hands were fidgety that way. He'd been known to have a touch of OCD all the way back to their days in the police academy. 'And talk to the nurse in private, away from the house. Sounds like she knows more than she could tell with everyone there.'

Lauren put that to the top of her mental checklist. 'I want Gunnar's phone records. I'd love to know if he was talking or texting with either of the siblings while he was here.'

'I can take the phone over to the Regional Computer Forensics Laboratory and try to dump it,' the kid volunteered. 'Your sergeant showed me the crime scene and evidence photos. He had an older model smartphone without the six-digit encryption. We should be able to get into it. It might take a while, but we should be able to crack it. And I can send the transcripts to our interpreters to translate, if need be.'

'You work in the computer lab, am I right?'

'Yes.' His face flushed a little. 'I just transferred here from the bureau branch in Dallas. But I have my master's degree in computer science from the University of Arizona. I'm originally from Green Valley.'

'So this is your first winter in Buffalo?' Lauren asked.

He glanced at the snow falling lightly outside of the sarge's window. 'It's my first real winter anywhere.'

The sarge clapped his hands together, signaling they should move the meet-and-greet outside of his office. 'OK then. Let's work together and get on top of this thing. Special Agent Lawton—'

'Matt,' he cut in.

'OK, Matt,' the sarge conceded. 'Matt here says they have a liaison in the Netherlands who will contact the Icelandic authorities and put us in touch with his family over there. And please call Doug Sheehan, he's been blowing up my phone since Matt arrived.'

'Your truck is in your regular spot,' Lauren told the sarge, then turned back to Matt. 'Let's see if I can find you a desk to work from.'

'Thank you and good work on the notification and the background info,' the sarge called as they were walking back out into the hall. 'At least we have a jumping off point now.'

Instead of getting rebuked like she thought she would, Lauren got an attaboy. And an actual boy.

He walked next to her with his hands shoved deep in his suit pants pockets. 'I'm twenty-nine, in case you were wondering.'

Off by a couple years, but she was in the ballpark. 'I wasn't,' she lied.

'I know I look a little young.' He looked a lot young. Matt looked like he should be playing college baseball, catching fly balls, not catching killers.

'So did I, once.' Lauren smiled at him, knowing what it was like to be judged for your looks. 'A long, long time ago, before this job sucked the life out of me. Don't worry, you'll get there.'

He laughed out loud at that. 'Thanks.'

She opened the door to her crew's office. 'You can take my partner's desk for now.' She led him over to Reese's workspace. 'He got a grazing gunshot wound in March, fell forward, and fractured his skull. He won't be back for at least another two months.'

'That sounds awful. Sorry to hear it,' he said, slinging the bag he was carrying onto the floor next to the desk.

'Not as sorry as I am.' Lauren straightened a picture of Watson she had displayed on Reese's desk in his absence. They had moved into the new police headquarters while Reese was still in the hospital. He'd never actually sat at his own desk yet. 'He and his dog are staying with me until he's cleared to come back to work.' She turned away from Matt. 'Cops make the worst patients and even worse houseguests.'

If Matt thought it was strange that she had her partner living with her, he didn't say anything. And she really didn't feel like explaining their relationship to him. Matt let that topic go and so did she. What would she say about it anyway? She wasn't sure how to categorize it herself anymore.

Matt sat in Reese's chair and surveyed the clutter. Reaching over, he touched the top of a Jim Kelly bobblehead perched on a stack of files with the tip of his finger, sending it bopping up and down. 'Do you think he'd mind if I—'

'Cleaned up a little? He hasn't even been in this new office yet. Just make a pile and stuff it in a drawer. I tried to recreate the actual paperwork tsunami that was on his desk. As you can see, it's in no particular order.'

Matt started to stack up the papers.

'This is my desk right here,' Lauren motioned to the next desk over. 'I have to return some phone calls. You good for now?'

He opened the bottom left drawer and slid a bunch of random items in. 'The sergeant made me copies of all the reports so far. I'll get on the family notification in Iceland. My boss has already been on the phone to the state department and the Icelandic consulate in New York City.'

'Thank God,' she told him. 'I had no idea who to contact. Believe it or not, foreign citizens don't get murdered much in Buffalo.'

'That's a good thing, right?'

'Right. But our investigations are usually a little more straight forward than this.'

Matt rocked back and forth, testing the chair. It was wobbly. 'You can wad up some napkins and stuff them under that leg,' she told him. 'That'll fix it.'

He looked like he was going to say something else about the condition of the office equipment for a split second, but thought better of it and instead asked, 'So what's our next move?'

'I want to bring the brother and sister in later, probably around four o'clock, give them time to stew and see if their stories change.'

'Suspicious of the family already?' He reached down into his bag, careful of the tilting chair and then plunked a laptop down in the middle of the desk.

'Homicide 101,' she replied, thumbing through her notes before putting them aside. 'Always clear the loved ones first. If you can. Then go on from there.' She picked up the receiver to the landline on her desk. She always used the old-fashioned phone when possible. Truth be told, she'd dump her cell phone altogether if she could. She hated feeling so *connected* all the time. Only the year before had her daughters managed to convince her to get on social media. She now had twenty-four friends on Facebook.

Matt didn't respond to that, and instead kept unpacking his things and she hoped he didn't think that she was talking down to him. Lauren didn't want them to get off on the wrong foot. She was only in her early twenties when she got into the police department, so she also had been hampered by looking young. She actually liked this kid already. He was eager and smart without being pushy. After almost twenty years on the job, Lauren was still working on the pushy part.

She punched in Doug Sheehan's number and waited while the phone rang in her ear. Just when she was about to hang up, Lauren heard a breathless, 'Hello?'

'Doug,' she grabbed a pen and started twirling it with her fingers, 'what's the emergency? I got caught up at the family's house doing the notification.'

'You're not still there, are you?'

'No, I'm at the office.' She bent forward over her desk and pulled her notebook to her. 'Tell me what Dr Heartly said.'

'Gunnar Jonsson had a total of seven separate blunt force trauma wounds: three to the face and four to the skull, effectively crushing it. Defensive wounds to both hands; scrapes and abrasions from trying to grab the brick. He was hit so hard a piece of it was lodged among the skull fragments.' In the background she heard some rustling, like he was getting out of bed. 'Did the father say he had a beef with anyone here?'

Lauren took a second to digest that last fact. 'The dad had no idea Gunnar existed until he showed up on his doorstep a week ago.'

'Really?'

'No clue. But his two siblings weren't too happy about it.'

'We got no idea who the assailant might be?' he asked. 'The family members check out?'

'I spoke to the brother and sister briefly,' she told Sheehan. 'They both gave weak alibis. I'm going to be following up on that angle.'

'Dr Heartly gave me her take on how the crime possibly went down. Want to hear it?'

'Let me guess.' Scribbling her notes as fast as she could, Lauren squashed the phone to her cheek with her shoulder and asked, 'Whoever did this struck him both in front and in the back?'

'Yes. From the stain pattern on his jacket and pants, the doctor theorized the killer knocked him to the pavement with a blow to the head. He must have managed to get on his back and tried to defend himself before getting up and trying to run away. The perpetrator just kept striking him. Vicious, is how Heartly put it.'

'And the brick? Any chance we can trace it?'

'Doubtful. Common construction grade. There are two sites within three hundred yards of the crime scene, doing repair work to buildings. It could have come from either of those. There must be thirty projects going on in downtown Buffalo right now.'

'You sound exhausted,' she told him, catching the hitch in his voice. Lauren was starting to feel the lack of sleep herself.

'I am. I'm at home. I just fell asleep when you called.'

'Go back to bed. The FBI sent someone here to help.' She saw Matt glance over at her. 'Come in when you wake up and I'll give you everything I've got so far.'

'Sounds like a plan,' was all he said and hung up.

Lauren took a minute to go through her notes before she turned to Matt, who was staring at her, waiting for her to address him. She wanted to make sure she had everything straight in her head before she spoke. Lauren used to tease Reese that he had no filter, so she started nagging him into practicing the fine art of pausing before he spoke, which sometimes made him appear like an idiot, other times like an ass, but it had saved him from countless embarrassments. Not all embarrassments, but enough.

'That was my temporary partner, Doug Sheehan. You'll meet him later, maybe. He went to the autopsy this morning. Our victim definitely died of blunt force trauma from multiple blows to the head and face.'

'I'd better call my boss,' Matt said, reaching for his cellphone on the desk.

'Just wait on that,' Lauren said, stopping him in mid-dial. 'Let's get the siblings in first. See what they have to say.'

He put the phone back down. 'You really like the brother or sister for this?'

'I really want to find out who did this to Gunnar. The siblings are the only leads we have right now. How long did you say it would take to get into his phone?'

He shrugged. 'Anywhere from a couple hours to a couple months, but I doubt it will take that long. Best guesstimate, with that brand of phone, a couple days at most.'

Lauren had to hand it to the Bureau, as much as local cops groused about having to work with them, they really did have access to so many more resources. 'I'm going to set up these interviews with Ryan and Brooklyn. Then we should take a ride to the hotel and talk to the cleaning staff. See what they remember about Gunnar.'

'I'll make sure the computer lab makes his phone a priority.'

Twenty minutes later they were in his spotless FBI ride heading back to the hotel. Both of the siblings tried to find excuses to blow them off, which was met by Lauren's cheerful offer to come pick them up, at which they kindly agreed to come in on their own. Ryan was coming in at four o'clock with his wife and would bring Brooklyn with them. She would divide them once they got to headquarters and interview them separately.

It never ceased to amaze Lauren how the light of day changed a crime scene. The mouth of the alley, which seemed so ominous the night before, now appeared as just a benign cut-through to the next street over. The crime scene tape had been removed and the news cameras long gone. She wondered if the hotel manager had sent someone to shovel away the bloody ice and snow that had clogged the walkway. *It's so easy to wash away the physical remnants of someone's horrific death*, Lauren thought. *But something always remains behind, doesn't it?*

'Park here in the fire lane,' Lauren directed, pointing to the spot next to the valet stand.

'We can't park there,' Matt said, eyeing up the no parking sign.

'Sure, we can. Watch.' Lauren unclipped her badge from her belt as the red-jacketed valet approached Matt's car. Rolling down her window, Lauren stuck the badge out. 'Buffalo Police, official investigation.'

The young valet nodded, holding his hands up as he backed away, retreating to the valet stand.

'If you get in trouble with your bosses, tell them I made you do it,' she said, gathering up her things.

'You made me? That'll go over with my SAC like a fart in church.'

'Your special agent in charge and I have known each other for a long time. He'll believe it.' She'd worked with his SAC on a detail years back, when she was in the Special Victims Unit, before he got promoted. He learned very quickly that Lauren's favorite tactic in getting her way was to annoy people into submission.

The hotel looked different in the December sunshine as well. Gone was the sparkle from the twinkling white lights strung up everywhere. Now evergreen wreaths popped in every window with bright red ribbons and holly berries. The grand tree in the lobby, which she hadn't paid attention to last night, seemed to loom over the front desk.

A young lady looked up as they approached. 'May I help you?'

Still with badge in hand, Lauren held it up for her. 'Detective Riley with the Buffalo Police Homicide Squad. This is special agent Lawton with the FBI. We're here about the murder last night.'

Her eyes went wide; her hand went to her chest. She leaned in toward Lauren and Matt. 'I saw it on the news last night. How awful. And the killer is still out there, right?'

'What's your name?' Lauren asked gently. She was definitely the easily traumatized, delicate flower type.

'Angela Nguyen. I'm the daytime front desk manager. Gunnar was such a doll. We loved having him as a guest here.' Her dark eyes started to look moist. 'I can't believe this happened to him.'

'You interacted with Gunnar a lot?' Matt threw in, trying to get her back on track. At least he knew the basics of interviewing techniques and how to apply them.

Angela's eyes turned to Matt. 'He was very nice. The quiet, friendly type, you know? He spoke perfect English. I must have asked him a hundred questions about Iceland the day he checked in. I wanted to go on an all-girls' trip there with my friends – because he said it was so safe.'

'Did he have any visitors while he stayed here?' Lauren asked.

'Just one, that I know of. The guy said he was his brother. Gunnar's husband came down from their room and the two of them had words in the lobby, then the brother left.'

'Husband?' Lauren asked.

'Mr Steinarsson checked in with Gunnar. Did you know that in Iceland women take their father's first name and tack *dóttir* on the back of it and men take their dad's name and stick *son* on the end? Even when you get married you don't change your last name.' She glanced around the lobby, a look of worry passing over her face. 'I haven't seen Mr Steinarsson all day. Is he all right?'

ELEVEN

'Are you sure he was Gunnar Jonsson's husband?' Lauren asked.

Now Angela stumbled a little. 'They checked in together. And after he explained about the Icelandic last names, I guess I just assumed.'

'But they were definitely a couple?' Lauren asked.

'Mr Steinarsson stayed in the room a lot while Gunnar was out every day. When Gunnar came back to the hotel, they went out together. They seemed very affectionate toward each other.'

The manager took a deep breath. 'Take your time,' Lauren told her. 'I know it's a shock.'

'I just never knew anyone that was murdered before. And right here, where I work. I can't believe someone would hurt him. He was so friendly and nice. He told me this was his first time in America, and he was so excited.' Angela sniffed and grabbed a tissue from under the counter, blowing her nose. The poor kid was probably right out of college, probably had never seen a fraction of the awful things people do to each other. The protective bubble of her middle-class world had just been violently popped.

'Can you check and see if Mr Steinarsson checked out? Maybe when you weren't working,' Lauren asked, thinking that one of the night managers might have assisted him when he learned of Gunnar's death.

She punched the keyboard in front of her. 'Mr Jonsson made the reservation. Requested a king-sized bed, but it looks like Mr Steinarsson was never put on the reservation.'

'And you're sure they shared the same room?' Lauren hadn't seen one indication of another man in that hotel room: not an extra tie, not two razors, nothing. If he had been staying with Gunnar, he had completely cleared out.

'He was staying in that room. I know that he called down here a few times to get more towels.' She gave a small, bittersweet laugh. 'That was the only thing unusual about them: they used a lot of towels.'

Lauren flipped a page in her notebook. 'Do you remember his first name?'

She shook her head. 'He was older than Gunnar, more formal. All I remember is him joking around that it's warmer in Iceland right now than it is in Buffalo.'

'Can you describe him to me?'

Fiddling with the top button of her pressed white shirt, she gave a good physical description: over six feet, blond hair that was graying at the temples, thin build and in his mid-to late fifties. 'And pale,' she added, 'but with ruddy red cheeks, like they were permanently wind burned.'

'Like a fisherman?' Lauren asked. It would seem like a crazy question but pretty soon Lake Erie would be crawling with ice fishermen. You'd drive by on Route 5 and they'd be walking across the ice with their poles and buckets to the little sheds they'd erected on the bumpy white-and-blue ice. Then you'd see them in the taverns later, faces and hands red, drinking beer or whiskey, trying to warm up. It was a sight to see once the lake froze over and people tramped out with their poles.

'Yes, but he wasn't like a local fisherman. He seemed very upper crust, if you know what I mean. Very sophisticated. And handsome. He was very handsome. Mr Jonsson hung on his every word.'

'When was the last time you saw him?' Lauren asked.

'Right before my shift ended yesterday,' she replied, still picking at the pearl button at her throat. 'He came down and asked where they could find a good chicken wing place within walking distance. I told him to try Giovanni's Wings and Subs on Main Street. That was a little before seven o'clock when I got off work.'

And less than two hours later Gunnar was dead, and the mysterious Mr Steinarsson had cleared every single thing connected to him out of their hotel room.

'I'll be able to check the Peace Bridge records, get a full name on who he crossed over with, and what time Steinarsson crossed back into Canada, if he left right after the murder,' Matt offered.

'Let's get on that right away,' Lauren agreed, then turned back to Angela. 'You said Mr Steinarsson came down and had words with someone claiming to be the victim's brother. Can you describe that man to me?'

'He was very nicely dressed. Brown hair. Average build.' She shrugged her shoulders. 'It got a little heated, then the man stormed out of the lobby. They didn't fist fight or anything like that.'

'Would you know him again if I showed you a picture?'

'I think so. Mr Steinarsson came to the desk after the other man left and told me that they did not want to be disturbed by that man again, and to tell him that Gunnar was out if he came back.'

'He wasn't extremely thin, was he?' Lauren asked, thinking maybe Brooklyn had tried to disguise herself somehow.

Angela shook her head. 'No. He was average. He looked like a businessman type. That's why I was so surprised when they started to argue. Why wouldn't Gunnar want to talk to his own brother?' Her brown eyes went wide. 'You don't think the brother killed him, do you?'

Time for damage control. 'Angela, it's really too soon to jump to any conclusions. And that's a serious accusation to make. Our investigation is still in the beginning stages.'

'OK,' she agreed, 'but I would definitely talk to the brother, if I were you.'

'I'm going to leave you my card,' Lauren told her, cutting her off before she launched her own investigation and put it on YouTube. 'Please call me if you think of anything else.' There was a gold business card holder on the desk in front of her. Lauren plucked one out. 'And I'll take yours.'

Angela took Lauren's card, studied it for a second, then looked back up. 'OK. Thank you. I hope you find the guy who did this.'

'We're going to try. Thank you for all your help.'

Matt gave her a thank-you as well and they turned to leave. 'Talk to the brother!' Angela called across the lobby, causing an older lady lugging several department store shopping bags to stop and stare at the retreating cops. Lauren raised her hand in an acknowledging wave. Seemed like everyone wanted her to take a closer look at Ryan Hudson.

TWELVE

'In the last six hours I've found out that my victim surprised his father with his very existence, was here with a man who has since disappeared, and the hotel front desk manager and Mr Hudson's nurse don't trust the brother, who apparently came and argued with the vanishing boyfriend.' Lauren let her head fall forward into her hands as Matt pulled out of the fire lane. She was starting to develop a migraine. 'And it's only three thirty in the afternoon.'

'Seventeen million dollars is a lot of reason to kill someone,' Matt pointed out.

'How does this mystery man factor in though? We should be able to see him leave when we get the hotel surveillance footage,' Lauren said as Matt turned onto Delaware Avenue and headed back toward police headquarters. 'None of the Hudson family mentioned anything about Gunnar being here with someone. And Ryan Hudson damn well didn't mention stopping by his hotel.'

Hands at ten and two on the steering wheel, Matt glanced over at Lauren. 'Sounds like both our victim and his family had some secrets.'

'Hopefully Hector Avilla came up with something on the video canvas,' she said. 'That would make life so much easier.' The new glass-and-steel buildings that had popped up on Delaware Avenue as downtown Buffalo revitalized itself over the last ten years seemed to loom over them on both sides. If someone had asked Lauren fifteen years ago about thirty construction projects going on simultaneously downtown, she would have laughed. For most of the eighties and nineties the city had been in decline, losing population and businesses. It never ceased to amaze her how everything had changed – seemingly overnight.

'Does that ever really happen for you?' Matt questioned with a slight smile as he checked his blind spot before changing lanes like a good motorist.

'For me, personally?' Lauren sighed. 'No, never. Not once.'

They found a parking spot in the police lot across from the building so poor Matt wouldn't have to worry about getting a demerit from his boss, or whatever the Feds did to rebuke their employees. Gathering up their things, they headed for the front door of the old federal courthouse-turned-Buffalo Police headquarters.

'I have a message for you,' Marilyn called out as soon as Lauren crossed the threshold into the Homicide office. 'And you're not going to like it.'

Lauren took a deep breath as she peeled off her coat and slung it over her arm. 'OK. Give it to me.'

Marilyn's glasses slipped down her nose as she read from a little rectangle of paper. 'Ryan Hudson called. He said he won't be coming in on advice of his attorney. He also said that his sister took off in her car, so don't expect her to come in either.'

'Son of a bitch,' Lauren muttered. 'I should have known better with those two.

Matt looked at Marilyn in disbelief. 'He called and cancelled, just like that?'

'Happens all the time, young man.' Marilyn poked her glasses back up, crumpled the paper in her fist, and let it drop into the trash can next to the desk. 'Welcome to the Homicide office.'

'So where do we go from here?' he asked, turning to Lauren. 'Our two main suspects just decided not to show up for their interviews.'

Lauren glanced at the time on her phone, then looked back up at Matt. It was five minutes to four. They'd made it back just in time to be told they'd been stood up. 'We write our reports. Then we go home. I had a long night yesterday, and I'm tired. Just because Ryan has a lawyer doesn't mean Brooklyn does. Hopefully she goes back to Mr Hudson's house. We'll pick things up first thing in the morning.'

Matt opened his mouth to protest, must have noticed the bags under Lauren's eyes for the first time, and snapped it shut.

'First thing in the morning,' she assured him, laying her

notebook on her desk so she could type up their activity report. 'Unless we get a call in on another homicide, then we'll be together for the rest of the night.'

She silently hoped the citizens of the city could behave themselves until morning.

THIRTEEN

'Hey! Pain in my ass, I'm home!' Lauren yelled as she stepped into her front foyer. Reese's dog, Watson, came tearing down the hallway from the kitchen, barking his head off with joy at her arrival.

'Good boy,' she said as she bent and scooped him up, carrying him into the living room where Reese was lying on her couch, watching a DVRed football game. With his head turned toward the big screen television, Lauren could see the railroad tracks of scars that crisscrossed his bald head. Sitting on the ground next to the remote was one of his numerous baseball hats. He used to wear them because he was a die-hard fan, now he wore them for camouflage.

'Hello, stranger,' he said, not taking his eyes from the screen. 'You didn't wake me up when you left for work this morning.'

Lauren allowed herself to slide into the overstuffed chair next to Reese, tossing her tote bag on the coffee table. 'I didn't want to disturb your beauty rest. I let Watson out, made us some breakfast, watched the news on my tablet, all without you missing a wink.'

Now Reese twisted around to look at her with his clear green eyes. 'I figured you caught a homicide. That's why I didn't bother you at work today. Thought you'd be deep in the zone.'

He was still handsome despite his scars, with his warm brown skin and killer smile. Almost six years younger than her, Lauren used to like to refer to him as the annoying little brother she never had. She hadn't said that in a while. Or thought it. Somewhere in the last few months her feelings had changed.

'You know me so well,' she exhaled, putting her feet up on the table. White lights twinkled on her fake Christmas tree. She'd always had a real one until last year, when Watson decided he liked to water it. Now, he snuggled against her while simultaneously licking her hand. 'Ew. No, stop, Watsy.'

'You must have had something good and messy for lunch. Watson approves.'

Lauren wiped her hand on her black pants, not worrying about ruining them. She had ten more pairs just like them up in her closet. 'Now that you mention it, I forgot to have lunch today.'

Now Reese sat up. 'Then it's a good thing I ordered a pizza already. It'll be here any minute.' He ran his hands down along his torso. 'I've lost so much weight I can't even harass you for your stick-like figure. We're getting to be Irish twins.'

'I don't think that means what you think it means,' she teased. He looked so comfortable on her couch in her living room in the five-bedroom colonial she'd gotten in her divorce settlement from her second husband. Reese had his own room with a private bath and separate entrance on the first floor. Built as an in-law suite, it was now home to Reese and Watson while he recovered. Lauren liked to needle Reese, but it was just the nature of their non-romantic relationship. With both her daughters away at college, the house had become too big and quiet. She appreciated the noise and chaos that Reese and Watson brought with them.

'I know what it means,' he countered, getting off the sofa and stretching out. 'Your daughters are less than a year apart. Irish twins. Me and you both look like skinny bean poles. And we're both part Irish, so there's that.'

'What about the fact you're biracial and I'm mostly Polish?'

He shrugged. 'Only one of us can be perfect. I guess that's me. I shouldn't have to be telling you this stuff after all of our years together as partners. It should be etched forever in your mind as fact.'

'Sorry, Mr Perfect.' She suppressed a smile; no need to encourage him. 'Do you want to hear about the homicide or not?'

The doorbell rang. Lauren lived in one of the only gated neighborhoods in the city of Buffalo. Reese must have called the guard and told them to let the delivery guy in. Watson jumped down and charged out of the living room, barking all the way to the door. 'I'll get it. I already set the table. Let's eat.' He clapped his hands and rubbed them together. 'I'm starving.'

Reese setting the table consisted of him putting two paper plates, two plastic forks and two folded up paper towels on the kitchen table. He and Lauren sat down and dug in while she relayed the facts of the case. He chewed loudly, with his mouth open, while dropping bits of crust to the waiting Watson. When she was done, he picked up the last slice and gazed over it at her. 'So why do you have that look on your face? You got two great suspects and seventeen million motives. That's more than we have with most of the homicides we get on the first day.'

'Last night was a full cold moon.'

Reese dropped his slice on the paper plate, wiped his mouth with his paper towel, and pointed at her. 'Don't you start with Billy Munzert. Do you hear me? Don't you do it.'

Lauren's pizza hovered in mid-air an inch from her mouth. 'What?'

'I took Watson for a walk last night and it was so bleary out you couldn't even see the moon.'

'That was later. After it got cloudy. I'm just saying there was one. A bright one. And when I went to do the notification with the dad—'

'Did the dad mention the moon?' Reese asked, tossing Watson a piece of peperoni.

'Yes.' She put her pizza down on the table.

'So you read into it and now, somehow, this case is related to Billy Munzert's?'

Lauren shook her head and pushed her paper plate with its half-eaten slice on it away from her. 'They aren't related. I know that. It's just I can't help thinking about Billy and how I promised his parents—'

'Which you never should have done.' Reese cut in.

'Which I never should have done,' she agreed, her face getting hot. *There's more to it than that!* she wanted to scream. *You didn't see the look on Mr Hudson's face, or hear how much he sounded like Billy Munzert's dad. It's not just about the moon.* 'But I did. And I owe it to them to keep trying.

And now I owe it to Mr Hudson to give this case everything I've got.'

'You always give every case everything you got. That's why between the two of us we've been stabbed, shot, and put in front of a grand jury. Lauren, you worked the Munzert case hard. You re-interviewed every person left alive in the file. You followed up on every lead. You can't keep banging your head against the wall. If a break is going to come in that case, it'll come. Someone will find his body, a snitch will talk in jail, or you might get a deathbed confession. But you've done everything you can do.'

Her appetite had completely gone. Lauren sipped some water out of the champagne stem Reese had put out. Her mouth was dry, her throat tight. Reese knew exactly what she was doing to herself. She'd seen Billy Munzert's father in Mr Hudson and was trying to atone for not solving his son's case.

'OK,' she said finally. 'But when you come back to work promise me we'll work on the Munzert case again.'

Reese reached down and let Watson lick his fingers. 'I don't have to promise you I'm going to do my job. Let's just do it, all right?'

She nodded. 'OK.'

'Have you heard anything on the DNA sample in CODIS lately?' he asked. When Lauren had all the evidence reprocessed, the lab techs had found a sample of DNA from an unknown male on the left handlebar of Billy's bike. Lauren had swabbed every single family member, childhood friend and neighborhood acquaintance, but nothing matched. The only thing she could do was have the lab put the sample into CODIS, the Combined DNA Index System. The national database, maintained by the FBI, contained millions of DNA samples. Once an unknown suspect's sample was submitted to the system, it was routinely run through to see if it would hit on another submitted sample.

'I called this morning. Don't look at me like that. I know they would have notified me right away. I just wanted to double check. And no, there was no hit.'

An awkward silence filled her kitchen. At one time it had been Lauren who told Reese how to run a case. She had broken him in when he first came to Homicide, taught him everything she knew about cold cases. More and more over the last few years their roles had changed. Now they were equals, but somehow that made Lauren uneasy. Because if they were equals, then she definitely couldn't put him in the little brother category anymore. And if he wasn't her little brother, what was he?

'So tell me again about this Hudson guy's nurse,' Reese said, breaking the silence. 'Erna? Is she hot?'

Lauren balled up her greasy paper towel and threw it at his face. 'She's old enough to be your mother.'

He ducked and smiled that thousand-watt smile of his. 'So what? You know I don't discriminate.'

'And a grateful nation of single women thanks you for that,' she replied, gathering up the paper and plastic products. Reese snatched a piece of crust off of his plate before she could dump it in the garbage, and slipped it to Watson. Maybe there was still some little brother in him after all.

FOURTEEN

'Good morning, Agent Lawton,' Marilyn called from the front desk. Lauren had left their office door ajar so she could see who was coming and going, anxious for Matt to show up. Finally getting seven straight hours of sleep was a blessing, but it also meant they had a lot to make up for. Every minute they'd spent at home the case had more potential to grow cold.

'Tired?' Lauren asked as he slipped through the door, shutting it behind him.

'Exhausted. The baby is teething. I couldn't sleep all night.' Lauren remembered those days. *Your babies will be grown and out of the house before you know it*, she thought, *and you'll miss these sleepless nights.*

'You'll get used to it,' she assured him.

'I thought the Federal Building's security was tight,' he said, hanging his coat on the rack in the corner. 'I had to swipe eight different doors and the elevator to get here, and this place is set up like a maze.'

'The security in our last building was non-existent. And you know this used to be the old federal courthouse, right?' She didn't know how long Matt had been in Buffalo, but she assumed he didn't know about her getting stabbed in her own office. She was grateful the brass had finally taken security measures seriously.

'I was informed by my bosses, but I didn't know what to expect.'

'Matt, what did you do before you got into the Bureau?' Lauren asked as she wiggled her mouse around to bring up the home screen on her computer. She'd already been in the office for a half hour, made some phone calls, and had coffee with the sergeant.

'I ran the Internet Frauds department for a bank.'

'I figured as much.' She took in his expensive suit and shiny black shoes. 'You don't look like a cop.'

'Just because I wasn't a cop doesn't mean I don't know how to work a case,' he said. Matt dropped his briefcase next to his temporary desk with a loud *thunk*. He was right to be a little pissed and Lauren knew it.

Seeing the deep frown creeping across his face, Lauren added, 'That's a good thing. I don't need a cop right now. I need a computer expert to track this mystery guy. Lucky for me the Feds sent me one.'

Placated, Matt gave her a half-smile and reached for the landline. 'I'll call and find out who Gunnar Jonsson crossed over the Peace Bridge with.'

'Thank you.' The gratitude in her voice wasn't exaggerated.

'I spoke to Erna, Mr Hudson's nurse, as soon as I got in,' she said. 'Brooklyn never came home last night.'

'So she's in the wind right now?'

'Junkies don't go far. Iceland is a lot farther. See what you can dig up.'

While Lauren worked on the numerous reports that went along with any routine follow up, Matt was making plays over at Reese's desk. Within a half hour he had the name, date of birth and citizenship of Gunner's traveling companion.

'Ragnar Steinarsson, age fifty-seven of Reykjavik, Iceland crossed the American-Canadian border with Gunnar Jonsson. He crossed back into Canada the night of the murder at 8:40 p.m.'

'We'd just made it to the crime scene and he was slipping out of the country,' Lauren said.

'Maybe not,' Matt said. 'Gunnar extended his stay, maybe this Ragnar guy decided to leave early. Maybe that's why Gunnar was by himself getting money out of the ATM.'

'Speaking of ATMs,' Hector Avilla came walking in with a sheaf of papers in hand, 'these are the stills from the one your victim visited. No one but him in the pictures.'

Lauren took the photographs from him, passing each one to Matt after she was done with it.

'Gunnar doesn't look scared or nervous,' Matt commented, handing the shots back to Lauren to add to the file.

'No, he does not. If he suspected Ragnar was going to beat him to death, he sure didn't show it.' Lauren turned back to Hector. 'Any other luck with the video canvas?'

'The security company from the hotel called. They got the subpoena and are getting the digital files together. The woman said they'll be emailed to you by the end of the day. Problem is, the company is in California and you'll be done for the day by the time that happens.'

Lauren wasn't in the mood for sitting in front of the computer all morning. 'That's hours of footage we have to go through. We can get to that later,' she told Matt.

'What about the city cameras?' Lauren asked.

'I got you some still photographs but they aren't going to help. That huge scaffolding is perfectly positioned to block the view all the way to the corner. You can't even see Gunnar approach the ATM, let alone the killer.'

'Figures,' Lauren replied.

Hector excused himself, grabbing his keys and jacket from his desk. 'I have to run to the holding center. There's an informant there with possible information on the case. Says he knows some things about some street robberies. He wanted to talk to someone right away. Could be related to Gunnar Jonsson's murder. I'll let you know. Oh, and Doug Sheehan called in sick. Good luck, guys.'

'Same to you,' she told him as the door shut. Hector couldn't sit still for more than a few minutes at a time. With his regular partner, Reggie, off on medical leave, Hector popped in and out of the office all day long, not content to even take a coffee break.

Matt hit some keys on his computer and Lauren could hear the copy machine outside their door rumble to life. He went out and returned in seconds, handing her some papers. 'I printed out the border crossing information from the Homeland Security database. I have a call into ARC – the Airline Reporting Corporation – and they should be able to tell us what airline Steinarsson left on, what flight number, right down to his seat assignment.'

Lauren nodded her head as she mentally tried to organize

that information. 'Good, good. All this is good. Maybe Hector's informant will pay off. If he knows about a guy doing street robberies, maybe he heard about Gunnar's murder and wants to make a deal.'

'Does that happen a lot?' Matt asked.

'More than you would think but we can't wait around and hold our breath. You have Gunnar's cellphone at your computer lab?'

'They're already trying to crack the code. It could be a couple hours or a month. There's no telling.'

Matt picked up his Tim Hortons coffee cup and took a sip. Lauren was glad to see that particular Buffalo fetish had rubbed off on him. 'Now what?'

'Now we go look for the sister. Let's take a ride over to Brooklyn's friend Lenny's house. Maybe he knows where she is.'

They gathered up their things, put on their coats and stopped at the front desk to let Marilyn know they'd be out on the street.

'Make sure you call it in!' Marilyn reminded Lauren as they walked out of the squad room door. Always the mother hen of the Homicide office, Marilyn felt it was her duty to try to take care of the infamous detective Riley. She rarely succeeded.

They took Lauren's detective car so as to not lose the prime parking spot for Matt's Fed vehicle. Also, the apartment building they were heading to was rough, so his pristine, polished ride would stick out like a sore thumb. It was too square to be a drug dealer's and too new to be a resident's. 'You know this place?' Matt asked as Lauren eased onto the Kensington Expressway.

'It's been a thorn in the E District's side for twenty years. It caught fire on New Year's Eve about eight years ago, but the out-of-state landlord rebuilt. It should have been demolished.' Lauren's eyes flicked from one mirror to the next as she watched the lanes of traffic. Rush hour was creeping up and the expressway was notorious for accidents.

Lauren pulled off at the Grider Street exit, heading left instead of right towards the Erie County Medical Center. She was silently grateful for that small thing. She'd already spent enough of her life in ECMC, between her getting stabbed and Reese getting shot. *Within four months of each other*, she thought as she pulled up to a red light. *We didn't even have the luck to have it happen on the same night.*

The building hadn't changed since the last time she'd seen it. Three stories high with its red paint peeling from the wood frame, it had once been a grand single house. Now it was chopped up into six shitty one-room apartments, each floor sharing a bathroom. Over the years Lauren had been there for a multitude of reasons: serving search warrants, looking for witnesses, arresting suspects. The faces changed, but one thing remained constant – it was a sad, awful, depressing place. The structure itself seemed to list to the side, as if the weight of the years and broken lives inside was dragging it down. An old shopping cart filled with a crusty layer of snow sat on the front lawn like a sentinel.

Parked out front was a brand new, cherry red Mustang.

'Brooklyn's here.' Lauren pulled across the street and threw her car into park. 'That car was parked in her father's driveway yesterday.' She typed a message to dispatch on her dashboard computer that they were on scene at the house on a follow-up. She waited for the dispatcher to reply with a message acknowledging, then she slumped down in her seat. Matt mirrored her.

They sat on the house for a few minutes, watching it. Lauren could see a well-worn path in the snow leading up the front walk onto the saggy porch. Foot traffic to the derelict building looked heavy. Sure enough, a rail-thin man in an old bubble coat came shambling out the front door. He looked left and right, pulled the coat tighter around himself then shuffled off the porch. He paused for a second to look at the Mustang and tried the passenger-side door handle. When he found it locked he made his way down the street, peering into every car window that he passed.

She unclipped her seatbelt and turned to Matt, leaving the keys in the ignition. 'Wait here. I'll go in and grab her. Then we'll take her to headquarters and get her on paper.'

'Hold up,' Matt said, brows furrowing. 'You want me to wait in the car while you go in there alone?'

'Look at yourself,' she countered. 'In that suit, with those shoes? You'll scare our witness. She's got to consent to come down. Besides, you want to bring roach eggs home to your baby? This will only take a minute. I'll be right back.'

The idea of cockroach eggs clinging to his shiny black shoes was enough to make Matt agree, with one condition: 'If you're not out in five minutes I'm coming in.'

'Give me eight.' She picked up her portable radio from the console and grabbed the door handle. 'I might need a minute or two to convince her.'

'Five,' he called as she closed her door on him.

Ignoring him, she crossed the street, looking both ways as the skinny crackhead had done. It was still morning but cloudy and overcast. The windows, with their make-shift curtains, gave no clues as to which apartments were presently occupied. She paused on the porch to look at the row of mailboxes, with names written on ragged slips of paper and taped on the front.

Leonard Able lived in apartment one. *Bingo*, Lauren thought, first floor. *Today's my lucky day.*

She twisted the outer knob and pushed the heavy wood door open. On either side of her she could hear the muffled sounds of people talking. From somewhere upstairs the smell of curry flooded the narrow hall.

Someone had tried to paint the apartment door a cheery yellow, but had only succeeded in making it look like the would-be artist had rubbed egg yolk all over the wood. A metal number one was nailed in the center, there was no peep hole. It had been kicked in recently, splinted wood had been roughly patched together to keep the door closed but it still sat slightly ajar. Using the butt end of her radio, Lauren knocked twice.

From inside she heard glass smashing. 'What the fuck? What the fuck is wrong with you?' Then someone else cried out.

She pushed the door open with her hip as she pulled her Glock out. 'Buffalo Police!'

Brooklyn was on the ground convulsing next to a ratty plaid couch, while a man with long hair pulled back in a ponytail and a thick beard knelt beside her. A broken bottle littered the bare, scratched hardwood floor by her feet. Another man stood slightly behind them, his head whipping up at the sound of the door flying open. He pulled a six-shot revolver from his waist band and drew down on Lauren.

'I ain't getting robbed again, bitch,' he growled. Brooklyn's mouth frothed with white foam as her eyes rolled back in her head.

'Buffalo Police!' she repeated. 'Put the gun down!'

'She's dying here, Devon!' the man who must have been Lenny screamed. 'Where's the fucking Narcan?'

'Did my probation officer send you?' A short guy, with shaggy brown hair, Devon had a face full of open sores. His position behind Brooklyn and Lenny didn't give Lauren a clear shot.

'No,' Lauren told him. 'I came to talk to Brooklyn. Drop the gun so I can help her.'

'The Narcan. Devon, where's the Narcan?' Lenny reached over and riffled through the trash strewn across a scratched up, garbage-picked coffee table. He grabbed a pink-and-white box, shook it and dropped it back down. It was empty.

'It's all gone, Lenny. I used the last of it two days ago.' Devon's eyes didn't leave Lauren. 'You go for that emergency button on your radio and I'll shoot you in the face.'

The fingers on Lauren's left hand had been searching for the little red button, while she was holding him at bay one-handed with her right.

'Drop the radio,' he told her.

She did, but only to bring her other hand up to double grip her Glock. The radio bounced on the dirty floor with a loud squawk. 'She's going to die,' Lauren told him. 'Put the gun down and let me help her.'

'Give her your fucking gun!' Lenny was desperately slapping Brooklyn's face and shaking her. 'She's dying.'

'I don't give a fuck. And I'm not going to jail for your bullshit.' Devon inched his way to his right, knowing the other two junkies were providing him with cover. 'She wouldn't have OD'd if she wasn't such a pig. That was the last of it.'

'Listen to me,' Lauren kept her voice even. 'I have Narcan in my police car. We all carry it. Drop the gun and I'll go get it.'

'No way,' Devon's eyes flicked to the open door. 'Drop your gun and let me walk out of here.'

Sweat glistened on his forehead and his hands were shaking slightly. Lauren wondered when he last shot up.

'Let her help my girl.' Lenny was pleading now. Brooklyn's chest barely rose under her black tank top. She was fading fast.

Devon shook his head, sending beads of sweat flying. He was dope sick and desperate, a volatile combination. 'Drop it now.'

It was an ultimatum, but Lauren knew you never give up your gun, ever. And their standoff had to end because Brooklyn couldn't wait any longer for that Narcan in her car.

Lauren had the best angle she was going to get. Her finger tightened on the trigger.

'FBI! Drop your weapon!'

Matt came in around the back of her, flanking Devon in on the left. Devon's gun swerved from Lauren to Matt as he tried to make sense of what was happening. Lauren squeezed the trigger. Devon fell backwards with a howl, revolver clattering to the floor next to her radio.

'You fucking shot me!' he screamed, clutching his right arm. Matt ran over and flipped him on his belly. The shot had gone through his upper arm, Lauren could see the bullet hole in the drywall behind him.

'Stay with us, Brooklyn,' Lauren said as she grabbed her radio. She quickly called for an ambulance, backup and a supervisor, not pausing to hear dispatch's response.

'Cuff him,' Lauren tossed Matt her handcuffs. 'I'm running out to the car to grab my Narcan.'

Matt, with Lenny's help, had pinned Devon to the floor. Brooklyn wasn't moving. 'Hurry,' was all Matt said as he yanked Devon's left arm behind his back. He clicked one cuff to his wrist, then clicked the other cuff around the leather belt holding up Devon's pants. Not ideal, but it would have to do.

Five minutes, Lauren thought as she raced across the street to her car. *The glorious little boy scout literally waited five minutes.*

If he had waited six minutes someone would be dead right now.

FIFTEEN

In all her years on the job, and all the trouble she had gotten into with Reese, Devon Crosby was the first person Lauren had ever shot. It was a through-and-through wound; the doctors at the Erie County Medical Center had stitched him up in no time. Poor Matt had his special agent in charge there at the hospital within minutes of them walking in the door, along with his supervisor from the computer task force. They'd led him away to grill him about what went down, leaving Lauren by herself to make sure Devon was treated, charged and sent upstairs to the ninth-floor lock-up – where the medical center had secure rooms for police prisoners – until Connolly showed up.

The homicide squad investigated all police shootings, even non-fatal ones, and the sarge had showed up to take care of business. Now they were waiting for Brooklyn to regain consciousness so they could talk to her.

Lauren's phone buzzed in her pocket and she checked it. Reese.

You sure you don't need anything?

She thumbed the tiny keyboard: *For you to feed Watson.*

Three dots and then: *I'll talk to you later.*

OK. She slipped the phone away. That had been the third exchange they'd had since she got to the hospital. A year ago she wouldn't have bothered to return Reese's texts. Now she made sure she always answered him in a timely manner. All it had taken was a bullet to his head to convince her he deserved at least that.

'Hell of a day,' the sarge said as they stood in the hallway of the emergency room. He was trying to fill in her silence with mindless chatter. Lauren could stand quietly for hours, and it unnerved some people, like her sergeant.

'It was legitimate,' she said. 'When Matt surprised him, I thought he was going to shoot.'

The sarge rubbed the colorless stubble on his face absently and looked at the closed door to the ER where they were still examining Brooklyn Hudson. Usually a good squirt of Narcan up the nose caused addicts to pop up like cork from a champagne bottle, but in Brooklyn's case she needed three doses just to bring her back to semi-consciousness. 'Good thing you only winged the guy or I'd have to place you on administrative leave.'

'Believe me, I would have rather he just tossed the gun,' Lauren said. She'd been placed on administrative leave at the end of March, and hadn't gotten back to work until she was 'no billed' by the grand jury at the beginning of August. It had given her plenty of time to take care of Reese, but she needed to be working. 'Are they going to take Matt back to the Feds?' She hadn't seen him since his bosses got to the hospital. As soon as his special agent in charge came through the sliding doors, Matt's face had fallen into a look of restrained worry, his forehead creasing, his eyebrows drawing together in a tight V.

The sarge shrugged. 'Who knows with the Feds? The poor kid is going to have a boat load of paperwork, that I can tell you for certain.'

A nurse in sky blue scrubs with white fluffy clouds on them stuck her head out of the exam room door. 'Detective? Miss Hudson is awake now. She's alert and she wants to speak with you.'

Raising an eyebrow at the sergeant, Lauren followed the nurse with him at her heels. They had Brooklyn Hudson propped up on a hospital bed, sipping water from a plastic cup, the thin gray sheet pulled up to her chin. She pulled the straw from her mouth and managed a weak smile. 'Hey.'

'Hello, Brooklyn,' Lauren said. Usually overdose victims whose friend you just shot weren't so happy to see you, or so Lauren had been led to believe.

'The doctor and nurses said you saved my life.'

Under the stark hospital lights, the dark circles beneath Brooklyn's eyes were in sharp contrast to her ghost-white skin. The track marks were red and infected in the crook of her exposed elbow. Her dark hair, so much like her deceased brother's, hung limply around her face. She looked older than her years and terribly broken. Lauren felt a pang of sadness at the state of ruin this young woman's life was in. She wasn't much older than her own daughters who were both thriving at college. 'I had to come looking for you when you cancelled your interview.'

'About that.' She put the cup down and covered her exposed arm with the sheet. 'I was ashamed and I didn't want to lie to you. My dad wouldn't give me any money and my bank account is way overdrawn. I took a ring that belonged to my grandma to a pawn shop, so I could get money to get high.'

'Do you remember which pawn shop?'

She nodded her head. 'If you look in my phone case, I put the receipt in there. I was going to get it back. If my dad knew I pawned that ring,' she took a deep, stuttering breath, 'he'd disown me for real this time. But I get so sick. So sick, you don't even know.' Tears ran down her cheeks and she tried to wipe them away with the corner of the sheet, smearing it with mascara.

Lauren turned to the nurse and pointed to the clear plastic bag sitting on a chair against the wall, 'Is that her property?'

'Yes,' the nurse said, reaching over and picking it up, 'and the phone is right on top.'

'Do we have your permission to open your phone case and look for the pawn slip?' the sergeant asked. He was all business. Until they established her alibi, she was still a person of interest in Gunnar's murder.

'Go ahead,' she sighed. 'I guess I don't have anything to hide anymore.'

Lauren took the bag from the nurse and fished out the phone. It was housed in a bejeweled plastic case that easily snapped off. Under the back cover was a single dollar bill, a torn piece of paper with a phone number on it, and a pawn shop slip. Lauren unfolded the slip and read aloud, 'December twelfth, seven fifty-five p.m., one twenty-four-karat gold ring with a ruby center stone, pawned for two hundred dollars at the Touch of Class Jewelry and Loan on Bailey Avenue.'

'I don't know what time Gunnar got killed but I went right

to my dealer on Seneca Street. I spent all two hundred there and then went to Lenny's. You can ask him.'

Lauren didn't tell her that they already had. The pawn slip just confirmed the story they had both given. 'Lenny's been very cooperative, and we appreciate that.'

'I heard someone say you shot Devon.'

Hospital big mouths, Lauren thought. Doctors and nurses could be worse than cops sometimes. 'You don't need to think about any of that. You just need to get better.'

Connolly moved forward a step. 'We'll need a swab of your DNA to compare to any evidence we might find.'

Brooklyn nodded her head, her hair falling over her eyes. 'You can have it. I know my fingerprints are already in the system, so you won't need those. I've been arrested a couple times.'

Lauren and Connolly both already knew that. 'Just a cheek swab,' he said. 'I'll send someone from evidence to come and do it.' Lauren usually took her own cheek swabs, but she didn't want to be carrying a box of evidence for a homicide around a hospital. When she took a sample she liked to get it into the evidence unit right away, either handing it off to one of the techs or putting it into the secure storage lockers at headquarters, to maintain chain of custody.

'Is my dad here?' Anxiety crept into her voice. *She isn't afraid he's here*, Lauren thought, *she's afraid he isn't.*

'He's on the way,' Lauren assured her. 'He might be here already. Erna had to get him up and dressed.'

She let her head fall forward and held her forehead with her hand. She was openly weeping now. 'This will kill my dad. First Gunnar and now this? I'm literally killing him. You should just lock me up.'

The nurse moved over to her bed side and put a comforting arm around her thin shoulder. The sarge cleared his throat loudly. He didn't do emotions very well.

'Nobody's arresting you. Only Devon is going to jail.' Lauren held up the pawn slip. 'We're going to hold onto this, if you don't mind. I'll check and see if your dad is here, OK?'

'Maybe you should have let me die,' Brooklyn sobbed, grabbing onto the nurse, clutching the clouds on her scrubs between her boney fingers. 'No one understands what it's like. I wake up and I'm sick. I never have enough. No matter how much I do. I'm not a bad person. I'm not. I just can't live like this anymore.'

The nurse shushed her, rocking her a little. The sergeant was practically out the door.

'I'm not here to judge you, Brooklyn,' Lauren told her, her voice softening in sympathy for the girl. 'I just want to find out who killed your brother. You're lucky that you have a father who takes care of you. Have they talked to you about going to rehab?'

She nodded, still weeping, into the nurse's shirt. 'I've already been there twice. I just got out. My dad thinks I'm clean.'

'Maybe the third time's the charm, honey. Don't give up. Get some rest. We'll talk more when you're better.'

'Thank you, Detective,' the nurse called as Lauren walked out with the pawn shop slip. She wondered how Brooklyn fell into heroin. It was everywhere now. Kids were dropping dead of overdoses every day, hence the police cars having Narcan stored in them. Her mind wandered to her own two daughters. She was sure at some point both of them had been offered drugs. She'd be naïve if she thought otherwise. Had one, or both, of them dabbled? Could one be hooked and hiding it? She'd seen both girls at Thanksgiving and neither gave any indication they were into drugs, but she hadn't been looking for the signs either. Seeing Brooklyn suffering in her addiction put the Hudson family dynamics in a new light for Lauren. Brooklyn was no threat to Ryan's inheritance. Gunnar Jonsson definitely had been.

Erna was waiting right outside with Mr Hudson bundled up in his wheelchair. 'Is she OK? The doctor told us she's OK.' Mr Hudson looked anxious and exhausted.

Lauren gave him a slight smile. 'She's all right. She wanted to know if you were here.'

'I'm here.' His good hand clutched the armrest of his chair. 'I'll always be here for my baby. Thank you for saving her life. I hope that bastard who pulled the gun on you goes to jail for the rest of his life.'

More like the rest of the month, Lauren thought, *but maybe a little longer if he violated probation.* 'He's in custody. I'm just glad I showed up when I did.'

'So am I. I told Ryan to get his ass down to police headquarters. I told him if he doesn't show up, he's out of my will.'

'That's coercion, sir,' the sarge piped up.

'Is it?' Hudson snapped. 'He can sue us all from the cardboard box he's living in. I want to know what happened to my son. And I have to make arrangements for Brooklyn to go right into a residential rehab as soon as she's released. If Ryan had anything to do with Gunnar's murder, I want to know, right now.'

Erna bent down and whispered something in his ear. He nodded in recognition and looked back to Lauren. 'Are you going to arrest Brooklyn or her boyfriend?'

'It's not illegal to overdose. And apparently, they used whatever dope they had, so there's no possession charge.' Lauren could see a little wave of relief pass over Mr Hudson's face. 'Only the fool with the gun is going to jail. I'm going back to headquarters now to talk to Ryan.'

'And do your statement about the shooting,' the sergeant reminded her.

'And do my statement,' Lauren repeated for Connolly's benefit, then she said to Mr Hudson and Erna, 'I'll be over first thing in the morning to talk to both of you.'

The cloud-wearing nurse stuck her head out again. 'Are you the father?'

'Yes.' He pulled himself up in his chair a little straighter. 'I'm Brooklyn's dad.'

She held the door wide open for him. Erna gave Lauren a grateful smile as she wheeled Mr Hudson past her.

'I've got to go find Matt,' Lauren told the sarge. 'I need that kid. If Reese is out of commission, I'll stick with him.'

'What about Doug Sheehan?' he asked, following her down the long corridor.

'He's ready for retirement. Matt Lawton proved today he's got my back. I need that.'

'Yeah, you do need that.' Connolly's face fell into a frown as he looked Lauren up and down. His gravelly voice lowered a notch. 'How are *you*? Are you OK?'

Lauren was unconsciously flexing her right hand, opening and closing it. She realized what she was doing and snapped it closed into a fist. 'I'm shook up. It's playing back in my head, you know? Over and over. What I did, what I could have done. I'm pissed off he made me shoot him. I'm glad he's alive.'

Connolly nodded as he walked the green line on the floor that led to the waiting rooms. 'Do you want some days off? Take a break?'

That was the last thing she wanted. 'No. I need to see this thing through for Mr Hudson.'

'That's what I figured,' he said. 'But if you need it, ask for it. You don't always have to go through everything by yourself.'

'I'm fine,' she replied. And she was. Or at least she would be. She'd been through worse in the last two years. Much worse. She wanted to tell Connolly she wasn't alone, she had Reese at home, but that might open a line of discussion she didn't want to get into right then.

SIXTEEN

Lauren and the sarge managed to find Matt with the special agent in charge of the Buffalo branch of the FBI near one of the comfort rooms. She'd known Sam Papineau for years, since he was a field agent and she was a new detective. He'd gone away to Washington once he got promoted, and then came back to head up the local office. They'd worked together on a joint human trafficking investigation when she'd been in the Sex Offense Squad years before, where they'd made six arrests. Lauren liked to joke with him, when they ran into each other, that that case was what had clinched his promotion. He kidded back that it was why he got returned to Buffalo, and not some place with palm trees. Lauren suspected that they were both right.

Sam Papineau was an average middle-aged guy: balding brown hair, not too tall, rounding belly, and an unmemorable face. The only thing distinguishing on him was his teeth. Extremely crooked and crowded and stained, Lauren could not figure out why he didn't get them fixed. *Surely the federal government has great dental?* She thought that every time she saw him. It was a struggle not to stare at his mouth when he spoke.

When he saw Lauren turn the corner, Papineau shook his head. 'I should have assigned someone else when they said it was you who needed help. Poor Lawton here just got off of probation.'

'I think he handled himself very well,' Lauren told him, trying not to be distracted by his teeth, as her sergeant reached over and shook Papineau's hand. 'He might have saved my life, actually.'

Papineau crossed his arms in front of his chest. 'I'm not worried about him; I'm worried about you. Did you step on a thousand cracks? Break a couple hundred mirrors? Let a whole herd of black cats cross your path?'

'I never took you for the superstitious type,' she countered.

'I'm not. But I've never heard of anyone having the bad luck you've had lately.'

Sergeant Connolly had no patience for Papineau. He cut right to the chase. 'Can she have Lawton back, or does the Bureau have to bench him for a while?'

'If he was the one who did the shooting, yes, his time with you would come to an end while we investigated. Since he was only a witness, he has some Bureau paperwork to do, then he's good to go.'

'We're going to need him to come down to our internal affairs and give a statement now,' Connolly said.

'I figured.' Papineau turned to Matt. 'Fax me copies of everything, Lawton. And don't forget to do a FD-302 as soon as you can.'

'Yes, sir,' Matt said. His voice sounded unnaturally stiff and formal. Lauren surmised he was still not at ease with his new superior. Papineau was a nice guy, but his humor tended to be on the dry side, so it took a while to know when he was serious or not.

'Are you both ready?' Connolly asked. 'I'm driving. I had a patrol guy bring your detective's car back to headquarters.'

Papineau clapped Matt on the shoulder. 'Not even twenty hours with Lauren Riley and you get involved in a shooting. That may be a new record.'

'Meaning what?' Lauren asked. They had a very good working relationship, but Lauren wasn't about to let him bust her balls without hitting back. It just wasn't in her nature.

'He saw you shoot someone today and this poor guy still has no idea what's about to happen to him.'

'What's going to happen to him?'

'You,' he smirked. 'The hurricane that is Lauren Riley.'

She shot Sam Papineau a side eye. 'My luck runs both ways. You know that as well as anybody.'

'That I do,' he agreed with a dismissive wave as he walked away from their little group toward the elevators. 'That I do.'

SEVENTEEN

Back at headquarters, Connolly went to the Homicide office, while Lauren took Matt and dropped him off with Michele Sutter, the captain of the Internal Affairs Unit. Sutter was waiting for him in a very crisp black pantsuit with a starched white shirt, her dark copper hair pulled back in a severe bun. The younger woman was always very squared away, not a wrinkle to be seen, not a hair out of place. Lauren wondered if that was how she made captain so fast – the whole 'dress for the job you want, not the job you have' mindset.

'Matt, I'll see you when you're finished.' Lauren told herself she was trying to maintain the confident façade she had put up for Matt's boss, Papineau, but what she was really trying to do was keep Sutter and Matt from noticing that both of her hands were shaking.

Ryan Hudson was sitting in interview room two when Lauren got back up to the Homicide office. It was almost ten o'clock at night, but his eyes were wide and alert. Lauren studied him on the monitor in the observation room, which was comprised of six little cubicles, each set up to watch one, or all, of the interview rooms. In the old police headquarters, you either had to stand in a narrow closet in the dark with the door closed, or cluster around a single monitor if there was more than one detective that wanted to observe the questioning.

Lauren watched him looking around, crossing and uncrossing his legs, trying to look comfortable and at ease, though he was clearly not. He had taken off his expensive coat and draped it over the back of his chair, showing off his red cashmere V-neck sweater and navy wool trousers. *He probably saw that outfit in a catalog somewhere and thought it would look good at the country club*, she thought.

There were no windows in the interview rooms, no clocks or decorations. They all contained two chairs and a desk, nothing more. There wasn't a thing to focus on except why you were in that room. And people's reactions were very telling. Sometimes Lauren watched a person for a half hour or more before she went in.

Poking the computer's touchscreen with her finger, Lauren brought up the other interview rooms. Ryan's wife sat in interview room three, scrolling through something on her phone, oblivious to her surroundings.

Ryan was definitely the one she wanted to talk to.

The good thing about videotaped statements was that there was no need to take notes. Lauren still carried a legal pad and a pen into the room with her, as well as a copy of his file. She wanted a visual reminder for Ryan that she had been working the case hard. And would still be working it, despite what had happened at his sister's boyfriend's apartment that day.

Ryan looked up when she walked into the room. 'How is Brooklyn?'

Sliding into the seat across from him, Lauren carefully arranged the items she brought in on the desk, purposely taking her time. She put the file labeled RYAN HUDSON on top of the stack. Before she'd gone in, she'd stuffed it with forty or so pieces of blank paper, making it look thick. Now his eyes fell on that folder and he stared at it, even after Lauren started talking.

'She's going to be fine. I left her with your father and Erna at the hospital.'

Ryan exhaled a breath of relief. 'I heard on the news there'd been a shooting there—'

'And you thought I shot her?'

'I didn't know what to think. The newscaster said it was an unidentified person, but then my father called and said I had better get my ass down here with my wife. I didn't know what to think,' he said again. 'The news shows don't always get things right.'

'On that,' Lauren said, 'we can agree. Brooklyn overdosed, someone else was shot.'

'Was it Lenny? I can't stand that leech.'

Lauren didn't bother to answer his question, throwing out

one of her own instead. 'Do you mind telling me why you cancelled our appointment? I would think you'd be eager to help me figure out what happened to Gunnar.'

He reached up and scratched the side of his neck. 'I talked to my lawyer and he said I didn't have to come if I didn't want to.'

'And now you want to?'

'I want to convince my father I had nothing to do with Gunnar's death. So yeah, I want to talk to you.'

Lauren slipped a Miranda card out of her pocket and read off the warnings. When she was done, she had him date and sign the card. Once that was out of the way, she put the card on the desk. Putting her hands on her knees, she leaned forward, cutting the distance between their faces in half. 'I know you lied about only seeing Gunnar at your father's house. I know you went to his hotel.'

Ryan put his hands up as if to slow her down. 'Whoa. I only went there to talk to him. I didn't lie. I never actually saw him. Some other guy came down.'

'Who was the guy?'

He shook his head. 'I don't know. I told him I wanted to talk to Gunnar, and he said no. I admit I was pissed. I had no idea who this guy was. Probably some goon who was in on the scam with him. He said he was Gunnar's companion.'

'You still think Gunnar Jonsson was trying to scam your father?'

Ryan's face colored as his agitation rose. 'I mean, yeah. Why else would he be dead? He probably brought that guy along to strong arm my dad and something went wrong. Maybe Gunnar tried to cut him out. Maybe a lover's quarrel. Who knows?'

'Did you out Gunnar to your father?'

He shook his head. 'No, because then I'd have to explain how I knew, just like I'm doing with you.'

'How did you know where Gunnar was staying? Did your dad tell you?'

Now he actually looked a little shame faced. 'I followed him. Not my finest moment but I needed to talk to him one on one.'

'Does your wife know you went to the hotel?'

'I told her I had to meet with the private investigator I wanted to hire.'

Lauren closed the gap even further. 'Seems like you lie to everyone. What else have you lied about?'

'Look, I told her I was meeting with a private investigator because I thought I could talk to the guy and figure out what his game was. When that backfired, I really did hire someone the next day and that's who I was with when you say Gunnar was murdered.'

'Can I have the name of this private investigator?' Lauren laid a hand on the file, as if she wanted to add that information to it.

He puckered his lips for a second, like a little kid who really didn't want to tell his secret, then spat out, 'Tony Borrelli. I was paying him his retainer and giving him all the background I knew about Gunnar, which wasn't much. I went straight from my dad's house at six and didn't get home until after nine that night. You want Tony's number?'

'I know Tony. He's a good PI. I know how to get ahold of him.' Lauren had let her own private investigator's license lapse almost a year before. Being a cop and a PI had gotten her into a lot of trouble over the years, and she had finally decided she was through with it for good. She still knew most of the players though, including Tony, who was a retired Transit cop and a really sharp guy. It would be easy enough to check out that part of Ryan's story.

'He'll tell you. I was at his office in Amherst on Sheridan Drive. There's no way I could have done it. I went right home, minus almost a thousand dollars.' He paused, shaking his head in disgust. 'Which now he says I can't get back. Can Borrelli do that? Keep my money?'

Reaching across the desk and throttling him was off the table, so all Lauren could do was remind him, 'A man was murdered. Your brother is dead.'

Ryan shrugged. 'I didn't even know him. I'm sorry he's dead, for my father's sake, but he should have never come here. What did he think was going happen?'

Lauren sat back in her chair wanting to put some distance

between herself and this repulsive person, interrogation techniques be damned. 'I'm pretty sure he didn't think he'd get
murdered.'

'Yeah, but that's what happens when you insert yourself
into other people's lives. Things go sideways.' He gestured to
Lauren. 'Look at you. You came looking for Brooklyn when
she didn't want to be found, and you shot someone.'

Lauren couldn't keep the disgust from creeping into her
voice. 'I saved Brooklyn's life. She was overdosing.'

A bittersweet smile turned up the corners of Ryan's mouth.
'You think you did her a favor?'

EIGHTEEN

L auren managed to wrap up the interview with Ryan
without strangling him. Surprisingly, he gave her a swab
of his DNA without an argument. 'If it convinces my
father I didn't have anything to do with it, take my DNA, my
fingerprints, whatever. I just want to be done with this.'

She talked briefly with his wife, who corroborated Ryan's
story. Finally, she got up to Internal Affairs and gave her own
statement about the events of that day. Matt had gone home,
probably figuring it was best just to get a good night's sleep
and start over again in the morning. Lauren imagined he must
be pretty shaken up as well, even if he wasn't the one who
pulled the trigger. She filed her activity reports, then texted
Reese and told him she was on the way home.

As Lauren packed up her gear, she couldn't stop running
the scene at the apartment through her head, thinking what
she could have done differently, second-guessing herself.
Ryan's interview had been a distraction from that. His cold,
heartless demeanor didn't sit well with her. She'd check with
Tony Borrelli and get Ryan's E-Z Pass records, but she felt
like she wasn't done with him yet.

It was almost one in the morning when she got in her car
and drove north to her gated community near Delaware Park.
As she pulled into her driveway, she could see her Christmas
tree was still lit and her living room lights were on. She was
just about to put her key in the lock when the door opened.
Reese was standing there in his Buffalo Bills red, white and
blue pajamas. He'd heard the car pull in. 'Shhh.' He put a
finger to his lips. 'Watson's asleep.'

He stepped back, letting her in, the warmth of her house
engulfing her.

'Come into the kitchen. I made you some tea.'

She followed him as he retreated toward the back of the
house. 'Is there whiskey in the tea?'

He looked over his shoulder. 'Of course. You think we're going to drink straight Earl Grey at one in the morning?'

Two steaming cups of tea sat on her kitchen table. They sat down in the chairs that had somehow each become their own when they started living together. It hadn't been a conscious choice, Lauren always sat facing the window and Reese always sat facing the door. Tonight, that little ritual held some comfort for Lauren as she wrapped her cold hands around the teacup. Reese had actually gone into the far cupboard and taken out the real teacups, instead of using his favorite Yankees mug or the Scooby Doo mug her daughter Lindsey had given her.

He'd also put a bottle of Jameson between them.

'How're you doing?'

She looked down into the cup, swirling the contents slightly. 'I know I did everything right and it still bothers me.' She laughed at herself. 'That's wrong. It doesn't *bother* me, it disturbs me. Or pains me or something I can't put into words. Like, it's bullshit he made me shoot him and did this to me.'

Reese waited a second for her to take a sip and then said, 'Do you think that's because of David Spencer?'

'I don't know.' She put the teacup down and opened her right hand. An angry-looking red scar crossed her palm from where a shard of glass had sliced through it. She'd had two surgeries immediately after the David Spencer incident, and although she'd regained full use of her hand, the scars would remain for the rest of her life. In more ways than one. 'I killed David Spencer. He'd murdered at least six people, shot you, and was trying to kill me. Everything that led up to it, all the shit that went down, it seemed like that was how it was supposed to end. With one of us dying.' She grabbed the bottle and added more whiskey to her tea. 'And then it would be finished.'

'You're still a cop, Riley. Cop shit is going to happen to you. It sucks, but you're tough. The toughest old broad I know.'

'If I was really tough, I'd punch you out for calling me a broad.' She gulped down the tea and whiskey mix.

'It's the thought that counts,' Reese said as he added more whiskey to his own cup.

Watson barked once in his crate from Reese's room and

they both froze like parents of a newborn, listening to hear if the baby was up or just fussing in their crib. When ten seconds of silence passed, they both let out the breaths they'd been holding. Once Watson was up, he was up for the day.

'Did you get anywhere on your homicide at least?'

'I don't know. I think the sister can be ruled out. But the brother?' She shook her head. 'He's got an alibi, but I can't clear him a hundred percent. I wouldn't put it past him to have hired someone to kill his brother.'

Reese ran his hand over his bald head, like he was feeling for the hair that was no longer there, tracing the lines of his scars instead. *Look at the two us*, Lauren thought, *beat up, marred and scarred*. But Lauren didn't feel too sorry for him. The scars on his head didn't deter women from constantly pursuing him.

'Murder for hire is rare,' Reese reminded her.

'I know. I'm reaching here. Hopefully we'll get some DNA off the brick or under the victim's fingernails. One of his gloves came off. But it will take weeks to get the results back.'

'You don't have any other suspects?'

Lauren recounted the story of the mysterious Steinarsson, whereabouts unknown. Even as she told him about the disappearing act, she knew what was going to come out of Reese's mouth before he said it. 'Put a pin in the brother, you need to find this guy from Iceland.'

Which was exactly what she was afraid he was going to say.

NINETEEN

Lauren knew something was going on as soon as she walked into the Homicide office. Marilyn looked up from her computer where she was inputting the payroll and whispered, 'All the bigwigs are here. They're in the War Room on the fifth floor. I think they're here for you.'

Lauren's eyes surveyed the Homicide squad. The hallway was empty and silent. Every single office door was closed. The usual morning ruckus was nonexistent, a sure sign that everyone was lying low. 'Is Agent Lawton here?' she asked Marilyn.

'He came in early and went into your office, but he must have gotten a text or phone call because he walked right back out. I think he's up there with the brass. He didn't take his coat with him.'

'Connolly?'

She pointed with her pen to his door. 'He's in there, waiting for you.'

Lauren tapped Marilyn's desk with her palm in thanks and headed for her sergeant's office. Everything could have changed overnight. The brass and the DA's office and the Feds might have decided that she was too much of a liability and needed to go. Swallowing hard, she rapped on Connolly's door.

He opened it with one hand while putting his suit jacket on with the other. 'Good. You're here. Everyone is waiting on us.'

'I got stuck in traffic,' she said, glancing at the clock over Marilyn's desk. She was only five minutes late.

'Doesn't matter. You're here now. Let's go.'

She held up her tote bag. 'Can I put my stuff away?'

He reached over, grabbed the bag, and threw it on the floor next to his desk. 'It's put away. Let's go.'

Marilyn's face was twisted in concern as Lauren walked past her, following the sergeant to the elevators. 'What's going on, Sarge?' she finally asked as they stepped into the empty car.

The sarge swiped the card reader and hit the button for the fifth floor. 'I got a call at seven this morning from the police commissioner that there would be a meeting at eight thirty with the district attorney, Papineau, and a representative from the mayor's office about the Gunnar Jonsson homicide.'

'Are they taking me off the case?'

The door slid open. 'I don't know,' he said gruffly, hands stuffed down in his pockets. Connolly hated the administrative part of his job. He just wanted to make sure his crew of detectives was doing what they were supposed to do and solve some homicides. Lauren knew what Connolly thought of the upper tier of the Buffalo Police Department: that they were politicians, not cops, and he made that sentiment known many times. Them making him and Lauren come to this meeting was an affront to his authority over his detectives. Lauren's shooting the day before had been properly handled, referred to internal affairs for review, and in his mind the decision to let her keep working the case should be respected, not second-guessed by upper management.

The War Room was the nickname they'd given to one of the old Federal Court's conference rooms, just off of Police Commissioner Barbara Bennett's office. It was smaller than the huge room the police academy had on the third floor, which was outfitted with audiovisual equipment for critical incident management. The War Room on the fifth floor consisted of a rectangular table with three chairs on each side and one at the head and foot. The chair at the head of the table was flanked on either side by an American flag and the flag of the Buffalo Police Department. A large window was positioned right behind the head chair, illuminating whoever sat there like some kind of law-and-order deity. Today Barbara Bennett was sitting there bathed in sunlight when they walked in, looking like some kind of avenging angel in her dress uniform, face set in a deep frown.

That was when Lauren knew it was serious. The brass only wore their dress blues for important functions or occasions. Lauren had just become an important function. Sitting to the left of Bennett at the table was Ansel Carey and Deputy Mayor Samantha Lloyd. On the right side was District Attorney Carl

Church, SAC Sam Papineau, and Matt Lawton. 'Detective Sergeant Connolly, Detective Riley, come in. Please,' she gestured to the only two open chairs. 'Have a seat.'

Connolly was ahead of Lauren, grabbing the chair next to the deputy mayor, leaving Lauren the seat at the end of the table. She realized she hadn't taken her winter coat off, or her gloves. Her knit hat was sticking out of her jacket pocket.

'I'm going to assume we all know each other and skip the formalities. We've had some developments in the Gunnar Jonsson case,' the commissioner began, folding her hands in front of her. 'Special Agent in Charge Papineau has been in contact with the State Department. Agent Papineau?'

Papineau cleared his throat and opened a small laptop in front of him. 'The Icelandic government has taken great interest in the case, for obvious reasons. Their consulate in New York City has been in constant contact with our office since the victim was identified as an Icelandic citizen. We've been keeping them updated on the case. Agent Lawton says that as of last night both the victim's siblings have alibis?'

The last question was directed to Lauren. Matt must have read the progress reports she filed the night before. She glanced over at him and he nodded ever so slightly. 'Ryan Hudson did give a statement last night that included an alibi witness. I haven't verified his story yet—'

'I have one of my investigators on his way to Tony Borrelli's office, and another to the pawn shop as we speak,' Carl Church said, cutting her off.

Lauren and Carl had a lot of history, not all of it good.

He had his hands clasped in front of him as well, leaning back, relaxed in his chair. Lauren used to tease Reese when he first started shaving his head that he looked like Church, but any resemblance ended at the bald head. Dark-skinned and fit, Church was a former marine who valued loyalty above all things. Lauren had violated that loyalty two years before with David Spencer, and was still trying to earn her way into his good graces again. Carl was a difficult man to read. Lauren didn't know if he was there to make sure she was off the case or on it.

'I don't understand,' Lauren said, looking around, resisting the urge to scratch her nose. The lemony scent of the wood polish the cleaners used on the table burned in her nostrils. They must have cleaned the room right before the meeting started. 'Why are your investigators working our case?'

'The consulate and powers that be in Iceland want this matter resolved.' Papineau's eyes slid to Matt, then back to Lauren. 'I've been keeping them abreast of the investigation. Agent Lawton's reports state that another Icelandic citizen was staying in Gunnar Jonsson's hotel with him and fled immediately after the murder.'

'Agent Lawton is pretty quick with forwarding his reports,' Connolly said. Lauren glanced at Matt again, who was concentrating his attention on his superior.

'The authorities in Iceland want' – Papineau looked down at his laptop screen – 'Ragnar Steinarsson either cleared or charged as soon as possible.'

'Wait a second, that's not how a murder investigation works,' Lauren protested.

'Do you have any other viable suspects?' Papineau asked.

'We're not done here. Hector Avilla was following up with a possible snitch. We haven't ruled out a street robbery. Hell, we haven't ruled out Mr Hudson's nurse, Erna, yet.' Lauren was pleading her case now, her voice rising an octave. 'They can't take over my homicide investigation. Commissioner,' she turned to Barbara Bennett. 'They can't take me off this case, can they?'

'They don't want to take it away from you,' the Commissioner assured her. 'They want you and Agent Lawton over in Iceland, following up.'

Sucking in a breath of surprise, Lauren's eyes went wide. 'Excuse me?'

'This is a very delicate matter,' Papineau continued, picking up where the commissioner left off. 'We have to consider that Mr Jonsson may have been murdered because of his sexual orientation, making it a hate crime. Murders are a rare event in Iceland. And the person who was with Gunnar Jonsson, Ragnar Steinarsson, is apparently a very well-connected businessman in Reykjavik. His country's government wants this matter handled expediently, effectively, and quietly, especially if Steinarsson turns out not to have been involved in the homicide.'

'I don't understand.' Lauren's head was spinning. 'They want us to go there?'

'There are less than four hundred thousand people in the entire country of Iceland. Right now, they are shocked and mortified one of their countrymen was murdered in America. To publicly name Steinarsson as a person of interest at this point would make matters worse.' Carl Church was speaking now, his baritone voice low, calm, and commanding. 'The Erie County District Attorney's Office in conjunction with the Federal Bureau of Investigation sent official letters rogatory to Iceland's Ministry of Justice this morning. We are expecting their reply within the next twenty-four hours.'

'Pardon my ignorance,' Lauren said, 'but what are letters rogatory?'

It was Papineau who answered. 'It's a formal request to the Icelandic Court system for judicial assistance in investigating Gunnar Jonsson's murder. In this case we're not asking them to take evidence from witnesses, we're asking for a police liaison to accompany you while you talk to witnesses. You'll want to speak to the victim's family, friends, coworkers. It'll go much more smoothly with a local detective with you. Ragnar Steinarsson is just another witness on the list at this point. If he, or any witness, is uncooperative and has to be compelled, then the liaison can help with that. You'll have no subpoena or arrest powers while you are over there.'

'Who is going to continue the investigation over here while we're gone?' Lauren was trying to process what they were telling her: somehow, she and Matt were getting sent to Iceland.

'Hector Avilla and Doug Sheehan will take it from this end,' Commissioner Bennett said. 'I'm aware that there were some street robberies that occurred the same night as the murder that need to be checked out, some assaults as well. The DA investigators will follow up on the siblings' alibis, talk to Mr Hudson's nurse, and go from there.'

'Am I allowed to follow up with them after you send me to Iceland?'

Bennett was twisting her wedding ring around and around

with the fingers on her right hand. She didn't like this anymore than Lauren did. They'd asked for assistance, not a hostile takeover of the case. 'Of course you can,' she said. 'I expect you to share your finding with your coworkers. Cooperation is the key in an investigation like this.' She'd stressed the word cooperation ever so slightly.

Samantha Lloyd, the deputy mayor, now piped up. 'The mayor and our office have been monitoring this situation closely. The victim's father is making arrangements to get Gunnar's body back to his half-brother in Iceland. We'll provide you with whatever resources you need to clear this case.'

Lauren felt like a pinball; she was being bombarded with information from all sides. 'It's almost Christmas. How long will we be gone?'

'You'll be gone for however long it takes to speak to all of the relevant witnesses,' Bennett told her. 'You two are traveling a long way. You wouldn't want to get back here and realize you missed something important because you rushed.'

Sergeant Connolly's gruff voice chimed in, 'I thought the US Marshals handled this kind of stuff.'

'Only if there's a warrant for a suspect's arrest. Then they travel to the foreign country for the extradition process. You're just going to interview witnesses. Who knows? Maybe while they're there, Hector and Doug will catch a break and make an arrest here. Then Lauren and Matt got a free vacation on our dime.' Sam Papineau was smiling, but it was a forced smile that didn't reach his eyes.

Lauren had to ask the literal million-dollar question. 'Why are you sending me when I just shot someone yesterday?'

Carl Church crossed his arms over his chest, the same forced smile Sam Papineau wore now gracing his face. 'Because John Hudson called my office last night and expressed sincere gratitude and total confidence in your ability to investigate this case,' he said. 'I believe he also expressed the same sentiments to the mayor.' Samantha Lloyd's head bobbed in agreement.

In other words, Lauren thought, *he's become a power player with his lobbying for work safety reforms, and he's a huge donor to you and the mayor's campaigns, and he demanded it. That's the only reason I haven't been benched. Carl and the mayor have to answer to their money. Politics in its purest form.* 'When do we leave?' she asked.

'As soon as we get the Icelandic court's response to our letter, you'll be on the next plane. Within forty-eight hours, no more than seventy-two, I'd imagine, with the time differences,' Papineau said. 'I'd start packing now, if I were you.'

'Look on the bright side,' Church said, opening his hands up in a welcoming gesture that didn't feel so welcoming to Lauren. 'It was two degrees warmer in Reykjavík yesterday than it was in Buffalo.'

TWENTY

M att left with Lauren and the sergeant when the meeting was over. Connolly waited until they were in the elevator before he turned to him and said, 'She was barely back from the hospital and you were forwarding reports to your bosses?'

Lauren jumped to Matt's defense. 'I set up the folders so that as soon as I add a document to the case file, Matt has access to it. The last thing we want is for anyone to think we're not being straight about something at this point. It sounds like a lot of people are interested in who killed Gunnar Jonsson.'

'Iceland is five hours ahead of us,' Matt pointed out. 'While we were sleeping, they were sending memos and emails trying to find out what's going on with this investigation. A foreign citizen killed on US soil is a big deal, Sergeant Connolly.'

Connolly waved off his protest with a meaty hand as the elevator doors opened to the second floor. 'I'm just pissed everyone wants to rush this. We can do it fast, or we can do it right.' That was one of Lauren's favorite sayings. She preached it to Reese all the time. 'We haven't even gotten the official autopsy report yet, and they want to send you two jet-setting around the world.'

'I want to go back and talk to Gunnar's father. Matt, I think you need to meet him.' Lauren trooped back into the office. Craig Garcia was making copies at the machine. He looked up, was about to say hello to the sarge, thought better of it when he saw Matt, and went back to it. A lot of cops didn't trust the Feds, and apparently Garcia was one of them.

'Do what you have to do,' Connolly told them. 'But document everything. We got the damned United Nations looking over our shoulders.'

Lauren and Matt stopped back in their office so Matt could grab his coat. 'Lauren, I'm sorry,' he began as he gathered up his belongings. 'Things are different in the Bureau—'

She held up her hand. 'Stop. This has nothing to do with you or the Feds. I've been around long enough to recognize when higher powers are at play. They want us to go to Iceland, we'll go.'

He let out a breath of relief. 'I just didn't want you to think I was undermining your investigation.'

'I don't think that at all.'

'The passenger manifest came in from ARC, the Airline Reporting Corporation.' Matt riffled through some papers on his desk and handed a paper-clipped report to Lauren. 'Steinarsson and Gunnar flew in on the same flight into Toronto, but Ragnar sat in first class and Gunnar sat in coach.'

She flipped through the paperwork. 'That's interesting. They shared a hotel room but didn't sit together?'

'I thought the same thing.'

She stuffed the pages into her folio. 'Maybe Mr Hudson can shed some light on this for us. Let's take a ride' – Lauren cranked the handle and held the door open for him – 'before we have to hop on a plane ourselves.'

'What am I going to tell my wife?' he asked, passing by her and back out into the hallway. 'The baby is teething and she's not getting any sleep as it is. And it's his first Christmas.'

Lauren shut the door behind her. 'Tell her you've become embroiled in an international conspiracy.'

He laughed out loud at that. 'I guess that's close enough to the truth.'

The ride out to the Hudson household was tricky. A nasty wind had whipped up over the lake sending sheets of snow flying sideways. Matt pulled his knit scarf tighter around his neck, even though he'd cranked the heat up in his vehicle. 'I can feel the cold coming through the windshield,' he said, fiddling with the controls on the dash.

'You've got thin blood,' Lauren said. 'And you don't know how to dress for the weather. What's with the dress shoes?'

'We have to maintain a certain standard in the office.'

'In the office, yes. But out on the street we wear boots. Hasn't anyone ever told you to keep your shoes in the office and change into your boots when you go out?'

'I'm not from these frozen parts, remember? I got here in September when the temperatures were in the high seventies. It was beautiful. Then the day after Thanksgiving all hell broke loose.'

'That was nothing.' Lauren recalled the six inches they got. In Buffalo six inches is a nuisance, not a crisis. The same could not be said of Matt's winter driving skills. 'Slow down, slow down! Turn into the skid.' Matt had taken the off-ramp corner too fast and sent them sliding on the ice toward a ditch. He corrected at the last second and they ground to a halt. A pick-up truck behind them blasted its horn before going around them.

Matt sat gripping the wheel, breathing hard for a second before easing back into traffic. 'You OK?' Lauren asked.

'I don't know how you live in this frozen tundra,' he muttered, keeping his speed well below the limit.

'I'd say the same thing about Arizona in August, I bet,' Lauren countered. 'One hundred and fifteen degrees in the shade does not sound appealing to me.'

'I guess it's all just what you're used to.'

'You better get used to this real fast,' she told him. 'They're sending us to an island called Iceland, remember?'

'How could I forget?'

'At least you can go on one of those *Game of Thrones* tours when we get there.'

Matt's face turned serious. 'Don't even joke about that. I loved *Game of Thrones* before it was cool.'

'Turn here.' Lauren pointed to the road that led to Hudson's development. 'It's going to be all the way on the end.' There was no need for further instructions because Brooklyn's Mustang was parked in the driveway radiating color into the snow squall like a huge red beacon. Mr Hudson must have had someone tow it back to the house overnight.

Erna met them at the front door. 'Mr Hudson was wondering if you would come today,' she said, ushering them in away from the cold.

'Did he think we'd left for Iceland already?' Lauren asked as she wiped her boots on a rubber mat.

'You can leave your shoes on,' Erna told Matt, who was

bent over, untying the laces on his right one. Lauren shook her head slightly and he struggled to quickly retie it.

They followed Erna to the kitchen this time, where Mr Hudson was eating. A peanut butter and jelly sandwich was cut up into pieces in front of him. He lifted his head when they came in the room. A little blob of grape jelly sat on his chin. 'Welcome back, Detective Riley.' He smiled with his half-wrecked face. 'Is this your partner? Sorry to have to meet you like this, with me eating a sandwich like a two-year-old.'

Erna zipped around the back of him and wiped his chin with a handkerchief she pulled from the front pocket of her scrubs. 'Thank you, Erna,' he said.

'Mr Hudson, this is Agent Matthew Lawton from the FBI. He'll be working with me on your son's case.'

'I'd shake your hand but I'm a little sticky.' He held up his good limb, wiggling his fingers.

'How's Brooklyn?' Lauren asked. Hudson angled his chair to get a better view of the both of them.

'She's on her way to a rehab in Michigan as we speak. I sent her boyfriend to one in Florida. She'll never get sober if he's not sober.'

'That's very generous of you,' Matt said.

'When it's your child, you'll do whatever it takes.' His voice had a certain edge to it, as if this was a mantra he kept repeating to remind himself of what was at stake. The sadness returned to his face and Lauren was immediately reminded again of Billy Munzert's father staring at her from the doorway of his living room. Like Munzert, despair seemed to radiate from Mr Hudson. They shared that same aura of extreme loss, a brokenness that could never be made whole.

As sympathetic as she was, it was time to cut to the chase. Lauren leaned against the countertop, crossing her arms in front of her. 'Were you aware that your son traveled here with a companion?'

Hudson looked confused. 'A companion?'

'Did you know,' Lauren repeated slowly, 'that Gunnar came to the States with someone?'

'No.' Hudson looked from Lauren to Matt. 'He never said anyone was with him.'

'Did he ever tell you he was homosexual?'

Erna put a hand on his shoulder protectively. 'I knew he was gay,' Hudson said. 'He told me the second day he came to see me. He didn't want me to tell Ryan or Brooklyn, since they already had enough reason to reject him. He wanted to let his existence sink in before he told them about his personal life.'

'How did you feel about it?' Lauren asked point blank.

'I was just happy to find him. I could have cared less who he was with. I think he was scared at first to tell me the truth because I asked right away if he was married or had any children. He said he wasn't and never had been, and no, he had no children. I think that's why he waited until the next day to tell me. I think he was afraid I was a bigot.'

'You have no idea who the man Gunnar came to Buffalo with might be?' Matt asked as he mirrored Lauren's pose next to her.

Mr Hudson shook his head. 'Gunnar said he wasn't married. He didn't mention a boyfriend. Maybe he really didn't trust me enough yet to tell me. Do you know who it is?'

'We have a name, that's it. He went back to Iceland, but you already knew all this, didn't you?'

His eyes cast down on his pieces of sandwich scattered across his green plastic tray. 'I knew a little. I knew you were looking for a man from Iceland, not that Gunnar came here with him. I know as soon as our courts get a reply from theirs, you're on a plane to Reykjavík.'

'You have good sources,' Lauren said.

His head snapped up. 'I learned a lot about politics and how they work during my civil case. I was a nobody then.' He gave a bitter laugh. 'I've been lobbying for reforms now for years. I've made a lot of connections. And money does talk, or at least gives you a voice. I'll spend every last penny I have making sure my son's killer is brought to justice before I leave this earth.'

'Why me?' Lauren was truly mystified. Of all the multitudes of resources available to Mr Hudson, he'd settled for Buffalo's less-than-finest.

'Because I know who you are, detective,' he said. 'I do have good sources and they told me all about you. I know what you'll do to solve a case. Or to save a life.' He handed the tray up and back to Erna, who took it without a word. She turned around, dumped the remaining sandwich bits in the garbage and slid the tray on top of the oven.

He turned his half-ruined face up at her. Once again Lauren was looking into the eyes of Billy Munzert's father. Her entire body tensed at the memory as Mr Hudson took a deep breath. 'I know you won't let this go until you find my son's murderer.'

Don't promise him, Lauren's reminded herself. *Don't make him any promises. You already made one promise you couldn't keep.*

'I'll try.'

'You're relentless,' he concluded with a grim smile. 'That's who I want investigating my son's murder.'

TWENTY-ONE

T wenty hours later, an Icelandair jet took off from New York City with an expected arrival in Reykjavik of 9:20 a.m., Icelandic time. Turns out the FBI had travel co-ordinators who made all the arrangements for both Matt and Lauren: flights, car, and hotel. Lauren found herself sitting in a window seat, with Matt squashed in the middle, of a five-and-a-half-hour red-eye flight.

How do I get myself into this shit all the time? she thought as the plane lifted off the runway, popping her ears. *I should be home doing last-minute Christmas shopping.*

Matt was busy next to her, trying to carve out a nest in his small space. While Lauren didn't take up much room, a man with shoulders as wide as a truck bumper sat on the aisle, unintentionally crowding him.

The flight had left at 11:55 – only five minutes late – and the captain assured the passengers that they'd make up the time in the air. It was a cold, clear night out; a million stars sparkled outside Lauren's window. Her breath fogged the glass slightly as she leaned closer to look, but her mind wandered back to her home as she lingered in that twilight between wakefulness and sleep.

Reese had not been happy with the strange turn of events. 'You know they don't send cops who just shot someone on all-expense paid vacations, right?' he'd asked her when she told him the news.

'I'm not in a position to say no,' she'd responded as they sat facing off in the living room – she on her chair, he on his spot on the couch. 'The commissioner could have just as easily put me on administrative leave until Internal Affairs comes back with their official findings.'

'This is why I need to get back to work.' Color was rising in his cheeks. 'You're out there, working with some rookie Fed—'

She waved her hand at him, cutting him off. 'I got in just as much trouble when we were partners. Matt's a sharp guy. You need to be one hundred percent before you come back.'

'Like you were?' he snapped.

'No, I wasn't, but I'm also not known for making the best decisions, right?'

He took a deep breath and exhaled before he spoke again. 'When do you leave?'

'It looks like they've got us on a red eye leaving from JFK tomorrow night at 11:50. I'll probably leave Buffalo around six p.m. or so.' Lauren studied his face for a moment, trying to decipher the emotions there. She didn't want to leave Reese and he didn't want her to go, but was she reading too much into his motivations? Or was she terrified she would see something that would change everything between them?

'Just be careful. Can you bring your gun? Do the cops carry guns in Iceland?'

'No, neither Matt or I can bring our firearms and the regular cops there don't carry them. There's a special unit called the Viking Squad that carry them, so they do have access to fire-arms if something extreme happens. What's funny is that Iceland has one of the highest per capita gun ownership rates among its citizens in the world, but almost no gun violence. It's a very safe country. Look it up.'

Reese wasn't convinced, even with all of Lauren's Iceland trivia thrown at him. His green eyes narrowed. 'You're going into an iffy situation without a safety net. Again.'

'We're just going to talk to his brother, Jakob, and try to find the man he came here with.'

'Who could also be the murderer,' Reese pointed out.

'Who could have conspired with the brother here to kill Gunnar. I'm not convinced Ryan isn't involved somehow.'

'You said the brother was fighting with your fleeing witness before the murder, so somehow they made up and are in cahoots? When I told you to find the witness I meant for you to have the cops in Iceland do it. The killer is probably some meth head running around downtown and they're shipping you off to a frozen island.' He shook his head. 'Maybe the district attorney does have it in for you. Maybe you're not the paranoid freak I'm always accusing you of being.'

'Carl Church isn't sad I'm leaving town,' she agreed, ignoring the paranoid freak part. 'I think he'd love it if I never came back.'

'Speaking of coming back, Lindsey and Erin will both be home on the twenty-first. What if you're still there? What if you get stuck over there for Christmas?'

Lauren's jaw clenched at the thought of her daughters being home for Christmas, and her not being there. Reese knew how to hit below the belt when he wanted to. 'Tomorrow's the sixteenth. Let's hope I can get this wrapped up by the twentieth.'

'The killer is here in Buffalo. They're sending you on a snipe hunt. Or a puffin hunt. Or whatever they hunt in Iceland.'

She threw a pillow at him, just missing his face. 'Stop it. Let me investigate. Just enjoy the holidays and get better. I already made arrangements for Dayla to stop in and check on you every day.'

He threw the pillow back, missing her completely and sending it gliding along the hardwood floor causing a dozing Watson to jump down from the couch, grab it, and give it some vicious shakes. 'If I wanted to be smothered with attention, I'd go stay with my parents.'

He'd lasted one week with his mom and dad after he got released from the hospital. On the eighth day Lauren found him standing on her front steps with Watson, his green army duffel and a plastic bag full of his medications. He'd been living with her ever since.

Lauren had recruited her neighbor from a few doors down to keep an eye on Reese while she was gone. 'Dayla has specific instructions on your care. I'm more worried about leaving Watson alone with you.'

Lauren deftly reached down, snagged the pillow from the little white dog and tucked it behind her back, slobber and all. Watson gave a bark of protest, but lay down in a huff at her feet.

'Just get back in one piece,' was how Reese ended the

conversation. Which was funny since Lauren felt like she was losing pieces of herself wherever she went lately.

As the plane hummed along, sleep finally overcame her, shutting out the memory of home, and she welcomed the darkness.

TWENTY-TWO

'Lauren.' A poke in her side woke her from a dead sleep. 'Lauren, wake up.'

She started at the unexpected prod to the ribs. Lauren's blue eyes fluttered open to the dimness of the cabin. Matt was leaning into her space, the large man on his right was snoring loudly with his head thrown back. The quiet was sprinkled with awed whispers.

'What's wrong?' she asked, going into her worst-case scenario default mode.

'Nothing,' he smiled, and pointed to the window. 'Just look. It's the Northern Lights.'

Her breath caught in her chest as she turned her head. Outside her window, ghostly streaks of green and pink and purple danced in the night sky. In all her life she'd never seen anything so magnificent, so magical. The plane seemed to be flying towards it and through it at the same time.

She felt small against its otherworldliness, yet blessed to be allowed to witness it, as if it were a gift bestowed on only upon a privileged few.

In that moment she felt that she was heading exactly where she needed to be going. That seeing the ethereal lights meant just as much as a full cold moon, maybe more. 'Thank you,' she whispered to Matt, 'for waking me up.'

'I couldn't let you sleep through this,' he whispered back, his cheek almost brushed against hers as he leaned in to get a better look. She glanced up along the row of windows to see the faces of other passengers pressed up in wonder against the glass. The people on the right side of the plane were either still asleep or straining to catch a glimpse from across the aisle. Lauren noticed the seat belt light on, preventing them from getting up and trying to get a better look. She turned her eyes back to the mystical show.

The silent symphony of light continued outside. She watched the swirling bands of color play across the sky until she somehow fell back asleep, dreaming in soundless shades and hues of greens and violets.

TWENTY-THREE

Lauren had woken up to the pilot's voice welcoming them to Keflavík Airport in English, what she assumed was Icelandic, and another language she didn't recognize. The time on her phone had automatically adjusted itself, telling her it was 9:35 in the morning, but no sunshine poured through her window. The sky was an inky twilight color, with just a hint of orange on the horizon as they touched down. All around her the other passengers were gathering up their belongings. She hit the Iceland app she had downloaded onto her phone. The sun wouldn't rise until 11:17 a.m. And it would set at 3:29 p.m.

'We have less than four and a half hours of sunlight today,' she told Matt, peering out onto the darkened runway as they taxied to the gate.

'I looked up all the sunrises and sunsets while we were waiting for the plane in New York City. I hope you're not afraid of the dark.'

She shook her head, standing up as soon as the seatbelt light turned off. 'I do my best work at night.'

'Let's hope so.' Matt waited for the large man to muscle his way forward, then stepped into the aisle to pull down both their carry-ons. 'We're not going to get too much daylight while we're here.'

'What's the name of our contact person again?' Lauren asked. They were stuck in the aisle, eyes forward, watching for the crew to open the cabin door. Matt's seatmate had lodged himself halfway up the plane, crowding a couple of touristy looking twenty-somethings with backpacks.

'Berg Arnason,' Matt replied. The door opened and they began to inch up the aisle. 'He's a detective for the Reykjavík Metropolitan Police.'

They followed the line out the narrow door, down the creaking hallway. Outside, a wicked wind buffeted the retractable metal.

'Did the Bureau send you his ID picture?' she asked as they stepped into the gate area.

'Of course. And I'm sure he has both of ours.'

The first thing that struck Lauren was how small the airport was in comparison to the sprawling JFK complex. The second thing was how clean it was. Everything was neat and tidy; no plastic wrappers on the floor, no gum stuck under the railings, no discarded magazines draped over the chairs. Lauren looked around the small bustling concourse lined with shops. A gift shop hawking Iceland souvenirs was just off to the left, selling not only T-shirts and spirits, but water, chocolates, and snacks. 'I need to grab a bottle of water. My mouth is like the Sahara Desert right now,' she said.

'I'll go to baggage claim. Watch for Berg,' Matt said, taking the handle of her rolling carry-on while adjusting the backpack on his shoulder. 'I'll meet you there.'

Lauren crossed the hall into the brightly lit shop. She grabbed two plastic bottles from a cooler against the far wall, then stood in line for the register behind an elderly white-haired lady in a gray parka. Lauren had Icelandic money in her pocket, coins and bills, but she wasn't sure which to pay with so she decided to use her credit card for her first purchase.

The lady in front of her leaned back conspiratorially. 'Only buy those first bottles and reuse them with water from the faucet. We have good water here. Right from the glaciers. Don't waste your money.'

'Thank you.' Lauren marveled at how the woman seamlessly went from perfect English to Icelandic as she turned to the clerk to pay for her purchases. Giving Lauren a wink, she took her bag and shuffled away into the terminal.

Lauren paid for her bottles, noticing they did, indeed, advertise themselves as being bottled glacier water, and went to look for Matt. Announcements in several languages over the loudspeakers kept reminding passengers to queue up for the next bus into Reykjavik. She saw a sign for baggage and followed the arrow.

Outside the windows that lined the terminal, the sky was still that crazy in-between-morning-and-night haze. She could see snow on the ground, but not much, maybe an inch or so, with a dusting blowing across the runways with the winds. She stopped to stare at a sculpture of what appeared to be a giant steel egg perched on some boulders in the middle of a pond. Coming through the side of the egg was what looked like the pointy tip of a wing. A group of tourists were taking pictures of it with their cellphones.

She made her way to the baggage area where she saw Matt standing near one of the carousels, next to a red-haired man.

That wasn't entirely accurate. He didn't just have red hair; he had fiery, flaming curls that framed an equally red-tinged face. Six foot one, with broad shoulders, he was about fifty years old, but it was hard to tell. Lauren guessed his complexion was what Angela from the hotel was trying to describe when she said 'like a fisherman.' He and Matt both turned toward her as she walked up. 'Detective Lauren Riley,' Matt motioned to his new companion, 'this is Detective Berg Arnason with the Reykjavik Metropolitan Police.'

Lauren's hand was engulfed in his as he shook it. 'Great to meet you, Detective Arnason.'

'Please, call me Berg.' His voice was deep and rich and his smile reached his eyes, which crinkled with deep laugh lines. Lauren noticed he had very straight, squared teeth with a yellowish tinge and the thought suddenly popped in her head, *This guy is a real life freaking Viking. I would not be surprised if he had a sword under that gray parka of his.*

'Berg is going to drive us into Reykjavík.' Matt swung his hard silver suitcase down off the carousel. 'It's a lot farther than I thought.'

'It's fifty kilometers from here,' he said. 'About a forty-five-minute drive, depending on the weather.'

Lauren tried to convert kilometers into miles in her head as she grabbed her own suitcase. *I should have paid more attention in math class*, she thought as she rolled her carry-on and her big suitcase behind her, one in each hand.

'Can I help you with those?' Berg asked, reaching out for her larger piece of luggage.

She smiled. 'I'm OK.' She didn't mind a man offering to help with her bags, but Matt was actually struggling with his, as one of the wheels was sticking and he was trying to balance his backpack on his shoulder at the same time. 'But thank you.'

Realizing Matt's distress, Berg didn't even ask his permission, he just slipped his arm up and snagged the backpack from him, slinging it over his shoulder. 'I got it, friend,' Berg said cheerfully, continuing to lead the way out of the automatic doors. Matt looked like a little boy trailing after his father, right down to the way his shoulders were slumped.

The wind hit Lauren full in the face as soon as she stepped outside. She'd always associated snow with a clean smell, like the rain and fog got a do over. Even so close to the runways, the air here smelled better, more *pure*, than the air during a snowfall in Buffalo. The cold stung her nostrils in a familiar way, but the scent made you want to inhale deeply, take it down into your lungs, and fill yourself up.

In contrast, Matt's whole body gave a shudder. While Lauren had dug out her brown parka with its detachable faux-fur-lined hood, Matt wore the same expensive wool coat and shiny black shoes he wore in Buffalo. It was clear he hadn't spent much time outdoors in the cold – probably just long enough to get from one heated space to another. Lauren also had multiple layers of thermal underwear packed in her suitcase. Layers were always the key in cold weather. Berg wore heavy black boots, dark pants and an unzipped, loose-fitting parka with no hood. The weather was nothing to him.

'Buffalo has cold, right? And snow?' he asked as he led them to an SUV in the lot.

'Lots of cold and snow,' Lauren replied. Matt's teeth were chattering.

'I went to Niagara Falls when I was a kid,' Berg said as he hit his key fob, opening the boot. 'I remember thinking there was a lot of snow.' He picked up each piece of luggage easily, sliding them into the back, putting Matt's backpack on top. He closed it with a bang. 'We've had some good weather the last two weeks. I'm hoping it lasts while you're here.'

'The weather reports said nothing major was expected,' Matt said, opening the passenger side door as Berg climbed in the front driver's side.

'The weather reports don't look out the window.' Berg turned in his seat to address Lauren behind him. 'If they did, then they'd know the weather in Reykjavik changes by the hour. Are you OK back there?'

'I'm fine,' Lauren replied. 'Plenty of room. I like that egg.' She pointed to the giant steel sculpture.

Berg laughed. 'The Jetnest? It is nice, isn't it? That's a jet's wing coming out, not a bird's. I love that it's the first thing I see when I come home from abroad.'

He motioned to more buildings in the distance. 'The Naval base Gunnar's father was stationed at was located here. We still have a small presence of your military. But now the barracks are used to house many of the foreign workers we had to bring in for the main airport.'

'Not enough people here for the jobs?' Matt asked.

'With the number of tourists we get now? No, my friend. It's like we get invaded every summer. There are literally more visitors than Icelanders. It's not so bad now in the winter months.'

Lauren watched the people pour from the airport doors and drag their luggage to waiting buses to take them into downtown Reykjavík. *They're outnumbered*, she thought as she watched the poor drivers struggle to load all the bags into the vehicles.

Berg put the Subaru Outback 4x4 into gear and pulled out of the lot. 'I was forwarded the case file from your Bureau, Matt. It's a terrible thing that happened to Gunnar.'

If she hadn't done some research, Lauren would have thought Berg knew the victim from the way he called him Gunnar. She had read that Icelanders rarely used last names when referring to people. It seemed the whole country was on a first name basis. That would take some getting used to.

Matt must not have read that Wikipedia page. 'Did you know the victim?' he asked.

Berg shook his head. 'No, I didn't know him. I'm familiar with Ragnar Steinarsson by reputation. His company is very successful. They've done quite well, even after the crash of 2008. He married Freyja Runarsdóttir, whose grandfather started it. She was a beauty queen when I was young. She was runner-up for Miss Iceland in the eighties.'

'Are they still married?' Lauren asked.

'I saw a picture of them from last month at a charity function in the online edition of the newspaper.' Berg shrugged his broad shoulders. 'But who can say what goes on between two people?'

'Our liaison spoke to Gunnar Jonsson's brother, Jakob. He confirmed that Gunnar worked for Steinarsson,' Matt said.

'I spoke to Jakob as well.' Berg's blue eyes met Lauren's in the rearview mirror. 'He said Gunnar's been Steinarsson's personal assistant for the past year. I told Jakob you'd be coming to speak with him. He's anxious to talk to you. He feels like his brother's murder isn't getting any attention since Erik Oddsson has come under suspicion of bribery.'

'Who's Erik Oddsson?' Lauren asked.

'A very beloved city council member who is being accused of being in the Russian mob's pocket. Very shocking. People are devastated. I was supposed to have a partner assigned to me to help you, but all resources were re-allotted to investigate Erik.' Berg let the SUV pick up speed on the highway. Lauren noted Berg's subtle accent; the Vs turned slightly into Ws in his mouth. 'It seems likely he could be arrested at any time.'

Lauren looked out at the serene, barren landscape stretching before her. 'It looks like we're on the moon,' she commented. The lack of trees was jarring, but the quiet stillness was also breathtakingly beautiful. 'I can't imagine a dirty politician somewhere so pristine.'

'Pristine to look at,' Berg replied grimly, 'but dirty under the surface. You'll see.'

TWENTY-FOUR

They discussed the homicide the entire way to the hotel, with Berg making them repeat things two and three times – not because he didn't understand, but because he wanted to be sure he was getting the story exactly right. 'We do have homicides here. One or two a year, mostly domestic situations or alcohol involved. But to be killed by a brick from a construction site? A crime like that is very rare in Iceland.' He seemed to mull it over in his mind while he drove. 'You don't have cameras on the city streets in Buffalo? We have them all over Reykjavík.'

'The view of the closest camera to the alley was blocked,' Lauren said.

'Let me guess,' Berg said, 'by construction equipment?'

'A huge scaffolding rig. It blocked the street view all the way to the next intersection,' Matt told him. 'The ATM camera at the bank showed Gunnar came into the vestibule alone, so that was no help.'

'Sounds like you haven't been able to catch any breaks yet,' Berg replied.

Lauren sighed. 'We're hoping this trip might provide us with one. We've come a long way to go home empty-handed.'

'Let's see if I can help you with that.' Berg's voice bordered on mischievous from the front seat. Lauren, who was usually excellent at reading people she wasn't romantically involved with, was having a hard time with Berg. He seemed deadly serious and recklessly merry at the same time. It was an oddly endearing combination.

The sun was just starting to peek from the horizon when Berg pulled into the crowded parking lot of their hotel, exactly forty minutes after they departed the airport. A modern four-story rectangular building, it overlooked Reykjavík harbor. It was squashed between high-rise apartments that must have had magnificent views. Across the icy blue water, the land seemed to bend around and get lost in clouds. On the other side of the busy street was a walking path that followed the coastline. People walked their dogs next to the snow-topped black rocks that made up the shore. Even though it felt like four in the morning to Lauren, it was almost the middle of the day for the Icelanders.

'You'll be tempted to go to sleep because it's dark out,' Berg cautioned as he helped get their bags out of the back, 'but don't. Take a short nap if you're tired, but set your alarm. Otherwise you'll be up and walking around at three in the morning. The dark of our winter days throws people off.'

'You'll be back around to get us?' Matt asked, accepting his backpack and grabbing the handle of his rolling suitcase.

'Make sure your cellphones and watches are correct. Don't forget the time difference. I'll be back at three o'clock to take you to headquarters. Maybe out to dinner after, if you're up for it.'

Lauren hadn't eaten since grabbing a burger at JFK during their layover. Nor had she had any coffee. A dull headache was starting to develop behind her eyes. She rubbed her temples, then grabbed onto the handles of her matching rolling bags, one significantly larger than the other. She was usually a very light packer, but her winter clothing was bulky right down to her wool socks. From everything she'd read about Iceland, its weather was even more unpredictable than Buffalo's. She had a feeling there'd be no Walmart handy to grab a new pair of thermal gloves if she needed them. The shops selling gear in the airport looked very high end. As fashionable as the clothes were, she'd make do with her own winter wear.

They waved their goodbyes to Berg and crossed the lot to the sliding doors leading to the lobby. Lauren had noticed in the airport a minimalistic aesthetic of pale wood, clean lines and white accents. The look was carried over in the hotel, but just like the Sussex back home, this hotel was done up in Christmas décor as well.

A handsome young man with hair so light it looked almost white was waiting behind the front desk for them. 'Welcome. Checking in?' he asked in perfect English.

Matt took the lead, as it was his Bureau's travel coordinators who'd booked their accommodations. 'Yes, thank you. Two rooms. Lawton and Riley.'

We must really look American, Lauren thought as she rolled her luggage up to the desk next to Matt. Behind the clerk, whose nametag read Oli, hung a large map of downtown Reykjavík. That set a light bulb off in her head.

'Do you have maps of downtown?' she asked as he handed her a key card.

'We do.' He bent over and pulled two maps from under the desk. He laid them on the pale wood and circled a spot on each map. 'We're here. All the landmarks and sites are clearly marked.' He went through them, touching each one with the tip of his pen, visibly proud of all his city had to offer.

'Thank you.' Lauren carefully folded her map and put it in her coat pocket. She'd examine it more closely in private once she got her bags upstairs.

'I'll meet you down here in the lobby at three. I'm going to try to FaceTime with Cara and the baby. Don't forget to set your alarm,' Matt said as they waited for the elevator.

'I'm not going to sleep. I'm ordering a pot of coffee.'

'Either way,' he said, 'I'll see you in a couple of hours. Welcome to Iceland.'

Welcome, indeed, she thought as she stepped into the elevator.

TWENTY-FIVE

Three o'clock came quickly for Lauren, especially after drinking the entire pot of coffee room service had brought up. She'd taken her contacts out after sleeping with them in on the plane and dreaded putting them back in. Finally, she decided vanity be damned, she was going to wear her black, square-framed glasses. She layered some cold weather long underwear under her usual black suit, opting for a light blue shirt just to add some color. Splashing some water on her face in the tiny bathroom, she looked at herself in the mirror. The usual bags under her eyes were minimal. She'd actually managed to get a couple hours of sleep on the plane, even with the Northern Lights show.

Running a brush through her short, dark hair, she mussed up the front a little. How different she looked from just two years ago when she sported long blond tresses and her vision was twenty/twenty. *Almost getting killed a few times makes you realize being over forty is a blessing, and all the baggage that comes with middle age is a necessary reminder that no one is promised another day.* She glanced down at the thick ropey line that crossed her palm. *I'm even proud of my scars,* she thought. But the mental ones, unfortunately, she was still working on.

Matt was waiting for her in the lobby, wearing the same expensive coat, blue suit with a white shirt and red power tie, a scarf that looked good but was paper thin, and those stupid shiny black shoes.

'I didn't know we were going on a photo shoot,' she said, joining him on a tan couch that arched around an oval ash wood table.

'Do you only have one black suit you wear every single day or did you spring for multiple sets?' he shot back good-naturedly.

She put her files down on the table and made a show of

running her hands down her unzipped parka. 'I have a great many black suits that all look exactly the same. People remember you better if you wear the same thing all the time.'

'Is there some science backing that hypothesis?'

'Possibly.' She eyed the coffee station across the lobby where a woman in a green sweater dress was pumping some steaming brown liquid into a white coffee mug. She was tempted to go over, but her heart was already pounding in her chest from the last cup she'd had. 'Did you talk to your wife? How's the baby?'

'She's good. Andrew is crabby, but extremely cute. It's his teeth. He wants to gum on everything.' Lauren remembered those days. It seemed impossible her daughters were twenty and twenty-one. In her mind it was just yesterday that she was bouncing one on her hip while the other cried to be picked up. She wished those days hadn't been so hard, flown by so fast, that she had appreciated them more instead of just trying to survive each day as a single mother.

The double doors slid open and Berg came striding in, snapping her out of her thoughts. Lauren appreciated the way he carried himself, broad shoulders back, chest out, oozing his personal blend of confidence and friendliness that made him so damn likable.

He squared himself in front of them, planting a fist on each hip. 'Did you have a nice nap?'

'No naps for me. I'm anxious to get started.' Lauren stood with her folio tucked under her arm.

'Yes, you do seem the type,' he commented with a smile. He had a day's worth of beard sprouting from his chin, just as red as his hair. 'How about you, friend? Get any sleep?'

Matt rose from the couch. 'I managed to squeeze in an hour. I forgot to close the shades and the sunlight woke me up.'

'Ah, yes,' Berg said. His coat was still unzipped, revealing a navy-blue sweater and black turtleneck. 'Window shades are very important here. In the summer it's light about twenty-three hours a day. Most of our windows have blackout shades.' He motioned toward the doorway. 'I checked in with my division commander while you were resting, told him I picked you up and we're going to see the brother today.'

'Aren't we going to Reykjavík Police Headquarters?' Lauren asked as they walked back out into the windswept parking lot. Unfazed by the wind whipping across the water, Berg's unzipped coat flapped on either side of him. Now that the sun was up Lauren could see mountains across the harbor ringed in white clouds.

'Not today,' Berg clicked open the doors to his SUV with the fob. 'I neglected to mention a few things to you this morning when I picked you up.'

Lauren got in the front passenger side this time. 'Such as?'

'The city council member being investigated . . . he's my cousin. I got called back to headquarters after I dropped you off. My division commander doesn't want me anywhere near the investigation or the detectives covering it until it's over.'

'Meaning what?' Matt asked from the back seat.

Berg threw the car into drive. 'They've been investigating him for quite some time. They say he had some police officials in his pocket. I didn't know anything about it, he and I were never close, but when the story got out two days ago, they gave me a choice: be put on a leave or be your tour guide. So here I am.'

'What about using your resources?' Lauren asked, forehead wrinkling in concern. 'Your local records, your databases?

'I can phone in whatever we need. I still have my departmental laptop. We're in good shape.'

'Can I go speak to your commander without you?' Matt's voice rose an octave. 'My superiors are going to want me to make contact with him.'

'They are in contact with him,' Berg assured him. 'As well as your State Department. And your police department, Lauren. Gunnar Jonsson's murder investigation is important, but the timing is terrible. I don't know how far my cousin's corruption goes, but if how they are treating me and you is any indication, it's a bigger scandal than they've let on.'

'So where are we going now?' Lauren figured it was just her luck. Or lack thereof. It seemed like everything that could go wrong with her investigation was going wrong.

'To Jakob Benediktsson's flat over on Sogavegur Street. He

lives over a clothing shop. I phoned him right before I picked you up. He's expecting us.'

Something struck Lauren as odd as they made their way through the narrow city streets lined with shops, restaurants and parked cars. 'Why are all the doors open?'

'We use geothermal power for heating. It's practically free here.' Berg expertly turned the car down a tight side street. 'The shops leave their doors open. It's welcoming, yes?'

Visions of her mother clutching her chest at such a thing filled her head. In Lauren's house growing up, the thermostat never went above sixty-eight degrees, no matter how cold it was outside. If you were cold, you put on another sweater. She and her sister were not allowed to touch the thermostat, ever, and heaven forbid she held the door open for a second too long. 'Do you think we're heating the outside?' her mother would screech from the kitchen.

'Very welcoming,' Matt agreed. 'And the Christmas decorations are great.'

'We take Christmas very seriously here.' Berg spotted a parking space and pulled up next to an impossibly tiny car to parallel park. 'We have thirteen Santa Clauses. We call them the Yule lads. Today Askasleikir, the bowl licker, comes down from their mountain home.' He put his arm around the back of his seat and guided the SUV into the spot with one fluid motion. 'He's my daughter's favorite. She puts food in a bowl and leaves it next to her bed. In the morning she'll wake up and it'll be licked clean. By me, of course, but she thinks it's magical. Tonight she'll get something extra special in her shoe.'

'Her shoe?' Lauren asked. They were parked in front of a store advertising real Icelandic woolen sweaters. The dummies in the front windows wore beautiful heavy cream-colored jumpers decorated with blue snowflakes and red zigzag patterns around the neck.

'Our children leave an old shoe on the windowsill. Now that I've told you, you'll see them everywhere. Each night until Christmas they'll get a small gift in their shoe if they've been good. If they've been bad the shoe gets filled with rotten potatoes.' He threw the truck in park and cracked the door. 'Jakob lives upstairs.'

'Did you ever get potatoes as a child?' Lauren asked.

The mischievous look came back over Berg's face as he smiled. 'Once or twice.'

Matt and Lauren followed Berg as he walked around the front of the shop and down a side alley to a metal staircase that led to the upper flat. The metal steps had rubber treads all the way up, clear of any ice or snow. A small shovel stood sentry next to the door. Berg pounded on the wood with one of his meaty fists.

Almost immediately the door opened. A short, thin man, younger looking than Gunnar, answered. 'Jakob? I'm Detective Berg Arnason. We spoke on the phone.' He motioned to the two of them behind him. 'These are the investigators from America.'

Jakob began to respond in Icelandic and Berg held up a hand, cutting him off. 'Please. In English. Can we come in?'

He nodded, seeming flustered he hadn't already invited them in. 'I'm sorry. I'm sorry.' He stepped aside. In one hand he held a mug with a tea bag string dangling from it. 'I just have so many questions. Thank you for coming.'

Berg let Lauren and Matt go in ahead of him. Jakob's kitchen was small, but had a very warm, cozy vibe. A teapot sat on the stove, steam curling out of its spout. A big orange cat sat on the kitchen counter eyeballing them. Jakob set his tea down next to the cat. 'Please. Let's go in the living room. We can sit there.'

Jacob's apartment wasn't much. In fact, from her seat on the taupe-colored couch in the living room, Lauren could see into every room of the apartment. Jakob grabbed a laptop off of the coffee table in the middle of the living room and tucked it away on some shelving behind him as he sat in the only chair, leaving the three of them squashed together on the sofa. 'I'm sorry,' he repeated. 'I tried to clean up. I can't seem to focus.' He shook his head as if to try to clear it. 'I can't believe this. I can't believe someone killed Gunnar.'

Lauren took the lead. 'Did you know Gunnar was going to the United States?'

Jakob nodded. He had the same small stature and delicate features of Gunnar, but the resemblance ended there. Jakob's

hair was blond and his complexion that mix of cream and
blush Lauren had seen on so many of the Icelandic citizens.
'Our mother married my father when Gunnar was five. He
was good to Gunnar, but I think Gunnar always wanted to
know who his real father was, especially because my mother
had no interest in contacting him.'

'Your mother never wanted to connect with John Hudson?'
Matt asked.

His eyes strayed over to a picture of a woman on the wall.
Painfully thin, she was looking straight into the camera and
smiling lovingly at the photographer, who was obviously
someone she cared very deeply about.

'Is that Katrin?' Lauren asked, gesturing with her head to
the picture.

He nodded. 'That was her right before she died. She told
us she only knew John Hudson for one night. Here in Iceland
there's no shame in being a single mother. She had a good job.
She had no need to find him. Then she met my father about
five years later. They married and had me. My father loved
us both. He treated Gunnar like he was his own. Then my
mother got sick.' Jakob paused for a moment, cupping his
hand around his mouth. Katrin's death was hard for him to
talk about. 'He moved closer to my grandmother when my
mother died. He came down to Reykjavík as soon as he heard
about Gunnar, stayed here with me. My father is heartbroken.
He just went back north yesterday.'

'What made Gunnar decide to seek out his biological father
now?' Lauren asked.

'When my mother died two years ago, Gunnar became
obsessed with finding out who his father was. He didn't act on
it for the longest time, I think because he didn't want to hurt
my father. But then it just sort of consumed him. He finally
gave one of those silly websites a go and a match popped up
right away. He was shocked. He ran into the living room and
held his phone under my nose, showing me the notification,
and telling me his father's name was John Hudson.'

'Have you spoken with Mr Hudson?'

Jakob gave a bitter laugh. 'Mr Hudson. My mother didn't
know his last name was Hudson. She didn't even know he

was John with an "h". That's why Gunnar's last name is Jonsson.'

Now he pressed his fist to his mouth, trying to keep himself together. Blinking back tears, he went on. 'I spoke to Gunnar's father two days ago. He's making all the arrangements to have Gunnar brought back here. I can't tell you how helpful that is for me. I had no idea how to get his body back from America. Mr Hudson said he can't travel to Iceland, but he wants to fly me and my father to the States after the new year for a memorial service. He seemed very distraught.'

'He is,' Lauren assured him. 'He was ecstatic to find out that he had another son and he's devastated by Gunnar's death.'

Jakob nodded, his mouth set in a grim line. 'Isn't that what every orphan dreams about? Finding their long-lost parent, and they're full of joy at their reunion? And now this.' He spread his hands out in front of him. 'Gunnar was murdered. Murdered.' He looked directly at Berg. 'How does this happen?'

'That's why they're here,' Berg told Jakob. 'To get answers for you and Gunnar's father.'

'I don't see how I can help.' The despair in his voice cut right to Lauren's heart. 'Gunnar was a very kind person. He never had an enemy. He kept to himself, minded his own business. No problems.'

'Tell me about his life here before he left for the States,' Lauren pressed gently, trying to keep Jakob on track.

'He worked for years for an IT firm. He hated it. So when the job offer to work for Ragnar Steinarsson came up, he took it.' His face became more animated now that he was talking about the good parts of Gunnar's life, instead of imaging how he died. 'It was hard work. He traveled a lot, with and without Ragnar. But Gunnar was a very organized person, that was his way. He was never late, he never missed an appointment, never forgot a birthday. It was like the job was made for him. He was very happy this last year.'

'What about his personal life?' Matt asked. 'Is there anything you could tell us about that?'

'I knew he was gay, if that's what you're getting at.' The anger crept back into Jakob's voice.

'Was he involved with anyone?' Lauren cut in, trying to ease the tension. 'We need to know who to speak with next.'

'I'm sorry,' Jakob apologized. 'I've always been very protective of Gunnar. I know you're just trying to find out what happened.' He took a deep breath and continued. 'He lived with someone for about three years. His name was Stefan. They broke it off about six months before Gunnar took the job as Ragnar's assistant. Gunnar moved out of their apartment and came to live with me. It's been tight, but Gunnar was hardly ever home.' The giant orange cat came creeping out of the kitchen, jumped up on Jakob's lap and glared at the three interlopers. Jakob absently stroked his head, used to the cat's intrusions.

'Can we get the ex-boyfriend's name and address?' Berg asked.

'Yes, but I doubt he'll be able to help you. My girlfriend and I saw him at a club here in Reykjavík the night before Gunnar was killed. He was with his new partner. They seemed very happy together.'

'You let us worry about who is or isn't worth talking to, my friend,' Berg told him. 'And don't try to play detective.'

'I'm a waiter in an Italian restaurant.' He reached behind him, feeling around on the shelf until his hand wrapped around a pen. Turning back without disturbing the cat, he scribbled something on a piece of paper he tore from a little notebook on the coffee table and handed it to Berg. 'I'll leave the detecting to you.'

Berg glanced down at the ex-boyfriend's information before pocketing it. 'Was Gunnar involved with Ragnar?' he asked bluntly.

Jakob seemed taken aback by that question. 'I don't know,' he said as if he was trying to figure it out on the spot. 'Gunnar worked six or seven days a week sometimes. I know he liked Ragnar's wife, Freyja. He did a lot of work for her as well. He never spoke about anything like that. Like I said, he was obsessed with finding his father these last few months. He'd spend hours researching on his laptop when he was home, printing out pages.'

'So there was no indication of a romantic relationship?' Matt asked.

Jakob shrugged helplessly. 'He didn't hide his relationships, but I didn't pry either. I never thought to ask. I just knew he was working a lot; long hours and business trips.'

'Can I take a look in his room?' Lauren asked.

'Yes, of course.' Jakob looked pained at the thought of this invasion into Gunnar's privacy. Lauren knew they'd have to wrap it up soon. Jakob was in a delicate state. 'It's the one on the left. He didn't have much. He wasn't one to collect things. Just a lot of new suits and good clothes. He had to dress well for his job.'

Knowing the three of them would never fit into the small area, Lauren stood up, giving the remaining visitors some breathing room. Then Jakob kept talking with Berg in Icelandic, asking him questions, while she crossed the living area into the tiny space that was Gunnar's bedroom.

She had to shut the door behind her to get fully inside. To her left was a closet full of suits, button-down dress shirts and pressed pants still in the dry cleaner's plastic. Several pairs of shoes sat on the floor in a neat line. To the right was a narrow bed topped with a single pillow in a teal pillowcase. It seemed too bright for the neutral décor of the room. Shelving on both walls held a few personal items: framed photos, a beer mug with a mountain graphic on it, some books. Against the far wall, under the window, was a blue-and-gray high-end mountain bike. A laptop sat on the small dresser next to the bed.

Bending over, she opened the drawers and riffled through the underwear, socks and T-shirts. The contents in the dresser held nothing of interest to them so she shut the drawers and turned her attention to the shelves above the bed.

She picked up a framed photo of Gunnar with his brother, mother and who she assumed was his stepfather. His mom was a petite little thing, with long blond hair and pale alabaster skin like Jakob. The resemblance was more pronounced standing next to each other. Katrin had an arm around each of her boys, both on the short side like her, but Gunnar's dark hair made him stand out. The taller man, who was Jakob's father, stood beaming next to the trio. A lush forest spread out behind them and Lauren absently wondered where the picture was taken. It was a loving family photo. She would have bet anything Gunnar's mother had given it to him framed as a gift. Lauren's mind flashed back to Billy Munzert's family. How broken his parents were. How maybe it was a blessing Gunnar's mother wasn't alive to go through the pain that Jakob and her husband were going through now.

She grabbed the laptop and went back in the living room.

The three men all stood. 'Do you mind if we take this?' Lauren held the laptop up.

'Go ahead. I don't know the password, but I'd like it back if there are pictures on it.'

'You'll get it back, friend,' Berg assured him, taking the computer from Lauren. 'I'll get this to our computer experts first thing in the morning.'

Jakob slowly walked the three back to the kitchen door, his shoulder slumped, his face a mixture of anguish and defeat. 'Aren't you looking in the wrong place?' he asked, as if he'd been wanting to ask that question since they showed up. 'Isn't the murderer in America?'

'We can't assume anything,' Lauren told him as Jakob reached past her and pushed the door open so they could leave.

'I can assume one thing,' he said as they filed out onto the metal steps. 'You won't find anything on his computer. He lived on his phone. If you want to know what was going on with Gunnar, check his phone.'

TWENTY-SIX

'Do you believe Jakob when he says he didn't know if Ragnar and Gunnar were romantically involved?' Lauren followed Berg back toward their vehicle as a light snow dusted down from the now dark sky.

'Maybe it was a strictly business relationship,' Matt said as they crossed the road. Berg got in the driver side and waited until both of them were settled before he blasted the heat for Matt's benefit. The temperature had plummeted with the sunset and Matt's lips were practically blue. 'Maybe we're barking up the wrong tree with that angle.'

'The day manager at Gunnar's hotel thought Ragnar was Gunnar's husband,' Lauren pointed out as Berg eased out of the space.

'But they didn't sit together on the plane,' Matt said. 'Ragnar sat in first class and Gunnar sat in economy.'

'I saw their passenger manifest,' Berg said. 'I knew four people on that plane with them. If they were trying to keep their relationship quiet, separate seats is a good start. And people see what they want to see. I think we need to talk to Ragnar tomorrow.'

'He has no idea we're here?' Lauren's stomach grumbled. She still hadn't had anything but coffee since the day before.

'I don't know what he knows. Everyone is connected to everyone in Reykjavik one way or another, and word travels. Which is the reason you got stuck with me, remember? Let's get you both something to eat. I don't want your boss to complain to my boss that I starved you.'

Not knowing where to go, Lauren and Matt had to put their trust in Berg for choosing a restaurant. 'I hope you like fish,' he said as they walked into a cozy little café on a side street near the harbor.

Lauren had seen signs out front of various establishments when they'd been riding over to Jakob's that advertised fermented shark, puffin, and whale – none of which sounded appetizing to her. When she voiced her concerns, Berg laughed out loud. 'Only tourists eat that shit. Go ahead and try the fermented shark. You'll stink like a rotting corpse for a week.' He opened his menu and stabbed it with his finger. 'This. Get the potatoes roasted in geese fat. It's what they're known for here. It's the house specialty.'

She and Matt both got fish entrées with the potatoes while Berg consumed a giant bloody steak. A candle in the middle of the round table threw shadows across the dark blue table-cloth. The place was packed, there wasn't a single empty seat to be had. When Lauren asked if they needed reservations when they walked in, Berg had cocked an eyebrow, smiled and said, 'I know a guy,' in his best American accent. He'd talked quietly to the hostess in Icelandic and they'd been seated right away.

'Tomorrow night my wife is making lamb for both of you,' he told them, shoveling a dripping piece of red meat into his mouth. 'My Anna's a wonderful cook. You'll see.'

Lauren wolfed down her dinner and even managed to eat desert. She knew she'd sleep better if she was full. The last thing she wanted was to lie in bed, staring at the ceiling while the minutes ticked by, like she did at home when she caught a case that came up short on suspects and leads.

Not only did Matt eat, he downed two beers with Berg in the process. With a teething baby at home, a three-course dinner and drinks were probably a rarity in Matt's life.

When the waiter brought the check Berg scooped it up. 'Sorry, friends. It's on the Reykjavík Metropolitan Police tonight.'

Even with the coffee she drank with dinner, Lauren was ready for bed when Berg pulled up to the hotel. 'We'll go visit Ragnar first thing tomorrow,' he called, leaning out of the driver side window. 'Get some sleep. And you,' he motioned to Matt's feet, 'go buy a proper pair of boots before I get here.'

'See you in the morning.' Lauren waved goodbye, trying not to laugh at Matt's ridiculous shoes.

It'll still be full dark when he comes around, Lauren thought as she and Matt walked into the lobby. It was barely nine o'clock at night, but the jet lag was pulling Lauren down fast.

'I'll be up at six and in the gym tomorrow, if you call in the morning and I don't answer,' he told her.

'I'll be lying in bed at six, and seven, and possibly eight with no intention of exercising anything. But have fun. I'll be in the lobby at nine.'

He slapped the door of the elevator as he got off. 'See you then, Riley.'

He's calling me Riley, a faint smile arched across her lips. *I guess I'm starting to grow on him. Poor kid.*

Lauren wanted to collapse on her bed, pull the covers over her head and just sleep when she got back to her room, but she glanced at the time on her phone. It may have been late in Iceland, but back home at the Buffalo Police department she was sure she could catch Hector or Doug Sheehan. Especially if the higher-ups had approved overtime for Gunnar's investigation.

Lauren decided to try Hector Avilla before she sat on the bed and passed out with all her winter gear on. He picked up on the second ring. 'Hey, Lauren!' Hector's voice filled her ear as she made her way over to the chair by the window. 'How are things halfway across the pond?'

'I think I'm more than halfway, but thanks for asking. I called to get an update. Any word on new leads?' She sank down into the chair, shrugging off her parka, the phone squashed to her ear with her shoulder.

'My jailhouse informant gave me a couple of names. One guy looks real interesting. His names is Michael Hoskins and he just got out of prison two months ago for a string of armed robberies. He did six years. He served his entire sentence so there's no parole or probation officer he has to report to. I talked to my friend who works at the prison, he said this guy's a real badass.'

Lauren's heart rate picked up a beat. 'Did you bring him in?'

'Yeah, but he knows the game. He lawyered up right away. We don't have enough on him to get a search warrant and he knows he's being surveilled so he's on his best behavior.'

'The commissioner sprung for twenty-four-hour surveillance?'

'The commissioner, the mayor, and the district attorney are giving us whatever we need.'

Putting Hector on speaker phone, Lauren laid her phone on the table so she could pick at the knots in her boots. 'That's impressive. Could you imagine if they did that for every homicide?'

He laughed into the phone. 'Yes, I can. The city would be broke. Unfortunately, throwing all that money at the case hasn't helped us catch a break yet.'

'You said "yet".' She kicked off one boot and started working on the other. 'You got someone else to look at?'

'Maybe,' Hector hedged. 'But you ain't going to like it.'

'What?' She lined both boots up together.

'The nurse? Erna? Turns out about twenty-five years ago she was indicted for embezzling from a church she worked at. She paid restitution so she was never convicted of anything.'

'Erna?' Lauren would have said she'd been a detective too long to ever be truly shocked but right then she felt blindsided. 'How did you find that out?'

'We brought her in today. She willingly gave a statement. She didn't try to hide it, if it makes you feel any better.'

Lauren sprawled face down on the table and thumped her forehead against the fake wood grain. *How can I have been so stupid,* she inwardly groaned, *I should have double-checked Erna the same way I double checked Ryan and Brooklyn's criminal backgrounds. She was also an heir. She had just as much motive as the siblings.* 'I can't believe I missed that.'

'They rushed you out of the country in the middle of your investigation.' Hector was trying to comfort her now. 'Mr Hudson is her alibi and I don't think he'd cover up Gunnar's murder for her, do you?'

'No,' Lauren agreed. 'But I know she had at least one grown son. Did you check into her kids?'

'I'm on it, Lauren. Of course, I did. This isn't my first homicide.' No, but it was starting to feel like it was hers. 'How are things on your end? Did you find your mystery man?'

'We talked to Gunnar's brother today. We're going to try to talk to Ragnar tomorrow.'

'Listen, the powers that be are getting the samples collected from Gunnar's crime scene processed for DNA right away. We should have preliminary results in two to three days. Even if we don't have a suspect, if we get a full profile, we can have them upload it into CODIS.'

Just like she'd done with the unknown profile found on Billy Munzert's bike. *A lot of good that did us*, she thought bitterly. *Maybe Ragnar will volunteer to give a swab of his DNA. Wouldn't that be a nice early Christmas gift?*

'I won't keep you,' Lauren said, rubbing her forehead where she'd smacked it against the table as she moved toward the bed. 'I know you probably want to get home.'

'No, I'm glad you called. I want you to know we are all over this case here. Just do your thing. I'll call you if anything breaks.'

And I'll be thousands of miles away if it does. 'Thanks, Hector. That means a lot to me.'

'Get some sleep, chica,' he paused, calculating the time difference. 'It's past your bedtime.'

'Thanks, Hec. Goodnight.'

He clicked off. She sat on the edge of her bed, staring at her phone.

Finally, she tossed the phone on the nightstand in disgust. *What the hell am I doing here?*

TWENTY-SEVEN

I t was the silence that woke Lauren, not the nightmare.

Sitting straight up, staring ahead into the darkness of her hotel room, she tried to remember the sound of her nightmare. Only there was no sound. Just Billy Munzert sitting in the chair by the window in his 1970s cowboy shirt holding a plastic *Star Wars* action figure in his fist smiling at her from across the room, his red hair so much like Berg's, and teetering on the edge of laughing out loud. Devon Crosby was standing next to him, smirking, with a gun in his hand pointed at Billy's head.

She was breathing hard, almost panting, heart pounding, expecting to hear the nighttime sounds of the city. But there was nothing, just the gentle whir of the heating unit. That barely registered as noise to her. Lauren's hand felt around the bedside table for the lamp. Switching it on, she saw she was alone. Billy wasn't there. Devon Crosby was gone. There was just her parka and next to the legs of the chair, her boots.

The room was warm; too warm. It was suffocating her. She had to get up, move around, make some noise. The next thing she knew she was pulling on her parka and boots. She didn't bother with her glasses, but she managed to remember to grab the key card off of the dresser. Lauren fled out her door and down the stairwell directly across from her room.

She felt her legs pumping as she rounded each landing, her breath quickening, her pulse racing. At least she could hear the blood pounding in her ears. That was something.

She hit the bar for the emergency exit and found herself outside, behind the hotel. The door snapped shut behind her and she closed her eyes, taking in a deep breath. The biting cold felt good, familiar. In the stillness she could hear herself breathing and tried to slow the rapid beating of her own heart.

'It's cold out, love. I hope you have a hat and gloves in your pocket.'

A voice from behind startled her out of her panic attack.

Lauren turned around to see an old man with a face like aged leather leaning against the side of the building, smoking a cigarette next to the exit door. She must have ran right by him. 'What?'

'I said' – he dropped the butt on the ground, stomped it with the toe of his boot and immediately lit another one – 'that you Americans are never prepared for the cold. I hope you remembered to bring a hat or gloves.'

She stared at him stupidly, stuck in the ridiculousness of the moment. Her having a panic attack in Iceland because it was too quiet, then jumping out of her skin when she heard someone. She fished into her front pocket, producing her knit hat. She held it out, showing it to him. 'Can I have one of those?' She gestured to the cigarette as she pulled the hat on.

He gave a snort of laughter as he shook one out for her. 'Nasty habit,' he said, cupping a hand around the top of his lighter as she leaned in. The tip glowed cherry red as she pulled back, inhaling. 'I feel like a criminal every time I light one up. That's why I hide back here, so no one can witness my crimes. It's good to have an accomplice on a night like this.'

Lauren hadn't had a cigarette in years, and definitely not whatever the brand was that he was smoking. She immediately began to cough but didn't put it out. *Just like riding a bike*, she thought, taking another longer drag. This time the smoke filled her lungs until she exhaled it. It was poison, but she felt her whole body relax as the smoke curled away from her lips. It amazed her at how easy it was to fall back into old bad habits.

'How do you know I'm American?' she asked. White haired, wearing a black knitted hat pulled over his ears, the man had on rubber knee-high fishing boots, like her dad used to wear when he'd go ice fishing on Lake Erie. The old man's were discolored and worn, like he'd owned them a great many years. His puffy nylon jacket had seen better days as well. She wondered if he was a guest at the hotel or if he worked there or was just stopping to have a smoke before he passed on by.

His watery blue eyes took her in. 'Ill equipped for the

weather. Not where you're supposed to be. And a general demeanor of reckless arrogance.' He laughed out a cloud of smoke. 'Everything about you screams American.'

'Is that good or bad?'

'It's three o'clock in the morning and a lady just rushed outside to smoke with this lonely old man. I'd say good for me. What about you?'

She looked up at the night sky and shook her head. 'I don't know.'

'Well, you've come a long way from home. You're either rushing into something or rushing away from something. Which is it?'

Her mind flashed back to her nightmare of Billy Munzert. 'Both, maybe.'

Suddenly, the night sky erupted with color. From the gap between the buildings, Lauren could see out over the harbor as the Northern Lights jumped and danced. *Like electric harp strings*, she thought, *being strummed high above in the heavens*. The cigarette began to shake between her fingers.

'Don't be scared,' the old man said. 'It just happens that way sometimes. People come here from all over the world to chase the Northern Lights and some never see them, no matter how hard or where they look. There's a lesson in that, somewhere.'

Lauren took another pull on her cigarette. It was almost down to the filter and it was making her sick to her stomach. 'What's the lesson?' she asked, not taking her eyes off the spectacle above her as she tapped the ash into a small pile of snow next to the door.

His deeply lined faced crinkled up in a smile as he gazed upward with her. 'When you least expect something, it pops up on its own.'

TWENTY-EIGHT

L auren finished her cigarette with the man, whose name she never did get. They walked together around to the front of the building so she could get back in the hotel through the lobby. The old man waved to her once she was inside the sliding glass doors, and ambled slowly toward the parking lot.

It took ten minutes of good scrubbing with her toothbrush to get the taste out of her mouth. Removing the smell from her pajamas was going to have to wait. She pulled them off, left them in a ball by the dresser and slept in a T-shirt.

When her cellphone alarm woke her at eight a.m. she wasn't exactly sure she'd gone outside the night before or she'd just dreamt it. She had to get up and smell her green pajama top to be certain. Sure enough, it reeked like smoke and she figured her hair must smell that way as well. Hopping into the shower, she was thankful she'd quit years ago but understood the pull it had, and still had, over her. If she wasn't careful she could fall right back into the habit again. Especially after conversations about the case with Hector and nightmares about Billy Munzert.

She thought about Brooklyn and her addiction to heroin as the hot water streamed over her face. It had taken Lauren seven or eight miserable tries before she finally quit smoking. She could only imagine what giving up a drug like heroin must be like. The struggle for Mr Hudson to keep his daughter alive was probably going to continue until the day he died, which wasn't that far off if both of his kidneys were failing.

She blew her short hair dry, styling it with some gel and her fingertips like her friend Dayla had showed her. Lauren was getting used to it being short, and darker – a light chestnut brown. If she went somewhere hot, the sun would bleach it blond again immediately. She still had light eyebrows. She liked the change in her appearance though. Her forties felt good and the new look reflected that.

She got to the lobby before Matt, attacking the coffee station and making small talk with a couple from California on vacation. 'Have you gotten to the Blue Lagoon yet?' The fiftyish woman asked, stirring her creamer into her coffee with a plastic straw.

'Not yet,' Lauren admitted. 'I'm here on business and we haven't gotten to any of the sights.'

'Don't miss that,' the woman's husband said, sipping from his own white mug. 'It's so strange to rush from the twenty-eight-degree air into the world's biggest hot tub. Very exhilarating.'

'It's on my to-do list,' Lauren smiled. Just then Matt came walking up, beads of water glistening in his hair from the shower.

'Good morning,' he said, glancing out the front windows into the darkness. 'I think.'

'It does take some getting used to,' the woman agreed. 'We've been here almost a week and it still amazes me how they carry on with only a couple hours of daylight.'

The sliding glass doors parted. Berg stuck his head in, holding his arm out to one side so they didn't close and decapitate him. 'Ready?'

'It was nice talking to you,' Lauren told the couple who raised their coffee mugs to her and Matt in return.

'Get to the Blue Lagoon!' the woman called after her as Lauren walked out with Matt.

'You want to go to the Blue Lagoon?' Berg asked. A wicked wind blew across the harbor through the hotel parking lot causing him to turn the collar up on his coat, but not zip it or put on a hat.

He hit his key fob and the three of them climbed in. Berg's truck was positively toasty after the wind tunnel of the parking lot.

'I want to finish this case,' Lauren replied. She then relayed the conversation she'd had with Hector the night before.

'It doesn't sound like your friends back home have much of anything to go on,' Berg said with an annoying look of doubt on his face.

'I can't help but feel we were *premature* in coming to Iceland,' Lauren replied as diplomatically as she could.

'You don't have quite as far to go today.' Berg said. 'Ragnar and Freyja live just down the road in one of the high-rises, almost directly across from the Harpa Concert Hall. If you look carefully on the way, you'll see the Sólfar or Sun Voyager sculpture. It was designed by a man with the last name Arnason, but he's no relation to me. It looks like a big Viking ship. It'll be on your right. The concert hall is just a short distance further.'

'I saw that ship on postcards in the airport yesterday,' Matt said, sliding over from the driver to passenger-side backseat to get a better view.

'I'll have to drive you past the concert hall when the sun is up,' Berg said. 'It's not the same if you can't see the sunlight reflecting off the glass.'

'I imagine an apartment overlooking the water and concert hall isn't cheap,' Lauren remarked, watching out the window for the metal sculpture.

'Not just an apartment, a *penthouse* apartment. This neighborhood is nicknamed the Shadow District. Sometimes I think it's because the people who live here have enough money to hide their vices.'

Berg's arm stretched across Lauren to point at her window. 'There's the Sólfar.'

The shiny metal skeleton of a Viking ship passed them by. 'That's the concert hall just ahead.'

The outside of the vast building was comprised of hundreds of glass panels that seemed to undulate in the reflected colored light cast on it. Set off of the main road into the harbor, it appeared to be floating on a reflection of itself in the water. 'It's breathtaking,' Lauren said in a hushed voice.

'It is nice, isn't it? It almost didn't get finished. They ran out of money.' He swung the car down a side street. Lauren craned her neck to watch it until they disappeared behind a building. 'But we managed to get it built and now it's a wonder.'

He came around the back of a huge high-rise building and slowly crept through the lot, looking for a parking space. 'Do they know we're coming?' Matt asked.

'No. I thought the element of surprise would be best.'

They zigzagged through the maze of parked cars to the back door of the apartment building. Lauren was surprised the door opened easily, forgetting that it was almost nine-thirty in the morning. They passed into a lobby where a young man in a suit, probably not even twenty years old, sat poised behind a desk. He wasn't staring down at his phone texting or checking his social media, he seemed genuinely alert and ready to do his job. He asked them a question in Icelandic.

'English, please,' Berg said, resting his elbows on the counter over the desk.

'Apologies. How can I help you?'

'We're here to see Ragnar Steinarsson.' Berg flipped open a wallet containing his credentials. The young man took it, looked it over and reached for the landline on the desk next to him. Berg put a hand on his arm. 'How about you just call the elevator for us, hmm? We'll see ourselves up.'

'Ragnar is off to work, I'm afraid.' He looked down at Berg's hand on his arm. 'Only his wife is in.'

'Freyja is an old friend of mine,' Berg told him, pulling his hand back. 'I want to surprise her.'

The kid looked from Berg, to Matt to Lauren, uncertain of how to proceed. Lauren gently squeezed in next to Berg and smiled. 'We only need a few minutes of her time. It would be better if we just went up. This is a very sensitive matter.'

'You're American.' It was a statement not a question. 'I knew it. You're here about Ragnar's assistant, Gunnar.'

'You knew him?' Lauren asked the wide-eyed desk attendant.

He nodded. 'Ragnar used to have his driver pick him up every morning. He brought Gunnar here and they'd go to Ragnar's office together. He was a very nice person. It's horrible how he died.'

He left out 'in America', Lauren thought, but kept up her reassuring smile. 'If you could just call the elevator down, we'll take it from there.'

'I shouldn't call up to Freyja first?'

Lauren was forcing him to break all of his rules. 'No, please. We'd rather just go up on our own. I promise you won't get in any trouble.' And there it was, one of Lauren's famous promises she had no way of keeping. Even in other countries she could still manage to throw them out like bombs ready to explode.

He smiled back at her and hit a button on a panel set into the desk. Behind them the elevator bonged. 'It's the top floor, penthouse suite. Hit the button marked 15.'

'Thank you. You've been a great help to us,' Lauren said, lingering just a second longer than the men.

Berg's laugh filled the elevator as soon as they were all ensconced and on their way up. 'You dazzled that poor boy. He will be heartbroken when you leave without saying goodbye.'

'I'm old enough to be his mother.' *And have you seen the women in this country?* She wanted to ask. *Every single one looks like a runway model.*

'You're an American policewoman, that's going to fascinate men, no matter how much you try make yourself look frumpy. And you,' his eyes flicked over to Matt, 'don't even say the words "FBI agent" out in a club. You may get swarmed.'

'My wife would love that,' Matt said watching the digital numbers climb as the car went up.

'Frumpy?' Lauren asked as the door opened to the penthouse floor.

Berg shrugged. 'There's clearly a woman underneath all those oversized clothes and messy hair and glasses, but she hasn't made an official appearance yet.'

Lauren didn't know if she should be offended or complimented. Her knowledge of Icelandic cultural norms didn't extend to what constituted an insult based on your looks. Was it appropriate to even say that to a fellow law enforcement officer on the job? Or was Berg just one of those people who had no filter?

She didn't have much time to ponder that question because Ragnar Steinarsson's penthouse took up the entire floor. The door to the suite was directly in front of them down a very short hallway. An evergreen wreath with red candles in the center decorated the taupe-colored door. It was obviously an expensive decoration and not meant to actually be lit, but it was beautiful.

Berg poked the doorbell and stepped back. Lauren hated that there were three of them. Three was definitely a crowd when it came to interviews, and a hindrance to creating a decent rapport with people.

A woman's voice speaking in Icelandic came steadily toward the door. The only word Lauren recognized was the name Ragnar. She was still talking when it swung open, revealing a tall, strikingly beautiful woman in her late fifties. Stunned at the sight of three strangers outside the door of her impenetrable fortress, the woman stood wide-eyed staring at the trio.

'It's not Ragnar,' Berg said. 'It's the police.' He gestured to Lauren and Matt. 'The American police as well.'

'You're here about Gunnar?' she asked, flipping to flawless English. Regal, sophisticated and poised, she held herself with a natural elegance. Freyja's blond hair was pinned up, away from her face. Her pink dress accented the hint of color across her high cheekbones.

Berg nodded. 'We came to speak to your husband. Is he in?'

She glanced at Lauren and Matt, drinking them in with her eyes, assessing them. Then she gave a dazzling smile of perfect, even white teeth. 'That's who I thought was at the door. I thought Ragnar forgot his keys again. He just left for work. I'm surprised you didn't pass him in the lobby.'

'Can we step inside and talk?' Lauren asked.

Her icy blue eyes narrowed just a touch, but her smile was still radiant. 'Please.' She held the door wide. 'Come in. Although it's not as if we have any neighbors to bother.'

They filed in and Freyja beckoned them to follow her into the great room. Floor-to-ceiling windows wrapped two sides, giving way to a spectacular view of the harbor and mountains beyond. The room was decorated in the same clean minimalistic style that Lauren kept running across. A huge fireplace crackled in the corner, throwing off a pleasant orange glow in the brightly lit room. The contrast to the murky darkness outside was warming and inviting.

Instead of being squashed together on one worn-out sofa, they sat in the three oversized cream-colored wing chairs arranged around a square coffee table and facing a matching sofa. Freyja was tall, taller than Lauren by a good two inches, even more with the heels she was wearing.

'Were you on your way out?' Matt asked, perching himself on the edge of his chair.

Freyja smoothed the silky fabric of her pale pink dress over her long legs as she sat on the couch. 'No. I was going to return some phone calls and emails. I have to go to the gym later to meet with my personal trainer, but that's not for a few hours.'

She's the type of woman who wakes up, gets dressed, and puts her makeup and heels on just to hang around the house, Lauren observed, *just on the off chance someone might see her.*

'Do I know you, detective . . .?'

'Berg Arnason. And no. We've never met, but I do remember when you were first runner-up for Miss Iceland.'

She waved her hand in a practiced, completely charming manner. 'That was ages ago. How would you remember me out of all those contestants?'

'My older sister loved the pageants. She made my mother take us to as many as she could. I remember you singing. Your voice was exquisite.'

'You must have been a little boy.'

'Not so little I didn't know a great beauty when I saw one.'

She expertly cast her eyes downward, then looked up at him through her thick, dark lashes. 'You know how to make a woman blush, detective. I know you didn't bring them' – she tilted her head slightly in Matt and Lauren's direction – 'all this way just to flatter me.'

'We actually came here to speak with your husband,' Matt jumped in. 'We understand Gunnar worked for him.'

Freyja's smile faltered slightly at the mention of Gunnar's name. 'It's such a tragedy. Gunnar was an excellent employee. My husband is devastated that he was murdered. And right after he left to catch a flight home. He can't help thinking if he'd just stayed in America for one more night Gunnar would still be alive.'

'You knew Ragnar was in Buffalo with Gunnar?' Lauren asked, trying to keep the surprise out of her voice.

Freyja's wide blue eyes fixed on Lauren's. 'Of course. They were there on business. Ragnar thought Buffalo's location on the Canadian border might make it an excellent place to open an office. We do a lot of business in New York City and Toronto, but real estate can be prohibitive in both of those cities. An office in Buffalo could have been a much more cost-effective option. But now' – she put her hand to her mouth – 'I'd never allow Ragnar to put a branch of our business there.'

'Is that why they flew into Toronto and not New York City?' Matt asked.

'Ragnar told me there was a four-hour layover between the New York City flight and the next flight to Buffalo on the day they wanted to leave. It seemed foolish to him to wait around that long for a fifty-five-minute plane ride when you can just hop in a rental car in Toronto and drive to Buffalo in less than two hours.'

'Have you taken that trip with Ragnar before?' Berg asked.

She smoothed back her satiny blond hair with her left hand. 'Of course. I've been to Toronto and New York City with him.' Her mouth turned upward in a half-smile at the thought of her trips with her husband. 'I prefer New York.'

'Did you know Gunnar personally?' Lauren asked.

Freyja nodded. 'I'm the one who hired him. I don't have much to do with the day-to-day operations of the company anymore, but I like to help my husband when I can. Ragnar's last assistant got another job and left suddenly, so I interviewed candidates for him. Ragnar insists on having a hand in everything, so he needs an assistant. Otherwise he'd never remember anything, which is why I thought he was at the door looking for his keys again. I called an agency to send over some candidates, but Ragnar says it's too soon.'

'Did he and Gunnar get along?' Matt asked.

'He got on better with Gunnar than his last assistant. That man was totally unreliable. I thought it was a stroke of luck when he decided to leave. And then an even bigger stroke when we were lucky enough to find Gunnar.'

'Have all of Ragnar's assistants been men?' Lauren asked.

Freyja's lovely face never faltered. 'I've been with my

husband since we were in our early twenties. We have three beautiful children. We have a lot invested in our marriage. Let's just say that the female assistants were more trouble than they were worth. That's why I took over the hiring process. I know my husband loves me, but the temptation to stray can be strong.'

'I find that hard to believe,' Berg offered before Lauren could press her on the details.

'Powerful men have powerful needs.' Her tone was still light and controlled. 'Sometimes preventative measures have to be taken for the good of everyone involved.'

An awkward silence followed that raw statement. Freyja sat with her hands folded delicately in her lap and her face never lost its serene composure as she waited for one of them to ask their next question. Finally, Berg cleared his throat. 'Do you know where your husband is now?'

'I assume he might be at his office already. I can call his secretary, Helga, and see if he's in yet.' She held up a shiny cellphone she'd extracted from a pocket hidden somewhere in the folds of her skirt.

'New phone?' Lauren asked.

Her smile was positively angelic as she answered. 'Ragnar thought it'd be best to get new phones once he got back. He's going through a cleansing moment. Throw away the toxicity associated with violence.' She looked down at her hands clasped in her lap. 'He wants to push what happened to Gunnar out of his mind. Forget everything about that trip and start everything fresh.'

'Do you think we could have your old phones to take a look at?' Berg asked.

'If we had them, of course, but you should know better than anyone the only way to make sure your personal information is safe is to destroy old phones.'

Berg stood, signaling for Lauren and Matt to do the same. 'Thank you. We'll take a ride over there. You don't have to trouble Ragnar's secretary. And we're sorry to have had to trouble you.'

'It was no trouble at all.' She led the way back to the entrance with her elegant, graceful gait. She turned back to the trio as she opened the door for them to leave. 'I hope you find out who did this to Gunnar. He was a very sweet man. It's just so unbelievable. I think Ragnar and I are still both in shock. If there's anything we can do to help, please ask.'

'Thank you,' Lauren said, still not sure how to address a married Icelandic woman. Mrs Steinarsson? Mrs Runarsdóttir? She had no idea how that worked. Matt thanked her generically as well.

'Don't you think we should have gotten more information on the former female assistants she was talking about,' Lauren asked Berg as soon as the elevator doors closed.

'It's obvious what she meant,' Berg said. 'And I'm willing to bet Ragnar is nowhere to be found when we get to his office.'

'You think she's going to tip him off that we're coming?' Matt asked.

Berg's usually expressive mouth was a straight line. 'I think she'll keep protecting what's hers.'

TWENTY-NINE

R agnar's office was located more toward the University of Reykjavik area in a nondescript two-story building. 'Ragnar and Freyja's company has multiple real estate holdings all over the country, but this is their headquarters.' At Lauren's request, Berg parked the car across from the building and the three of them sat watching the front door.

'I thought it'd be bigger.' Lauren squinted her eyes, trying to make out the writing on the glass.

Berg snorted back a laugh. 'This has been their headquarters for thirty years, at least. Remember, Freyja's grandfather started the business in the 1970s.' Berg was slouched in the driver's seat so Matt could see over him. 'They own a business complex on the opposite end of the waterfront from where you're staying, where the day-to-day operations of the company happen. It's very a modern collection of buildings, all windows and mountain views, but this is where Ragnar keeps his personal office.'

'How did you find that out?' Matt asked.

'You should know by now,' Berg's smile reached his eyes, 'I know people who know people. This was easy. It's not like Ragnar is trying to keep his private office location a secret. He probably just prefers to do his work without the prying eyes of his underlings on him, day in and day out.'

A brand-new black BMW X5 with tinted windows was parked on the street directly in front of the building. 'Do you think that's Ragnar's car?' Lauren asked.

'I'd say so,' Berg replied. 'Let's go inside and find out.'

Inside, the lobby had been remodeled into a sleek, modern workspace. A white puzzle-piece-shaped light fixture hung from the ceiling by thick wires casting a subtle illumination down onto the receptionist. Seated behind a long marble-topped counter, she stopped typing on her computer when they walked in. The woman's face was half hidden by her computer monitor until she slid to the side in her black-and-chrome ergonomic office chair. Lauren knew from the tight, pleasant look on her face Freyja had called the moment they'd left her apartment. Any remaining doubt she had was erased when the receptionist asked in English, 'May I help you?'

'We're looking for Ragnar Steinarsson.' Lauren figured she'd skip the pleasantries and get right to it. 'Can we speak to him?'

The sixtyish woman poked her silver-rimmed glasses up her nose with her index finger. She had a large, slightly crooked hooked nose. Lauren suspected she was another of Freyja's hires. 'He's not in the office now. If you'll leave your names and contact numbers, I can pass those on to him when he gets back. However, he rarely sees people without an appointment. Can you tell me what this is about?'

Berg had also picked up on the English greeting and lit into her in Icelandic. The woman's boney face flushed red as they went back and forth. Berg put both hands on the counter and leaned in, speaking in a low harsh tone. She seemed to shrink away from him with every unsatisfactory answer she gave. At one point he slapped his hand down causing her to jump. She quickly added something in Icelandic, pointing at Matt and Lauren, then outside.

After that the tone changed between them; it became almost conspiratorial. She kept glancing behind her, then back to Berg, as if she was sharing corporate secrets with him instead of the whereabouts of her boss.

After the extended exchange seemed to be over, Berg pulled a business card from his back pants pocket and dropped it on the woman's desk. 'Have him call me as soon as he gets back. Do you understand?'

She nodded, picking up the card. She scanned it quickly, then tucked it away in the breast pocket of her mustard-colored blouse.

Berg turned to Matt and Lauren. 'Let's go. He's gone.'

'Sorry to trouble you, ma'am,' Matt said as they were about to walk out the door.

'Wait,' she called, stopping all three in their tracks. She looked toward a hallway on her right that led back to more offices, making sure no one else was within earshot, then said, 'You need to speak with Bjarni Egilsson. Don't tell Ragnar or Freyja I told you.'

'Thank you, Helga,' Berg's voice softened.

'Do you know that woman?' Lauren asked as they walked with Berg across the street.

Berg looked over his shoulder at the building. 'She was married to a childhood friend of my father's. I haven't seen her since I was a little boy. She didn't recognize me at first.' He waved his hand in a dismissive gesture, like he wasn't about to let her get away with not knowing him.

'Do you know every single person in Reykjavik?' Lauren cut in, thinking about his 'know people who know people' statement earlier.

'There's less that 400,000 of us in the whole country. We actually have an app for our phones so that, when you meet someone in a bar, it can tell you how closely related you are. That way you won't sleep with your first cousin.'

'That's nuts,' Matt said.

Berg gave a shrug. 'That's Iceland. Anyway, Helga tried to pretend she had no idea who we were or why we were there. I made it clear we were investigating a murder and I wouldn't put up with her obstructing me.' He jerked a thumb at the BMW. 'That's Ragnar's work vehicle. She said his driver is in the back break room. Apparently, Ragnar left in his personal vehicle after Freyja called, and told his driver to go home for the day if he's not back in two hours.'

'You think he's running from us?' Lauren asked from the backseat.

Berg waited until everyone was buckled in and started the car. 'Hard to say.'

'Then let's find that Barney guy she mentioned.' Matt said.

'Bjarni,' Berg corrected, enunciating it carefully. 'There's a coffee shop around the corner. You two can get something to eat while I call the district house and get Bjarni's information and Ragnar's license plate. Helga says he's driving a white Skoda Octavia right now.'

'Helga turned out to be a wellspring of information.' Lauren noticed a muscular man in his twenties come out of the building and lean against the BMW's front bumper as they pulled away. 'I hope we didn't get her in trouble.'

'Helga has always been as tough as they come.' Berg pulled out onto the road. 'I've seen her in action. Believe me, she'll be fine.'

THIRTY

Lauren couldn't get over two things in the Blue Whale Coffee and Tea Shop as she sat sipping her Java with Matt: the front door was wide-open, and two baby strollers were sitting on the sidewalk in front of the picture window. Ordinarily that wouldn't be cause for concern, except both young mothers were inside drinking their beverages, while their babies slept outside in the strollers. Granted, they were sitting together right up against the window where they had a perfect view of their sleeping infants, and nobody else in the shop seemed alarmed, but it could not be legal to leave your baby outside in the cold while you gossiped.

'Excuse me,' she pointed to the window for the thirty-something waitress with hair cut so severely short it almost looked like a buzz cut. 'Is that OK? Them leaving their babies outside?' In her mind she flashed back to Billy Munzert's face and the frantic search his parents must have mounted in the neighborhood once they realized their boy had disappeared.

The waitress gave Lauren a knowing smile that said *poor, silly American*. 'It's perfectly fine,' she said, putting the sandwiches they'd ordered on the table. 'The babies are bundled. They sleep better in the fresh air. The heat from the doorway reaches them. You'll see babies napping outside everywhere. No worries.'

Lauren looked back at the children, still worrying. *All it takes is a second*, she thought, *one momentary distraction and they could be gone.*

'Excuse me, miss?' Matt stopped the waitress as she tried to leave. 'I can't seem to connect to the internet. Can I have the Wi-Fi password?'

It was the waitress' turn to point. This time to a small chalkboard sign. Something was written in Icelandic on it in bright Day-Glo colors and punctuated with a smiley face. 'That says "There is no Wi-Fi here. Talk to each other instead."'

She walked over to the serving area and began gesturing to the young man behind the counter. She jerked a thumb in their direction and they both started talking in earnest. Lauren wondered if everyone in Reykjavík knew who they were, or if she was just being paranoid. Except for Helga, every single person they'd met had been friendly and accommodating. But even Helga seemed more concerned than angry, like Berg had said. *Protective*, Lauren thought, *that's what Helga was being, protective. The question is: protective of who?*

Berg came inside, wiping his boots on a black mat in front of the door. 'Put that thing away,' he told Matt. 'There's no service in here.'

Matt tucked his phone into his jacket pocket. 'We just heard. Thanks.'

'Any luck on Bjarni or Ragnar?' Lauren asked Berg as he waved his arm at the same waitress. She picked up her fish sandwich and took a bite. It tasted heavenly.

'I have a license tag number for Ragnar's car and Bjarni gets his mail delivered to a bar called the Wolf's Den. It's in the seedy part of town. Not a lot of tourists, but plenty of rich folks from the Shadow District's pricey addresses like to keep the bars down there in business.'

The waitress knew Berg and brought a tall brown coffee mug over. 'Thank you,' he told her, then made a circle motion to include Lauren and Matt's food and drinks. 'Put it all on my bill.'

She said something back in Icelandic and sauntered off to another table.

'You come in here a lot?' Lauren asked. Matt was wolfing down his own sandwich, not even bothering to look up as he chewed.

Berg nodded and took a drink. 'They stay open late. I like working nights. It suits me.'

'I think we might be looking at the wrong angle here,' Matt managed after swallowing the last bite of his sandwich. 'Both Jakob and Freyja were very convincing that Ragnar and Gunnar just had a working relationship and nothing else.'

'Then why is Ragnar ducking us?' Lauren asked.

'Maybe the business they came to look into in the States

wasn't entirely legal. Maybe that's why Ragnar dumped his phone.' Berg scooped some raw sugar out of a bowl on the table and stirred it into his coffee. 'Maybe Gunnar wasn't the lover, but was covering for her, whoever she might be. Did your hotel clerk talk about any women they might have met up with?'

'No,' Lauren admitted. 'Then again, we never asked.'

'Went right for the obvious,' Berg chuckled. 'Never checked to see if Ragnar was spending his time in a lady's room in the same hotel while Gunnar was out finding his family.'

Matt put his hand to his forehead. 'We didn't. How could we have missed that?'

Lauren wanted to pound her head into the table again. How could she have missed something so basic? The answer was that in her haste to make Ragnar a suspect, she'd been sloppy. She'd missed double-checking Erna as a suspect and missed pulling all guest records. All the awards and accolades she'd garnered over the years for solving cases meant nothing if she could fail Homicide 101 so easily.

Lauren was tired of sitting around rooms and talking. It was time to *do* something. They needed to get a concrete lead. 'Matt, get on the phone when we get back to the hotel and have our DA's office get a subpoena for the name of every person that stayed in Gunnar's hotel the entire time he was there. Right now, I want to find this Bjarni guy.' She pushed back from the table. 'Or Ragnar. From here on in, we've got to be absolutely thorough. So may I suggest we check out the bar?'

Matt and Berg both stood. 'I'm on it, Lauren. I'll double-check the airline passenger manifests too. Expand our search.'

She made a bitter sound through her gritted teeth. 'Maybe we'll get lucky and Ragnar will get stuck at a red light in front of us on our way to his office.'

'She's a charmer, isn't she?' Lauren heard Berg say to Matt as she headed past the gossiping moms. She didn't wait around to hear Matt's reply.

THIRTY-ONE

This is all a waste of time. Lauren's head was filled with discouraging thoughts as Berg bumped them down the narrow streets. The sun had set, which should have made the shops and storefronts inviting to her. Instead they just reminded her how far she was from home. *The police department and district attorney's office rushed us all the way here to try to finish off a half-assed investigation. We're just spinning our wheels here and when I come back empty-handed, the department will hang me out to dry for messing the whole thing up.*

Which made sense. What does a police department do with a detective who consistently falls into trouble? Who they consider a liability? Find a reason to fire her. Or create one, if they had to.

Reykjavik's seedy part of town in no way resembled a seedy part of town in the States. The street was lined with bars and electronic shops and vapor emporiums, but there were no hookers milling about, no junkies on the corner, no homeless drinking out of paper bags. It seemed positively tame. Granted, the evening was still young, but the vibe was more of a lower-end suburban strip mall, than a haven of dens of iniquity.

There was no name across the front of the bar Berg pulled across from, only a red neon wolf's head blazing above the door. Loud techno music pumped from inside every time it opened. Instead of a burly bouncer, a scrawny guy stood by the entrance, hands clasped in front of him, his stringy brown hair ruffling in the night wind. A man and a woman in their thirties stopped and talked to him before the skinny guy gave them the nod to go in.

'It doesn't look like much,' Matt said.

Berg still gripped the wheel with both hands. 'It doesn't

have to,' he said, craning his neck to look up and down the street. 'This establishment has quite a reputation. They say you can get your hands on anything in there: drugs, weapons, sex. Rumor has it my newly disgraced cousin had connections to this bar.'

'Do they know you here?' Lauren asked.

Berg shook his head, giving her that mischievous smile of his. 'I've never been in the place. For some strange reason, the crime that happens inside doesn't get reported to cops like me.'

'It's a good thing me and Matt aren't a cop like you then,' Lauren said.

'Maybe so,' Berg laughed. 'Maybe so.'

For the third time that day, they exited their vehicle as a trio with Berg in the lead, Lauren on his heels and Matt bringing up the rear. They weren't in a hurry. The street was empty, the door to the bar was closed, and the unimpressive bouncer was fiddling with his phone.

The sound of a car engine revving angrily behind them filled the street. A squeal of tires and the roar of the engine froze them in place for a half-second, like deer, in the middle of the road.

A pair of headlights blazed out of the darkness. Berg and Lauren managed to throw themselves over the curb, both falling face down on the sidewalk. Lauren's glasses flew off her face and skittered over the ice. One pace behind them, Matt was not so lucky. The vehicle hit him squarely on his left side, sending him flying ten feet forward. He landed on the pavement with a sickening *thunk*.

The SUV didn't stop. It barreled around the corner and out of sight.

Reaching out and snatching her glasses, Lauren stuck the dripping spectacles on her nose as she scrambled over the ice and snow on the curb and into the street to get to Matt. He was lying on his right side, softly moaning.

'Stay with him!' Berg jumped up and ran across the road to their vehicle. Lauren could still smell the exhaust fumes from the SUV as he hopped in and gave chase.

She knelt by Matt's side, the snow soaking into the knees

of her black pants. 'Matt? Can you hear me?' Lauren didn't want to move him for fear of a head injury.

The skinny doorman ran over and knelt next to them. He started speaking in Icelandic and Lauren cut him off. 'Get on the phone! Call an ambulance!'

'Riley, I'm OK.' Matt tried to sit up, sucked in his breath and screamed out in pain.

'Don't move. Just stay still.' Lauren could see his left forearm was bent at an unnatural angle.

The doorman whipped out a cellphone as people began to trickle out of the bar.

'What happened? Is he all right?' A chorus of voices rang out in multiple languages all around Lauren and Matt. She could see the crowd pressing around them, leaning in to get a better look.

She steadied Matt as best she could on the icy pavement, trying not to move him too much. 'Did you see what kind of car it was?' Lauren called back to the bouncer.

He pulled his gaunt face away from his phone to answer her. 'No. It came out of nowhere. I think it was black.'

'Was it a BMW?' she asked.

He shook his head helplessly. 'I'm sorry. I was texting my friend. I didn't see.'

It was definitely a dark-colored SUV. It had happened so fast that that was all Lauren could make out.

'I am in so much trouble with my wife.' Matt's voice was weak and shaky.

'Are you kidding me? No one is ever going to want to ride with me again. It's an express ticket to the hospital.' Lauren tried joking to keep herself from losing it right there in the middle of a frozen street in Iceland. She brushed his dark hair back out of his eyes with her scraped-up hand.

Matt was shivering uncontrollably. A man standing next to her gave Lauren his jacket, which she draped over him. Then she shrugged off her own Parka and put that over him as well.

The SUV had hit him so hard one of his black dress shoes had come off and was lying in the street three feet from him. 'You lost your shoe. Now you really will have to spring for some boots,' she said as she sheltered him from the wind with her body.

Matt managed a pained smile, his eyes rolled up in his head, and he passed out.

In the distance, a siren sounded.

THIRTY-TWO

An ambulance took Matt to the hospital. Lauren now waited on the sidewalk, surrounded by uniform officers and the white police vehicles with yellow-and-blue striping that brought them. She was shivering and holding Matt's shoe. One of the car's overhead lights revolved lazily with the siren off, bouncing blue light off the bar and neighboring businesses. *Just like home*, she thought, hugging the single shoe to her chest.

Berg finally pulled up, blocking a driveway to a closed tattoo shop, got out and stalked across the street to her.

'It's like the truck disappeared.' He was breathing heavily, almost panting.

'Was it the BMW?' she asked. Once Matt had been taken away the crowd had quickly dispersed. The only other person who had been outside the bar when Matt was hit was the bouncer, who now stood by the door giving the uniform cops his statement. Other cops milled around, gossiping, shooting Lauren sideways glances. And she knew what they were thinking: *There's the American cop who came to Iceland and almost got her partner killed. Look at her. How does she sleep at night?*

'I don't think so, but I'm no expert on cars.' He looked on the ground all around them. 'I don't see any broken glass from a light or mirror, do you? Maybe the license plate fell off.'

She'd already combed the area while she had been waiting for him to come back. 'There's nothing.'

'Does this bar have cameras out here?' he yelled to the bouncer.

The doorman and the patrol cops looked up. 'The only cameras are inside,' he said.

'None on the door?' Berg demanded. 'None on the street?'

'Street cameras are the city's, not ours. And no. There aren't any cameras out here that I know of.'

Berg swore under his breath. 'I'm going inside and see if Bjarni is here.'

Lauren was soaked through her black pants, long underwear, suit coat and white shirt. Her parka had gone in the ambulance with Matt. Berg noticed her lips quivering, shrugged out of his coat and draped it over her shoulders. 'Let's go.'

She and Berg marched past the cops and doorman into the dimly lit bar.

It was your typical dive bar, like you'd find in any American city. Framed posters of famous rock bands lined the wall mixed in with neon beer signs. A few tables were set up around the small room dominated by the long, polished wood bar along the back near the restrooms. The only other distinguishing feature was a DJ booth built into the wall above a slightly raised dance floor. A bored-looking millennial with dreadlocks stood in front of a double turntable staring at his phone, while that same brand of techno music played. There were plenty of people bellied up to the bar, but no one was dancing.

Everyone stopped talking and stared at them as they crossed to the bar. *The only way this could be more cliché is if the DJ scratched the record to a stop*, Lauren thought and then mentally kicked herself for letting random observations into her head when she needed to focus on what just happened to Matt. And what just happened to Matt could very well be linked to Bjarni.

Berg pulled his identification out of his back pocket and slapped it open on the bar. 'Speak in English so my friend can understand you,' he growled.

The lone bartender stopped polishing a pint glass and tucked it under the bar. He wore a tight black shirt with a red wolf logo stretched across his muscular chest. 'Can I help you? We don't want any problems.'

'Is Bjarni here?' Lauren noticed the bartender's tattooed hands never stopped moving. They were now wringing the dishrag between his fingers.

'He was. He left about an hour ago. Ten minutes before the man got hit outside.'

'Was he here drinking or working?' Lauren asked, still clutching the lone shoe.

The bartender's eyes flitted over to Lauren. He blinked twice trying to control his surprise at this soggy, freezing woman asking him questions. She knew she looked a mess but didn't care. 'He works the door a couple nights a week, but tonight he was drinking. Is he in trouble?'

Berg ignored that. 'Did he say why he had to leave?'

The bartender ran a hand through his floppy brown hair and shook his head. 'No. He got a phone call and left. Is he involved in something?'

Someone tipped him off we were coming, Lauren thought. *The only question was who: the guy leaning on the BMW, or someone else inside the office they hadn't seen.* 'Where does Bjarni live?' Lauren asked.

Berg reached over, stuck his hand into the inside pocket on the coat draped across Lauren's shoulders, and pulled his notebook out. He slid it across the bar. 'Write it down.'

'He stays mostly with his mother.' The bartender quickly scribbled the address and shoved the notebook back at them like it was radioactive.

Berg handed it to Lauren, who tucked it away. 'What kind of car does Bjarni drive?'

'An old white Toyota Corolla. If you think Bjarni ran that man over, I'd think again. He'd hurt the car more than the person if he hit someone with that piece of shit.'

'Thank you for your time,' Berg said, effectively dismissing him. He and Lauren turned to walk out. The music turned up a few more notches.

'I need to get to the hospital,' Lauren said as she pushed the heavy door open with her hip. 'I need to make sure Matt is OK.'

'I'll drop you off, take care of my statement, and see if I can get more background on Bjarni. We need to find him.'

The night air quickly refroze any part of her that had briefly thawed out in the warm bar. 'Text me when you're done,' she said, trying to keep her teeth from chattering again.

'What are you thinking, Lauren Riley?' Berg asked.

She looked over at the spot where Matt had laid sprawled on the ground. 'Someone just sent us a message.'

THIRTY-THREE

M att was sedated and getting prepped for surgery when Lauren got to the hospital. The stocky doctor with his hands shoved into the pockets of his white lab coat explained to her that Matt had a compound fracture in his left forearm and a broken clavicle. 'He's lucky,' he told her. 'We have to reset the bones in his arm, but there are no internal injuries. The clavicle is a clean break. Other than that, just a lot of cuts and bruises.'

He then pointed out that Lauren had scraped up both of her palms pretty badly. She'd forgotten about her hands, but once the doctor brought it to her attention, they began to throb and sting. She'd given Berg his jacket back when he dropped her off and turned over the lone shoe to the attending nurse to put with Matt's possessions. Now she didn't know what to do with her aching hands.

The emergency room of the National University Hospital, or Landspítali, as the attending nurse had sounded out for her, was sadly a familiar-looking place to Lauren. Even the waiting room chairs were very similar to the chairs at the Erie County Medical Center. Both were made with a wood frame and spongy blue fabric cushions, although the Icelandic chairs were vastly more comfortable. The biggest difference was the quiet. The emergency room was almost empty, a far cry from the nightly chaos at the Erie County Medical Center back home.

That same nurse had retrieved her parka and brought her a scrub top to wear. She had quickly peeled off her wet jacket and top in the meticulously clean waiting room bathroom, and replaced it with the stiff greenish-colored hospital wear. She stood at the sink and carefully washed her hands. The thick scars across her right palm looked raw and bloody again. Lauren dabbed them dry with a paper towel, knowing she'd have to get some gauze to tape them up. She couldn't be running around Reykjavík with bloody hands.

Back in the waiting room, Lauren sat down and tried to focus on how to find out who did this to Matt. The room was pleasantly warm but her pants were still soaked, causing her to shiver. Lauren draped her parka over her legs. The outside shell of the parka was damp but, thankfully, the lining was dry. She furiously began fielding texts and calls from her superiors, Matt's superiors, and the district attorney's office. Inwardly, she was grateful for that because it put off the inevitable of having to talk to Matt's wife, Cara.

That gratitude only lasted a few minutes. Her cell buzzed and a call came across her screen: *Cara Lawton*. As per her commissioner's instructions, Lauren had put Cara's number in her phone and Matt had put Reese's number in his as their emergency contacts. Lauren never believed they'd actually have to use them, although with her track record she should have guessed they'd be needed. Commissioner Bennett obviously had.

Lauren stared at the phone for a second, then told the assistant district attorney she'd call him back.

'Cara?' She'd never spoken to Matt's wife before. She flashed back to the picture he had on his desk. It was him, his baby boy, and his pretty wife, all smiling into the camera. The perfect young family.

Lauren knew that the accident hadn't happened because of her, but she still felt responsible. It was irrational, but she was getting good at blaming herself.

'What happened to Matt? Is he all right?' In the background, a baby howled. She pictured Cara with the phone wedged between her shoulder and ear, bouncing the wailing baby on her hip as she paced around her living room.

'He's going to be fine. A couple of broken bones. No internal injuries.' Lauren tried to sound optimistic and reassuring. The panic in Cara's voice was real. She'd pick up on any hesitation on Lauren's part and read the worst into it.

'But what happened? His supervisor said he was hit by a car.'

Lauren took a deep breath before she spoke. 'We were crossing a street here in Reykjavík, when a car came from out of nowhere and clipped Matt. It was a hit-and-run.'

'Did they catch the guy?'

'As of right now, no.'

There was a long pause on Cara's end, then: 'No one will tell me anything. Is he conscious? Is he in pain? Oh my God, what is going on?' she cried from a world away, making the baby bawl even harder.

'Cara, he is being prepped for surgery on his arm.' *Keep your voice calm*, Lauren reminded herself, *don't feed her panic.* 'He has a compound fracture of the forearm, so they had to sedate him for the surgery to reset the bones. He also has a broken clavicle. The doctor doesn't seem as concerned with that injury. He said it was a clean break. He assured me Matt is going to be fine.'

She heard Cara take in a deep breath and try to soothe her baby with a *shhh shhh shhh.* 'He's going to be OK?'

She nodded as if Cara could see her. 'He's going to be fine.'

Now Cara let loose with straight up sobs of frustration and anger. Lauren wasn't sure if that frustration and anger was aimed at her or not. She gave Cara the name of the doctor she'd spoken to, cautioning her that Matt was probably in surgery now.

'Thank you. Thank you,' she panted, sucking in her sobs. Lauren heard another woman's voice over the line, gently trying to comfort her. At least Cara wasn't alone. 'Please keep me posted. Please.'

'I'll do my best,' Lauren said. Matt's distraught wife clicked off without saying goodbye.

Lauren sat staring at the phone in her scraped-up hand for a moment. It kept buzzing with incoming calls that she ignored. If it wasn't Berg or Reese, she didn't want to talk. She put the phone face down on the chair next to her, tilted her head back and closed her eyes to rerun the scenario over and over in her mind. It was all she could do.

It was ten o'clock when Berg showed up at the hospital. It felt like it was five in the morning to Lauren, who was nursing a two-hour old cup of coffee.

'How is he doing?' The snow caught in his red curls quickly melted into droplets in the warmth of the waiting room. He ran his fingers through both sides of his hair causing Lauren to get hit with the spray that came flying off.

'Out of surgery,' she answered. 'The last I heard from one
of the nurses was that he was in one of the recovery rooms.
We won't be able to see him until the morning.'

Berg reached down, putting his hand on Lauren's shoulder.
'We have excellent doctors in this hospital. Your friend will
be fine. There's nothing more you can do here.'

She nodded in agreement, or more like surrender, and Berg
removed his hand. 'Take me back to the hotel. I'll grab an
Uber or a cab first thing in the morning and be back here
when Matt wakes up.'

'No and no,' he corrected her. 'My wife made enough lamb
to feed an army. I know you haven't eaten since the coffee
shop. So we're going to go back to my house. You'll meet my
wife and daughter. Anna is letting Elin stay up late to meet
you. We'll eat, have some drinks and soak in the hot tub to
sooth your nerves.'

Lauren blinked at him in surprise. 'How can you think of
drinking or eating or sitting in a freaking hot tub after our
colleague just got run down in the street?'

'First of all, you need to eat,' Berg said in a maddeningly
patient voice, like he was talking to his daughter and not a
forty-year-old police detective. 'Second, you really, really
need a drink. In fact, I don't think I've ever met anyone who
needed a drink more than you. And third, we Icelanders use
our hot tubs year-round. We soak in them to clear our heads
and loosen up our muscles. They are great stress relievers,
believe me.'

Even though she didn't appreciate his tone she couldn't
argue with Berg's strange logic. 'Did they find Ragnar or
Bjarni yet?'

'No. And half the Metropolitan police force is out looking
for both of them. Ragnar never came home, Bjarni's mother
doesn't know where he is. As for the car,' he continued, 'I
went over to Ragnar's office to check it out for myself. The
BMW is still parked there. It was ice cold and there wasn't a
scratch on it.'

'He owns an import/export business. I'm sure Ragnar has
access to a lot of vehicles.'

Berg answered Lauren's next question without her having

to ask. 'I made certain they put all the collision shops on notice. If anyone tries to get front-end damage fixed in the Capital District, I'll get a call.'

'Thank you.' It came out in a whisper, lower than she intended.

'Don't thank me until you have my wife's lamb.' He held his hand out to her. 'And let's grab something to bandage you with on the way out. You look like you tried to warm up your hands with a cheese grater.'

THIRTY-FOUR

Lauren wished she could have just leaned her head against the window and closed her eyes like she'd done on the plane to Iceland. But every nerve in her body was firing off now that she was outside of the hospital. She found herself staring at every car coming toward them, wondering if they were about to take a head-on hit. Every pair of headlights that appeared behind them was suspect. In front of her, lines of text on Berg's police computer kept slowly scrolling down, the calls going out and patrol cars putting themselves back in service, she assumed. Not all that different from Buffalo. Outside, it was lightly snowing. The flakes hit the windshield and immediately disappeared. This place was so foreign and yet so familiar.

'I live in a very nice, quiet neighborhood,' Berg told her. 'It's called Mosfellsbær. It's only about fifteen minutes from downtown, but if feels like you're out in the countryside. I hope you get to see it during the day. The Valley of Mosfellsdalur is quite beautiful. They say in the Icelandic sagas that the great hero Egill Skallagrimsson buried his treasure in the valley.' He gave a chuckle, staring straight ahead at the road. 'No one's found it yet, though.'

Once they got out of the greater downtown area, the roads became desolate. Berg hummed to himself as he drove, tapping his fingers to his own tune, to fill the silence, Lauren supposed. Unlike her, Berg seemed to need to be doing something, saying something, or moving around constantly.

The sparsely populated road started to turn into the beginnings of a town: more houses, a gas station, a convenient-type store, the white steeple of a church.

Berg pulled off down a side street, then made another turn. The houses were square, boxy dwellings with two levels, spaced far apart. Whoever had built this neighborhood wanted to make sure that every resident had their privacy.

'In a snowstorm it can be a bitch to live here. It takes some time for the local officials to plow everyone out. But we make do. We're accustomed to it.'

'That sounds like Buffalo,' Lauren said as they turned up a long driveway. Set back at least sixty yards from the main road, Berg's small house was lit up like a beacon against a field of newly fallen snow. In the front window she could see a Christmas tree strung with white lights.

'You have Christmas trees here.' She'd seen one at her hotel, but she thought that was just for the tourists' benefit.

A woman in a long, full skirt and festive wool sweater appeared in the doorway. Her arm was draped around a little girl of about eight. Both were smiling, but Lauren could see the strain in Berg's wife's face. The stress of being a policeman's wife was universal.

'Welcome,' she called, waving at them. 'I have dinner waiting for you on the table. Come in, come in!'

Lauren crossed the threshold, while Berg stopped for a quick kiss from his wife and daughter, hugging them close to him on either side. 'Anna, Elin, this is Lauren,' Berg announced, still holding onto his family.

'Hello,' Lauren said, wandering further inside. The living room was warm and inviting, decorated in that Scandinavian chic aesthetic: clean lines, soft blues and natural woodwork. The smell of the lamb filled her nostrils as soon as she stepped in, making her mouth water. Had it really been hours ago since she had eaten that fish sandwich?

Giving Elin an affectionate rub on the head, Berg walked from the small entryway into the living room. He spread his arms wide. 'Welcome to my castle. If I know my wife, she's anxious for you to try her specialty: roasted leg of lamb and steamed vegetables. It's an old family recipe handed down for generations—'

Anna swatted Berg on the shoulder to shut him up. 'It's literally roasted leg of lamb and vegetables. No magic recipe, but it's good, I think. Please, come and sit in the dining room. What can I get you to drink?'

Berg led Lauren to their dining room. Simple green valances hung over the drawn pleated window shades. The rectangular table was covered with a white lacy tablecloth. It was done up like a royal feast: three plates of leg of lamb, a huge platter of carrots, cauliflower and potatoes, and a giant gravy boat sat waiting for them. 'This is too much,' Lauren said as Anna poured wine for everyone but Elin. 'You shouldn't have gone to all this trouble.'

'It's no trouble. Elin here already ate ages ago but said she wouldn't be able to sleep until she saw the American policewoman.'

Putting the bottle down on the table, Anna disappeared into the kitchen, coming back with a plate of flat round bread. 'This is *laufabrauð*, or leaf bread,' she said. 'See the little designs? They're supposed to look like leaves. Please relax and enjoy yourself.' Lauren took a piece and set it on her bread plate. It was almost too pretty to eat.

'Thank you.' She pulled at the edge and nibbled at a bit. It was delicious. Anna fluttered around the table, placing things here and there, while Elin sat across from Lauren staring at her with Berg's same look of mischief on her face. It was all so normal.

Too normal.

Lauren bit back the words that immediately sprang to mind. Lauren knew she was putting her frustration in the wrong place. Someone had tried to kill them today. They'd almost succeeded with Matt. Lauren could sense Anna was upset as well, putting on a strong face for her daughter. Someone had attempted to kill her husband, the father of her child, and there she was trying to be accommodating and understanding. *I need a class in empathy*, Lauren thought, sliding around in her seat, willing herself to be comfortable. *This woman probably wants to lock Berg inside this house and cry and here I am being ungrateful.*

Elin still stared at her with wide, round eyes. Finally she asked, 'Are you really a policewoman in America?'

Reaching out, Lauren grabbed her wine glass and took a drink before answering. 'I really am a policewoman in America. My name is Lauren. And you must be Elin. Your father has told me so much about you.' That was a lie, but Lauren could understand why Berg didn't go on about his family. She tried to keep her own daughters as separate from her police life as possible, volunteering nothing about them if she could help it. Sometimes she was afraid just being their mother was danger enough.

'Do you have a partner?' Elin asked. She flashed the same crafty grin she'd inherited from her father.

'Elin!' Anna cried, mortified at her daughter's boldness.

Lauren was confused for a second, then remembered that she had read in Iceland you could have a partner or be married. They were two separate categories for couples. The child wasn't asking about work relationships.

'No, I don't. I do have two daughters. They are both away at their universities now, but I plan to see them as soon as I get home, hopefully in time for Christmas.'

'I want to go to the university and be a biologist who studies whales.'

'That's a good thing to want to be,' Lauren agreed. From across the table Berg beamed at his daughter. Anna sat next to him, ladling the vegetables onto their plates one at a time from the serving platter in the middle of the table. Anna was at least ten years younger than Berg, maybe thirty-eight, with thin shoulder-length brown hair that hung straight down on either side of her heart shaped face.

Lauren forced herself to eat as much as possible, she didn't want to seem rude but the effects of seeing Matt sprawled on the pavement in pain had made her appetite disappear. She did her best to chew the lamb, which was delicious, very slowly before she swallowed to drag out the meal as long as possible. Elin sat recalling the events of her day to everyone around the table. She had hung out with one of her friends and played on a new app the friend had gotten that could turn your own face into a cute animal's. 'I made myself a duck. I even had a duck's bill,' she said, then asked, 'Can I get that app?'

'We'll see,' Berg told her, then added something in Icelandic. The three of them all laughed. It was still odd to Lauren to hear them flip from English to Icelandic like it was nothing. She'd taken four years of Spanish and the only thing she remembered was hello, goodbye, and how to ask where the bathroom was. She'd always wanted to try to learn Spanish as an adult but had never found the time. *Maybe it's time to make the time*, she resolved to herself. *I'm not getting any younger. And I came really close to not getting any older today.*

Lauren sipped hot herbal tea, while Berg put his daughter to bed and Anna cleared the table, refusing any offer of help. From upstairs the sounds of laughter drifted down, mixing with the sounds of dishes clanking together in the kitchen. She took a better look around. The living room flowed into the dining room in a kind of open floor plan. Family pictures adorned the walls of both rooms, mostly pictures of Elin and her various milestones. The love they had for her was evident everywhere.

A big screen TV sat on a console in the living room, dark and black, reflecting Lauren's image back at her. She was a mess. Pushing the hair out of her eyes, she stared at the gaunt person reflected in the glass. One of the lenses of her glasses had gotten scratched when they flew from her face. She slipped them off, polished them with the hem of her shirt and put them back on. Out of the corner of her right eye she could still see the scratch.

It wasn't her fault that Matt had gotten hurt. In her head, she knew that. Someone was trying to sabotage their investigation. But it sure felt like it was her fault.

Anna began to sing as she rinsed dishes and put them in neat rows in the dishwasher. 'I hope you don't mind wearing one of my old bathing suits,' she called over her shoulder. 'It might be a little big on you but it's very modest. I never went in for the tiny bikini look.'

'Me either.' Lauren wanted to wrap her hands around the tea mug like she usually did but looked down at the bandages and decided that wouldn't be the best idea. Fresh blood dotted the white gauze as her palms throbbed and stung.

A door slammed upstairs followed by a chorus of giggling. Berg came down the stairs with a huge grin stretched across his face. He stopped at the foot of stair, clapped his hands together and asked, 'Who's ready for the hot tub?'

Anna brought Lauren a simple black one-piece suit, exactly

the type she would pick out for herself. She changed in their downstairs bathroom; thankful she'd shaved her legs in the shower that morning. When she stepped out into the hallway, Anna and Berg were waiting for her. Anna had a similar one-piece suit on in a rust color and Berg had on tight boy shorts, like boxer briefs, for which Lauren was thankful. She'd heard European guys like to wear Speedos and while she was no prude, she wasn't sure she was comfortable with seeing that much of a colleague.

It was hard not to stare though. Berg was an extremely hairy man, made worse by the fact that it was curly, flaming red, covering him from head to toe. He noticed her trying not to notice and put a fist on each hip. 'I'm a hairy man. Like the Abominable Snowman. But I never get cold and Anna here loves it!' He gave his wife a playful squeeze.

Anna smiled and gestured to the back door through the kitchen. 'The hot tub is right out there. Please, let's relax for a while.'

'Take off those glasses.' Berg patted the kitchen counter. 'They'll fog up right away.'

Lauren pulled them off and left them folded neatly next to the microwave.

One of the couple had taken the time to put candles around the large eight-man hot tub that sat bubbling before them. Lauren had no robe, but neither did Berg or Anna. The steam rising from the roiling water hung above the tub like a dense fog. 'The trick is,' Berg said from the doorway, 'to just get in. No hesitation. Just drop in up to your chin, and the water and steam will keep you warm.'

To demonstrate this he charged out onto the wooden deck barefoot and catapulted himself over the side, sending a deluge of water slopping over the edge. 'Ahhh. That feels heavenly,' he murmured sinking down until only his face from the nose up was visible.

Anna was next, demurely slipping into the water. She beckoned Lauren to come in. 'It's fine,' she promised. Berg popped up and sat with his arms stretched out on either side behind him. 'Don't bother to shut the door.'

Lauren took a deep breath and plunged into the freezing

cold, not stopping until she was crawling over the side of the hot tub. She plopped herself in, marveling at how the rising steam made it feel like she was on a sunny beach in Jamaica, instead of a hot tub in Iceland at midnight.

'It's nice, right?' Berg asked, pouring wine from a bottle stuck in a small pile of snow into glasses Anna must have set out prior to them getting home.

'And good for you,' Anna said, leaning against Berg's hairy chest. 'Glacier water is good for your skin and hair and whatever else ails you.'

'This is unbelievable,' Lauren said, looking around. Berg's backyard stretched into white covered nothingness. His neighbors on both sides were nothing more than small rectangular window lights in the distance. 'You have trees,' she marveled, looking up at the pairs of spruce trees on either side of the yard.

'I planted those when I first moved in,' Berg said. 'That was sixteen years ago. Before I even knew this one.' He splashed some water toward his wife who laughed and gave a playful splash back. 'They came in nice, I think. When the Vikings arrived, they used up a lot of the natural forests here. We're still trying to bring back the trees.'

'They're beautiful,' Lauren said, wiping away the sweat that was beginning to bead on her upper lip with the back of her damaged hand. They sat in silence for a few moments, soaking in the hot water and breathing in the soothing steam.

'I know you feel responsible for your friend, Matt,' Berg began, 'But you can't think like that. Tomorrow we are going to go see him, and then we're going to find out who did this to him. I promise.'

'Don't promise. Some promises you can't keep, no matter how hard you try,' Lauren said to him, maybe just a little too sharply.

'Fair enough,' Berg conceded. 'We will try our best and with great luck we will succeed in finding out who did this. Better?'

'Better,' Lauren agreed, taking a drink of her chilled red wine.

'Without your glasses on you look more like I thought you

would,' Berg told her. 'I googled you and Matt before you came. There was nothing on Matt. But you? Page after page with your picture splashed across them.'

Lauren was glad the steam would obscure some of her reaction. 'Buffalo may be a big city, but it's more like a small town. Or Iceland. Everyone knows everyone.' She took another gulp of wine. 'I had a few very high-profile cases. It seemed like every time I turned around a news camera was in my face.'

'So you chopped your blond hair and started wearing glasses.' It was statement, not a question.

She nodded. 'I was tired of people recognizing me in the grocery store. I wanted to go out to dinner with my daughters without people gawking.'

'I'm sorry I called you frumpy,' Berg said. Anna whacked him with the back of her hand at that revelation.

'I'm not,' she smiled. 'It means my disguise is working.'

'So Lauren,' Anna began, trying to change the subject, 'is there someone special in Buffalo?'

Like mother like daughter, Lauren mused. But still, she hesitated before answering. 'No. I'm not involved with anyone.'

'But you said earlier today you had to check on your partner at home,' Berg said. 'I thought you didn't want to get personal in front of Elin. She can be a little aggressive with her questions at times.'

Lauren laughed. 'I meant my *work* partner, Reese. A few months back he caught a grazing bullet wound to the head while we were working. It was during one of those high-profile cases I was just talking about. He fell and fractured his skull.' Looking down into her wine glass she went on, 'There were complications. He's been staying with me since he got out of the hospital.'

'You blame yourself for that incident as well.' It was another statement, not question, from Berg.

She nodded. 'It was absolutely my fault. I did a series of stupid selfish things that led directly to his being shot.'

Berg took a drink. 'Somehow I think there's more to the story.'

'Much more, but you don't have all night,' Lauren said.

'But there is no romance between the two of you? At all?' Anna asked hopefully. Lauren could tell she was the romantic type, wanting to see flowers in the ice.

'Strictly platonic,' Lauren replied hoping to close the subject.

'Do you want it to stay that way?' Berg got the hint but couldn't help but be blunt.

A bead of sweat ran down her forehead. She'd been asking herself that very question a lot lately. 'I honestly don't know how to answer that.'

They let the silence of the night enclose them, broken only by the bubbling water and humming of the tub's motor. The snow had stopped and the light on the backyard made the ground glitter like a blanket of diamonds.

'See there.' Berg pointed to the sky. 'It's cloudy tonight.'

'Many times we sit out here and the Northern Lights come out to play,' Anna said.

'Just because you can't see them,' Berg explained, searching the night sky for a moment, 'doesn't mean they aren't there.'

Lauren swallowed hard. The words she wanted to say were stuck on her tongue, because once she said them, once she admitted to the feelings she'd been having, they'd be out there in the world, and there was no way to take them back. It was better to swallow them whole.

'Cheers.' Berg held out his wine and the three of them touched glasses.

THIRTY-FIVE

B erg, Anna, and Lauren polished off the bottle of red wine before Berg drove Lauren back to the hotel. Even though she loved it, red wine always gave Lauren a headache, and her head was throbbing as much as her hands when he dropped her off.

Berg said he'd be back to get her at nine a.m. sharp. Lauren doubted she'd get that much sleep, or any sleep at all, even with the wine. Sure enough, it was another night of her lying in bed, rewinding the events of the day, trying to figure out where she went wrong.

She was showered, dressed, and ready at the agreed upon time. No use dicking around – Berg was a man in perpetual motion. Somehow Lauren knew that if she tried to sleep in, Berg would have pounded on her door until she was awake. Resistance seemed futile against that guy.

He came strolling into the lobby as she finished her third cup of complimentary coffee. 'I thought I drank too much of that stuff until I met you,' he said as she put the empty cup upside down on the serving tray provided for dirty dishes.

'It's the only thing keeping me sane right now,' she shot back.

'Is that what this is?' he asked, grabbing her wrist and lifting her shaking hand.

She pulled away but couldn't help but smile at his nerve. 'Let's just get to the hospital.'

'There's been a change of plans,' he told her, walking with her through the early morning gloom to his vehicle. 'We're going to Bjarni's mother's house. I have a feeling he doesn't have many places to stay, or else why would he use the bar as his mailing address. It's nice and early for his kind. Let's see if we can roust him out of bed.'

'What do you mean "his kind"?'

Berg extracted some paperwork from the inside of his jacket.

'The criminal kind. He has arrests for drug possession, petty theft, fraud, and assault.'

'Son of a bitch,' Lauren whispered as she looked over the record that Berg had so kindly printed out in English for her. A mugshot was paperclipped to the front. Like Gunnar, Bjarni had dark, almost black hair, but the resemblance ended there. Where Gunnar had soft features, Bjarni looked like he was carved from a block of granite, all sharp angles – from his cheekbones to his chin. He was also listed as six foot one.

'He's a big man,' Lauren commented as Berg began to drive. 'Do you carry a gun?'

Once again, he laughed at the absurdity of her American thinking. 'No, I don't have a gun on me. I hope it never gets so bad here that I have to carry one on duty. Certain cars are equipped with weapons if a critical incident occurs, but us everyday investigators have to use our wits and charm to subdue criminals.'

Lauren arched an eyebrow. 'What a novel concept.'

'Why would someone fight with me? We're on an island. Where are they going to go?'

Board a boat, hop on a plane, or jump on a snowmobile, Lauren thought as the city streets rolled by. *Maybe people can disappear here, go up into the mountains and never come down.* Berg had told her all about the trolls his people still believed in. *Maybe they're just people who've made so many mistakes they don't recognize themselves anymore and hide away in the hills.*

As much as she wanted to allow her thoughts to take her to dark places, she had to stay sharp. She'd been an American cop for too long to disregard violence as a response to her presence. She would have thought Matt getting run down in the street would have driven that point home to Berg. He was still singing softly to himself as they pulled up in front of Bjarni's current residence.

Bjarni's mother lived in a rundown-looking building not far from the Wolf's Den. Lauren made Berg wait while they watched the two-story building. He was not the wait-and-observe type of person, fidgeting with the keys, just like Reese used to do when they were on stakeouts. 'An old lieutenant of mine used to say you should watch a house for at least ten minutes before you knocked on a door.'

'Is he still alive or did he die of boredom?'

'It's funny you should say that because now he works as a maintenance guy at a cemetery.'

Berg nodded in agreement. 'Sounds like a fitting place for a man such as that.'

'I don't see the car he was supposed to be driving last night.' Lauren scanned every vehicle parked up and down the street. For the life of her, she could not figure out how people fit into the little boxy type cars that were so popular here. They looked like the toy cars Lindsey and Erin used to push each other around in when they were toddlers.

'It looks like there's a garage in the back. His mother's apartment should be back there too, according to the report the uniforms who came here last night filed.'

'Let's go then. And watch your back,' she warned, holding up her freshly bandaged hands for illustration. 'Someone tried to kill us yesterday.'

It was a four-unit apartment house with four separate entrances. Every pair of headlights on the street was suspect now. Lauren listened for even a hint of an idling motor, but all she heard was the soft moaning of a light wind through the row of apartment buildings.

Bjarni's mother lived in the ground-floor apartment directly behind the building. A fire escape led to another door on the second floor, but Lauren wasn't sure if that was the main entrance or not. She wasn't sure what was considered up to code by Icelandic standards. A rusted metal 3 was nailed into the door at eye level. Berg waited until Lauren was bladed to the side and gave three good knocks.

From inside there was a shuffling sound, like old slippers on a worn floor, and when a tired-looking woman pulled the door open that's exactly what it turned out to be. She greeted them unenthusiastically in Icelandic, her eyes narrowed in suspicion as she looked them both up and down

Berg responded in his gruff but endearing way, not bothering to ask her to speak English. Lauren could tell this poor woman, who was maybe five years older than herself, was barely making ends meet. She yanked the door open and let them in.

The apartment was as shabby as the building, but clean. The living room and kitchen were one big room divided by a breakfast bar. In one corner of the kitchen a small television set was on, playing a cooking show. A mixing bowl with a wooden spoon sticking out of it sat on the counter. They had interrupted her making breakfast.

She turned her eyes to Lauren. 'He's in his bedroom. I'll go get him.' Then she shuffled off in her flowered housecoat down a side hallway.

'What did she say to you?' Lauren asked.

'She told me the police had been here last night and Bjarni wasn't home. She asked me if I'd come to take him away.'

'What did you tell her?' Lauren could hear Bjarni's mother knocking on a door and calling to him in Icelandic.

'That all we wanted to do was talk to him. She seemed miffed at that. Apparently, he doesn't help her out much.'

A second later she came scuffling back down the hall with a man who was about thirty at her heels. He was the guy from the mug shot Berg had just showed Lauren, no doubt, right down to the Viking runes tattooed on his neck.

'Can I help you with something?' he asked Berg in English.

'I think you know why we're here,' Berg said, squaring up with him. Bjarni was very fit and muscular, with dark hair that hung down to his broad, tattooed shoulders. 'So don't start playing stupid right off the bat.'

'Look,' Bjarni dropped down onto the worn brown sofa, as his mother made her way back around the breakfast bar to grab her mixing bowl, 'I got a call from Helga. She said three police officers were coming to see me and I'd better clear out. So I finished my drink and went to a friend of mine's house for a few hours. Then I hear that one of the cops got hit by a car on the way into the Wolf's Den.'

'Helga called you?' Lauren asked. *Why would Helga tip off the very guy she made it a point to tell them to seek out?*

'Yeah, what of it?' he asked, his handsome face tilted upward in a little show of defiance. 'She always liked me when I worked for Ragnar, but she'll deny it. She'll want to keep her job. I took off because I heard about what happened to Gunnar and I don't want any part of your investigation.'

'That's not exactly the actions of an innocent man,' Lauren said.

He snorted. 'You? An American cop telling me what I should do to protect myself? I read stories about what you do to your citizens every day. The last thing I want to get myself involved in is an American murder investigation.'

'How long did you work for Ragnar?' Lauren asked, trying to get back on track.

'Almost a year,' he said, the words highlighted by his Nordic accent. It was different from Berg's. Thicker, somehow.

'What was your relationship like with Ragnar?' Berg asked.

He put his hands out in front of him as if to slow things down. 'I respect you, but my *former* relationship with Ragnar is none of your business.'

Red rose to Berg's cheeks. He wasn't used to getting told no by a criminal, even if it was the nicest no Lauren had ever encountered in police work.

Lauren cut in to try to defuse Berg's temper. 'Have you left the country in the last four weeks?'

Behind them, Bjarni's mother dropped her mixing spoon and swore loudly before picking it up. Bjarni smiled. 'I've never left Iceland. Ever. But I'm sure you have ways to check that. I can also tell you that I was in Akureyri all last week working on a friend's barn roof that collapsed. It turned out to be a five-day job just trying to save the horses. I can give you my friend's name and number, and about six other men who were working there with me.'

'Can we see your car?' Berg asked, his agitation now in check.

'If it will put an end to all of this, of course. It's in the garage.' He wiped his hands on his jeans and stood up. 'Follow me.'

Sure enough, his white Toyota Corolla was parked in the cramped wooden garage. The old car was surrounded by spare tires, broken car parts and random junk. One thing was certain as they examined the car: the bartender at the Wolf's Den wasn't kidding when he said that if Bjarni hit anyone with it, he'd damage the car more than the person.

'You didn't drive this to Akureyri, did you?' Berg asked, running his hand along the rusted hood. Lauren was surprised the thing had made it into the garage.

'Of course not. The weather was good, so my friend sent me the money to fly in. He raises champion Icelandic horses. He needed that barn fixed right away.'

Lauren crossed her arms and leaned up against the driver's side door. 'Are you sure you don't want to talk to us about you and Ragnar?'

Bjarni wagged a finger in Lauren's direction with a smile. 'I like you. You're tough, like a TV cop. I've been waiting for you to pull your gun out and read me my rights. Maybe you'll slap the cuffs on me.'

A crooked smile formed on Lauren's lips. 'Don't believe everything you see on television. Believe some of it, but not all of it.'

He seemed to accept that answer. 'All I'll say is this, we parted on good terms. I miss working for him. I haven't been able to find a job like that since. Now, if you both will excuse me, I have things to do.'

'Give me your buddy's name with the horses.' Lauren tried to write down the Bjarni's friend's name in her notebook, causing Berg to grab it out of her hand and cross out what she wrote.

'That is not an "A",' he lectured her as he corrected her Icelandic, 'and this letter is . . . never mind, I'll do it.'

'Is he always so forceful with you?' Bjarni asked Lauren, suppressing another smirk as Berg wrote.

'I don't know. We've only known each other three days,' she replied. She couldn't help returning the grin. Bjarni may have been a cocky asshole, but he was charming in his own way.

He raised an eyebrow at her. 'That doesn't bode well, I think.'

Not even pretending to be amused, Berg handed back her pen and notebook and walked out of the garage without a glance back or a thank-you to Bjarni.

They weren't even halfway to the hospital before Berg said out loud what Lauren had been thinking all along. 'Why would a serious professional like Ragnar hire a rough, petty criminal like Bjarni to be his assistant?'

THIRTY-SIX

auren's phone buzzed in her pocket as they pulled into the hospital's parking lot. She pulled it out and looked at the screen: *Connolly*. Holding a finger up to Berg she said, 'Give me a minute, I have to take this.'

He gave her a gruff nod and dug his own phone out while she answered. 'Detective Riley.'

'Riley, it's Sergeant Connolly. What time is it over there?'

She looked out the windshield across the parking lot bathed in the soft light of the Icelandic morning. 'It's 11:31 a.m.,' she said, checking the time on the bottom of her phone.

'That's one easy question answered. Now the tough one: what the hell is going on over there? We send you to one of the safest countries in the world, and you still manage to get yourself in trouble.'

'I got one of my partners in trouble, you mean.'

'Don't start boo-hooing on me now. It was rhetorical.' Before she could tell him she didn't think that word meant what he thought it meant, he told her, 'I've actually got some good news for you.'

Her eyes slid to Berg, who was fully engrossed in texting something to someone. 'Don't keep me in suspense. Spit it out.'

'The FBI managed to get in Gunnar's phone. I just got the call. They're sending the data to their translators as we speak.'

Lauren sucked in a breath. 'This could be the break we're looking for.'

'And it could be nothing. But I'll say one thing, those FBI people must work around the clock. It's barely six thirty in the morning here and I just got the call from Matt Lawton's boss.'

Silently, she wondered if Matt getting hit by the car lit a fire under their asses or if the FBI was just that good. Maybe it was a little bit of both. 'Did they give a timeline? I need to know how long it's going to be to have Gunnar's text messages and emails translated.'

'No idea. But they do this forensic computer stuff all the time. Cracking the phone was the hard part, translating it should be a breeze.'

'I'm at the hospital right now, about to go in to see Matt. Call me as soon as you hear from Matt's people.'

'I'm on it over here on our end. Just you keep yourself safe, got it?'

'Got it. Bye.'

Lauren turned to Berg, who looked up from his own text conversation and told him, 'The FBI managed to get into Gunnar's phone. They're sending the contents to be translated now.'

'I heard. Why don't they just forward all his texts and emails to me? I'll translate them right now and we won't have to wait.'

'I wish the world worked according to Berg,' Lauren said. 'But it doesn't. If it's any consolation, my boss said he doesn't think it'll take long.'

Berg grumbled something under his breath in Icelandic and got out of the car.

Matt was awake but groggy when they came into his hospital room. Propped up by pillows, he was staring at the television mounted on the wall, his left arm was in a navy-blue splint held close to his body by some kind of contraption. He gave a weary smile. 'Hey guys,' he said. His face was sickly pale, his eyes looked like he'd gone ten rounds with Mike Tyson.

'How are you feeling?' she asked him, moving around to the right side of his hospital bed while Berg planted himself firmly at the end.

'I broke my ulna and radius. One of the bones went through the skin. It's pretty ugly under there.' He gestured with his chin to the split.

'What about your clavicle?' Lauren asked.

'The doctor told me that's the least of my worries. They had to reposition my bones in surgery and now they're being held together with metal plates and screws. They really have to monitor me for infection right now. That's the biggest danger.' He tilted his head toward the IV bags pumping him full of fluids. 'They've got me on some heavy-duty stuff.'

'Are you in pain, brother?' Berg asked.

'I think the anesthesia hasn't worn all the way off yet, but yeah, it hurts like hell. Every time I breathe in it's like two nice, sharp little knives sticking me in the shoulder and arm.'

He looked so young to Lauren, lying there like a middle-schooler who fell off the monkey bars at recess. Lauren's stomach clenched in the familiar knot of guilt. 'Cara called me last night,' she said.

He nodded. 'She told me. I got off the phone with her an hour ago. She stayed up all night, waiting until I was able to talk.'

'I'm glad they let you use the phone,' Lauren said, suppressing the motherly urge to pull his thin blanket up higher.

'We FaceTimed, actually. The nurse had to hold the phone in front of me. My right arm is fine but when I try to move it or reach for something . . .'

'You feel it on the other side,' Berg finished for him. 'I had a broken shoulder as a kid; not as bad as your injury, but I swear I felt it all over my body those first couple days. Don't fret, it gets better.'

'Cara is so upset. She wanted to jump on a plane and fly here. I told her not to. My little guy needs her there. And I'm still working. I can still work from this bed, see?' For the first time Lauren noticed a hospital food tray angled under his right arm. His phone, a pad and a pen were positioned on it. 'I can answer calls by putting them on speaker and take notes and relay information to the both of you.'

'I don't think your doctor is going to want you to do that,' Lauren cautioned.

He shook his head, forehead creasing in frustration. 'They aren't taking me out of the game. No way. They tried, but I'm still in this investigation, no matter what.'

Lauren gripped the rail of Matt's bed with both hands. 'We do have some good news though.'

'They got in Gunnar's phone, your people,' Berg told him. 'We're just waiting for them to have everything translated.'

A genuine smile stretched across Matt's face. 'Gunnar's brother said he lived on his phone.'

'Right,' Lauren agreed. 'And we just talked to Bjarni. He said Helga tipped him off we were coming, which makes no sense. He's got an alibi for Gunnar's murder that we still have to check out, but I don't think he's our guy.'

'Which brings us right back to Ragnar,' Matt said.

'It's possible he was in his office the whole time and Helga was protecting him,' Lauren said. 'For a supposedly innocent man, he sure is making himself look like a suspect.'

'I don't trust a word out of Bjarni's mouth,' Berg said, his red hair even more fiery under the bright florescent lighting. 'I want to go back to Ragnar's house. This time check to see if he's holed up in there.'

'Freyja will just protect him,' Lauren countered.

'Guys?' Matt said, making Lauren and Berg focus on him again. 'I know I just had surgery a couple hours ago and my mind is still in a fog, but we were focusing on people close to Ragnar and they've circled the wagons. Maybe you should talk to the one person who doesn't have a personal stake with Ragnar in any of this.'

Berg's eyebrows drew together in a questioning V. 'Who?'

A wave of pain hit Matt, causing his whole body to go rigid and tense up. It took a second to pass and then he let out a staggered breath. 'The ex-boyfriend Jakob told us about. I think you should talk to him.'

THIRTY-SEVEN

Berg had to squint at the piece of paper Jakob had scribbled on for a minute before he was confident he knew where he was going. Stefan Johansson lived in a trendy neighborhood near the university, close to all the best bars and restaurants, Berg told Lauren. His flat was located in a very modern apartment complex complete with underground parking. 'This place is a great mixture of students and young professionals,' he said as they pulled up. 'This is a very sought-after neighborhood. Close to everything. My niece lived on the next street over while she was going to the university.'

'Shouldn't Stefan be at work?' Lauren asked.

'This close to Christmas,' Berg ran his fingers through his crimson curls in the rearview mirror, trying to make himself look presentable, 'most non-service businesses are closed. When I ran his name, the computer said he works for a software company now, so we should be in luck.'

The lobby of this building was very different from Freyja and Ragnar's waterfront high-rise. Twenty-somethings were hanging out in the lobby, talking and laughing. One had a very handsome-looking dog on a leash, who sat obediently at his heel while his owner carried on a conversation with a pretty brunette in a business suit, parka and snow boots.

'This is an Icelandic sheepdog,' Berg said, bending over to pet him. The couple stopped chatting and the man exchanged a few words with Berg. Lauren knelt down, let the tan-and-white dog sniff her hand, then scratched him behind his ear. It wasn't a big dog, maybe twenty-five pounds, but he was thick and muscular with a tail that curled over his back.

'We had one named Thor until three years ago,' Berg said straightening up. They headed for the stairwell. 'I loved that dog. When he died, I just couldn't bring myself to get another one, even though Elin begs me.'

'I have a dog,' Lauren offered, then immediately backtracked.

'Actually, Watson is my partner's dog, but he's living in my house with us.'

Berg raised an eyebrow as they tackled the first landing. 'Sharing a dog together is a big commitment.'

'Don't read into it,' she said, pushing the door open to the second floor. 'It was a package deal when he moved in.'

'And yet you think it's your dog . . . together. Interesting.'

She felt her mouth pull into a straight line. The smirk on his face was infuriating.

Apartment 233 was almost right in front of them when they stepped out of the stairwell. 'Don't read into it,' she repeated, straightening her brown parka. 'Stay focused.'

'I am focused.' His mischievous grin was still there, teasing her. 'I just didn't know it was so easy to get a rise out of you.'

Instead of a nailed-on number, 233 was painted in fancy gold script. Berg gave his signature three knocks and they waited in silence, Berg smirking and Lauren trying not to appear annoyed at him.

The door swung inward, revealing a tall, thin man with square brown glasses, a blond beard and short, close-cropped hair. He greeted them with what sounded to Lauren like 'golden dying?' but what she had come to realize was Icelandic for 'good morning'. Berg pulled out his identification and held it up while responding in his usual manner. 'Please, friend, my colleague here only speaks English.'

Stefan smiled, almost like he was embarrassed, but warmly. 'My apologies. I heard what happened to Gunnar. I assume that's what this is about.'

'Can we come in?' Lauren asked.

He swept his hand behind him and they moved into his apartment. Unlike the other homes she'd been in, Stefan's did not adhere to the traditional décor in Iceland. The apartment was decorated in bright reds and blues. Black-framed jazz posters filled his walls along with abstract art. His living room couch and chairs were also blacked-framed with brightly colored throw pillows. A huge flat-screen smart TV hung over a gas fireplace, next to which was a funky silver Christmas tree decorated with round gold bulbs. The smell of freshly brewed coffee hung in the air, making Lauren's stomach rumble.

Maybe he heard the growl, or maybe he was just as kind and sensitive as he appeared to be, but Stefan leaned over, touched Lauren's arm and asked, 'Can I get you something? A cup of coffee? Anything?'

'I'd love coffee,' she replied, letting her guard down for an instant.

He pulled his hand away, asking Berg, 'And you?'

'I'll take a cup as well.'

'Have a seat.' Stefan gestured to the couch. 'I'll be right back.'

Normally, Lauren's instinct would have been to watch him go make the coffee, suspicious he was leaving the room, suspicious he'd do something to her drink. This man seemed to radiate kindness. Nothing in his demeanor put her on guard, so Lauren merely watched as he disappeared into the kitchen. She could hear him singing as they sat down on his funky modern sofa.

Berg's coat flapped open as he sank into the cushions. 'This thing is too mushy for me,' he complained, trying to sit himself up.

'It's a beautiful place,' Lauren commented, pleased that he was uncomfortable. Her eyes wandered over to a sculpture in the corner that appeared to be bundles of branches made out of concrete and steel.

Before he could reply, Stefan appeared, carrying a metal tray with a bone-colored ceramic coffee service on it, including a creamer and sugar bowl. He placed the tray on the glass coffee table, picked up his own cup, and settled himself into a lounge chair. 'I've honestly been hoping you'd show up. I thought about going to the police station, but I just couldn't bring myself to do it.' His voice cracked a little with emotion.

'Why did you want to come to the police station?' Berg asked, putting his elbows on his knees and clasping his hands in front of him, giving Stefan his full attention.

Wiping his eye with one hand, he choked back tears. 'Because I wanted answers. I heard what happened to Gunnar and I wanted to know how someone could harm such a caring, loving soul.' Tears flowed freely down his cheeks. 'He was a good man. A gentle man. He didn't deserve this.'

'Do you have any idea who may have wanted to hurt Gunnar?' Lauren asked.

That question seemed to confuse him. 'I thought it was a street crime. I thought it was some random robbery. That you were here to tell me . . .' He shook his head. 'I don't know what I thought you were here to tell me. I didn't think I had anything *I* could tell *you*.'

'Did you stay in contact with Gunnar after the two of you broke up?' Lauren asked, lowering her voice a notch.

Stefan set his coffee mug on the floor and rubbed both of his eyes with the heels of his hands. Taking a deep breath, he managed, 'It was an amicable break-up. The relationship just ran its course. We still texted each other and met for coffee once in a while. Then I met my current partner, Olaf, and Gunnar was so happy for me.' He pointed to a picture above the fireplace on the mantle. 'Oli just ran out to get some things to make dinner. He's part owner of a fitness gym. Tonight is his only night off this week.'

'Did Gunnar ever talk about his relationship with his boss?' Lauren asked.

Stefan seemed puzzled by the question. 'Of course, he did. They were in love. Deeply in love. Haven't you talked to Ragnar?'

Berg's eyes widened. It was the first confirmation they'd gotten that there even had been a relationship. 'No,' Berg said. 'He seems to be busy every time we come around.'

'Did you go by his house in the Shadow District?'

'Yes, we did,' Lauren told Stefan. 'We spoke to Ragnar's wife.'

Stefan nodded his head. 'That's explains it. The last time I spoke to Gunnar on the phone, he and Ragnar were going to the States in a few days. Gunnar finally found his birth father and Freyja had just learned of their affair. Ragnar's ex-lover had called her up and told her everything.'

'Ragnar's ex-lover?' Lauren asked, trying to keep the disbelief out of her voice.

'Bjarni.' Stefan's handsome face screwed up at the mention of the name. 'Ragnar fired him and broke his heart. Bjarni blamed Gunnar for his and Ragnar's break-up. He tried everything to win Ragnar back and when that didn't work, he resorted to calling Freyja up and revealing the affair.'

Berg and Lauren both sat in stunned silence for a moment. Lauren was used to being lied to. She got lied to by suspects every time she stepped foot in the interview room. She got lied to when she asked suspects what time it was. She didn't expect two people who appeared to have nothing at all to gain by lying to do it. Yet Bjarni lied about leaving on good terms and Freyja never mentioned Bjarni's phone call. The only thing that made sense was that they were lying to protect Ragnar. Freyja because she wanted to keep her husband and Bjarni because Ragnar was now free to pursue their affair.

'I think we need to talk to Freyja again.' Lauren's tone had turned grim with the revelation.

'Did Gunnar's brother Jakob know about his relationship with Ragnar?' Berg asked, not bothering to reply to Lauren's obvious observation.

'No. He was afraid his brother wouldn't approve of him being involved with a married man, especially his boss. I think that's why he rang me up in the first place to tell me about it. He wanted someone to know he was in love, with no judgments attached. He wanted to share how happy he was that he finally found his father and someone to spend his life with.'

'Is there anything else you think we should know?' Berg asked.

Stefan looked around the room, as if trying to pull the right words, words that wouldn't come to him, out of the air. Finally he said, 'I know Ragnar is worth millions. But it's his wife's millions, from her family business. If she cut him off, he'd have nothing.'

THIRTY-EIGHT

'Well, that takes our investigation down a different path,' Berg said as he sipped a beer. They'd stopped at a local restaurant a few blocks over. Berg had pointed out to Lauren it was after six o'clock, they didn't actually have a clock they had to punch and they both needed to eat and drink. The hostess, who knew Berg by name, had seated them at a table that overlooked the street. Looming in the darkening sky was the illuminated steeple of a strangely ominous-looking church Lauren had noticed during their drive downtown the day before. 'You see that?' Berg had said as they cautiously crossed the road. 'That's Hallgrímskirkja Church. If you use that as a landmark downtown, you'll never get lost.'

'It's actually the path we were on to begin with,' Lauren corrected, salting her broiled fish. 'I suspected Ragnar from the start, but I always try to gather all the evidence I can before I make a conclusion. Unfortunately, my evidence fled the country and here I am.'

The interior of the restaurant was dimly lit with fancy tea light candles placed on every table and a huge Advent wreath on the wall. Every seat in the house was taken, full of people talking and laughing, shopping bags piled at their feet, enjoying the holiday season. Over the sound system Christmas music played, but it wasn't anything Lauren recognized. *Maybe it isn't even Christmas music, maybe Icelanders like to put the sleigh bells in their compositions*, she thought. *Even being used to the snow and the temperatures, I am so out of my element here. I feel like they shipped me to another planet.*

'I know you like plans, so how about this one: we get up early, go sit on Ragnar's house, like you Yankees seem to like to do, and see if he slips up and comes home. I have a patrol crew sitting on the complex now, but maybe if we send them away, he'll think we've given up and show himself.'

'Can we stop and see Matt first?'

Berg swallowed a huge piece of red meat and immediately shoveled in another. 'I don't see why not,' he said, chewing with his mouth open. Lauren had an urge to call Reese and tell him she'd met his soul mate in Iceland. 'And if we see Ragnar, he's coming down to the station with us.'

Lauren carefully sawed into a small piece of steak with her knife. She had ordered the fish and beef special, forgetting about her damaged hands. 'Like you said, we're on an island. There's only so many places to go.'

'I've got the word out at the airports. If he uses one of his ships, we're out of luck, but no one ever leaves Iceland forever. Have you ever met an American citizen who emigrated from Iceland? I'm sure they exist, like your bigfoots, but I've never known one. Everyone comes back, sooner or later.'

'Can I get you more drinks, Berg?' The young waiter had been happy when the hostess sat them in his section and had been especially attentive since they came in. Lauren figured Berg must be a good tipper. She fingered the money in her pocket she hadn't had a chance to spend yet and tried to remember if Iceland was one of those places where you weren't expected to tip.

'Two more beers.' He raised an eyebrow to Lauren. 'You could use a beer, yes?'

'Yes.' Lauren smiled and lifted her water glass in a cheer. Berg clinked his empty beer bottle to it. 'I also approve of your plan.'

THIRTY-NINE

Pulling the hotel bed covers up to her chin, Lauren dialed Reese's cellphone. The alarm clock on the nightstand said it was only nine o'clock, but that only made it four in the afternoon back home in Buffalo. The phone rang until it went to voicemail.

'Hi, this is Shane Reese. Leave a message.'

Clean, clear and simple. Just like his brain, she would have joked if he were with her. 'Hey, Reese, it's me. Just checking in with you. Anyway, I'm good. The investigation has finally picked up some traction over here, I think.' *And there are a million ideas I want to bounce off you*, she wanted to say, but held her tongue. 'Take care of Watson. I'll try to call you tomorrow, if I have a chance.'

She hit the END button and put the phone face down on the nightstand. Reese was probably napping. Or maybe getting ready for a hot date. It shouldn't matter why he hadn't picked up, but it did, more than a little.

She wished she had brought her sleeping pills with her. She'd been afraid to bring them on the plane. Afraid some TSA agent would have pulled them out of her purse, held them up and asked, 'Are these prescribed to you? Pretty heavy duty, aren't they?' She'd been afraid to stash them in her luggage for fear it got lost, only to be found and opened. She wanted to keep that dirty little secret to herself. She told herself there was no shame in needing medicine, but anyone on the police department would say she couldn't handle her shit. Or that she was crazy and that's why crazy things were always happening to her. They would *blame* her. It wasn't fair, but she had made the choice to do without it rather than risk being labeled, like so many people did every day for different reasons.

She folded the covers back and went to the window. She'd remembered to pull the heavy blackout shades across the glass earlier, like Berg had told her, even though it had still been dark every morning she had gotten up since she'd been there. Now she pushed them aside and looked out at the night sky. The harbor front was lit up with boats and buildings and the road that snaked along the water was dotted with the headlights of passing cars.

She searched the sky for the Northern Lights but it was cloudy. Not even the moon was visible.

She slipped back under the covers and stared at the ceiling. Sleep was going to elude her, she knew. But at least she wouldn't have any nightmares.

FORTY

'Freyja packed up the white Skoda Octavia and left the penthouse in the middle of the night,' Berg told Lauren as soon as she got into his police car. It was different from the one he'd been driving since she arrived. He'd told her the night before he was going to switch. He didn't want to tip Ragnar off in case he had people watching them. 'I got a call from the patrol unit watching the house last night. They wanted to know if they should follow her.'

'What did you tell them?' Lauren asked.

'I told them to keep watching the apartment. If Freyja had the Skoda that means that Ragnar came back to the penthouse after we stopped at his office. The officers said she was upset and crying. He must have slipped into the underground parking lot before I sent a patrol car to watch the premises. So he's been holed up there all this time.'

'What do you want to do? Go and grab him out of the apartment?'

'That's what I want to do. But you Americans have all those Miranda warnings and possible cause—'

'Probable cause,' she corrected.

'Yes. That.' He shook his head as he drove with one hand on the wheel and the other fiddling with the computer on his dash. 'No. We can knock all day long, but we don't have a warrant and we don't have enough evidence to get one. We need to put Ragnar in the car that hit Matt. That's the only way to force his hand.'

'You want to sit on the apartment complex and wait?' Lauren frowned. Ragnar could hole up in there for days. 'We could be there for a long time.'

'It's almost Christmas. His three children are all grown, but they all still live in Iceland. I assume that they get together as a family. All of this must be a terrible stress and burden on Freyja right before the holiday. I imagine Freyja and Ragnar must have had a terrible fight. As a married man I can say that if it were me, and my wife had the power to put me in prison for murder and attempted murder on two continents, I'd be hauling my ass to wherever she was to either smooth things over—'

'Or kill her,' Lauren finished.

He nodded, his mouth set in a grim line. 'If Freyja dies, all of the business assets, the money, his reputation, remains intact. She's worth more to him dead. I told the patrol crew who relieved last night's people that if Ragnar leaves the building, to follow him. But only take him into custody if it looks like he's meeting with Freyja or trying to flee the country. I don't think he'll make a move until he sees patrol leave. We'll take over for them when we're done at the hospital.'

'We just have to make sure we get to Freyja before Ragnar.'

'He'll wait,' Berg said. 'He'll see the patrol car leave, wait an hour or two and then go after her. He's been running this whole investigation. It's worked for him so far.'

Lauren saw the bright lights of the University Hospital appear before her. 'Now his luck is about to run out.'

Matt was awake when they came in, anxious to tell them what he'd found out. 'We should have some of the translations today. I'm also waiting for someone to email me the documents I requested before I got hit.'

'We got the call yesterday evening,' Lauren told him and his face fell. 'But you need to stay on top of all of that. Listen to what we found out.' She went on to tell him about their conversation with Stefan; how Freyja and Bjarni lied to them.

'Wow,' he sat back against his pillows. 'And I thought I had big news.'

'You did, brother,' Berg assured him. 'We're going to need you to forward everything to us. If things go the way I think they're going to go, we're going to need you to keep us in the loop.'

'I met your director last night,' Matt told Berg. 'He stopped in for a visit, asked if there was anything I needed. He's a very nice guy.'

'Too nice, I think, sometimes,' Berg replied.

'He's handling the press on Gunnar's murder well,' Lauren said. 'I thought we'd be swamped with reporters.'

'I've been watching the news reports,' Berg said. 'The press is demanding answers from him about the political scandal. They want to know how it could have been happening for so long right under the Ministry of Justice's nose. Millions of dollars are missing. Criminals have been lining their pockets for ages, as well as my cousin. It's bad. Worse than I thought. Worse than the director thought. Which is good for keeping the press off our backs while we investigate.'

The machine behind Matt's head beeped. 'I need another bag of fluids,' he explained. 'Don't look at me like I'm going to die, Riley.'

I've been on that bed and I've seen my partner on that bed, hooked to those machines, making those noises, she wanted to say, but held her tongue. *You can't erase those sounds, sights and smells. They'll always trigger fear for me.*

But fear also meant you were hyper-aware and that was exactly what she needed to be. 'I just have to make sure you're OK. I wouldn't want Cara coming after me.'

'I'm on the phone with her ten times a day. She called right before you came in. I told her my SAC, Samuel Papineau, is flying in tonight. That seemed to make her feel better.'

Lauren should have known Sam would fly over. One of his men was almost killed, he'd want to be directly involved.

'How are you feeling?' Lauren asked, realizing she hadn't yet.

'I'd shrug my shoulders, but I'd probably pass out,' he joked. 'They have me on a lot of pain medicine for the arm. The way they have my shoulder taped and my arm splinted there's no way I can move my left side, so the collarbone only hurts if I try to look behind me or twist around.'

'When can they send you home?' Berg asked.

'A couple more days. The doctor still wants to make sure there are no infections, and that I won't grow a blood clot on the plane. But I have to tell you, I don't know how I'm going to be able to sit in an airplane seat for five and a half hours with my arm like this.'

Looking at the way they had his arm immobilized, Lauren suspected Matt might need two, if not three seats, to get home. She kept that thought to herself. 'The airlines have to figure these things out all the time. I wouldn't worry about that now, if I were you.'

'Listen, brother,' Berg told him, 'We have to go. Stay in touch. And update us with any information you get.'

He held up his phone with his good hand. Lauren immediately flashed to Mr Hudson in his wheelchair. 'I'm ready,' he said.

'Good. Let us know when you find out about that phone, eh?' Berg tapped the metal rail of the bed and Matt flinched. 'Sorry! Sorry!'

'It's fine.' He managed to smile. 'Just go.'

FORTY-ONE

'Ragnar and Freyja have four cars registered to them.' Berg squinted in the morning darkness as he began to read off a printout. They were parked in the far corner of the outside lot belonging to Ragnar's high-rise. 'The BMW, which is still at his office, the white Skoda Octavia, which we know Freyja left in last night, a blue Toyota Land Cruiser and a green Toyota Rav4.'

Lauren eyed the entrance to the underground parking ramp. 'Do Ragnar and Freyja have assigned spots down in the ramp?'

Berg folded up the papers and stuffed them in the visor above his head. 'Two.'

'I'm going to assume the patrol guys didn't look in the underground lot for their vehicles.'

'No. But we're going to.' He put the car in gear and headed for the entrance. 'If Ragnar has a vehicle, it's stashed under there.'

'And maybe the truck he used to hit Matt with as well.'

Berg called out to a man heading for the interior doors carrying a sack of groceries. When the man stopped and looked, Berg gave him a wide, helpless smile and launched into an Icelandic explanation. The man nodded, smiled back, walked over and passed a plastic swipe card in front of the reader. The wooden bar immediately lifted.

Berg yelled what sounded like 'Tak fee,' at the man, which Lauren had come to know meant 'thank you' in Icelandic. He gave a friendly wave and disappeared inside the building.

'What did you say to him?' Lauren asked.

'I said I forgot my pass card and my wife was about to kill me. The fierce look on your face was very convincing.'

Lauren swallowed the comment she wanted to make because he was probably right.

'Would this pass your probable cause test?' he asked, pulling through the gate.

'I don't think so,' she answered, but kept her eyes on the passing vehicles as they crept through the ramp, looking for the Land Cruiser and Rav4. 'Let's just see if they're here and we can retreat outside again.'

Berg grunted and turned the corner. He slammed on the breaks, causing Lauren to lurch forward against the seatbelt. 'There,' he pointed. 'That's their Rav4.'

A green Rav4 sat next to the only empty parking space in the row. Berg pulled the paperwork down to double check. 'Yes. That's it,' he said, passing the read-out to Lauren.

'So where's the Land Cruiser?' she asked, looking at the space.

'Where indeed,' Berg said and immediately pulled forward and headed toward the exit. 'We'll wait across the street. The marked unit has only been gone about thirty minutes. He'll want to leave before the sun comes up.' He checked the time on his phone. 'He's got less than an hour and a half before sunrise. I bet wherever he goes, the Land Cruiser is.'

For the first time since she got to Iceland, Lauren was the one who was losing her mind having to wait. They'd been out drinking, eating, having coffee, basically taking the slow road because Ragnar was ducking them and now they were within reach of him and they had to sit on their hands. Berg liked to talk about jumping right in, but Lauren realized that life in Iceland moved at a dramatically slower pace than in Buffalo. The pace of their investigation matched the Icelandic lifestyle.

Berg found a spot across the road from the lot that had a perfect view of the exit of the underground ramp. As soon as that green Rav4 came up, they'd be able to slip quickly and quietly behind it. Berg was unusually still and silent, making things even worse for Lauren. She wanted noisy traffic, people cussing each other out on the street, loud, pumping music. Instead, all she could hear was the quiet hum as each car passed them on the street. No one in a hurry. No one laying on their horns. It was maddening.

She looked around the unmarked Hyundai Santa Fe. She could see why Berg wanted to swap out the brand-new Volvo. Once people knew what kind of car the police drove, criminals could spot them a mile away. For years, the only unmarked detective vehicles they had in Buffalo were Chevy Caprices. Even now, when Lauren saw someone driving an old Chevy Caprice, she got a feeling of déjà vu. The Hyundai was an older model; the computer had been removed leaving just the bracket. Lauren figured this car was probably going to be put out to pasture soon. She knew from experience that ice, snow, and salt wreaked havoc on cars. The odometer showed it had over a hundred thousand miles on it. She hoped the old girl was ready to go on one last adventure.

A pair of headlights lit up the exit. The gate lifted and the green Rav4 appeared in the outside lot. She'd only seen pictures of Ragnar, and it was still dark and hard to see, but Lauren was certain it was him, even before Berg swore in Icelandic. They both slumped down in their seats. Ragnar would have to pass right by them. Berg waited patiently with the lights off, until Ragnar pulled onto the main road and turned.

Traffic was almost nonexistent, so Berg waited a good ten seconds before pulling onto the street. He followed a good distance behind, keeping Ragnar's taillights in sight, letting cars pull in front of them, hanging back.

'Where could Ragnar be going?' Berg asked himself. He wasn't speeding, or madly trying to pass other cars. It was like he was on a Sunday drive. All she knew was that they were headed away from the airport.

'You said Ragnar and Freyja owned a lot of properties,' Lauren said.

'They do. All over the country. Mostly by the ports, where their goods would be coming in and out. He's heading northwest. Go into that folder in the backseat and see what properties they own northwest of Reykjavík.'

Lauren twisted around and scooped up a thick blue folder with LOGREGLA stamped above a gold shield in the top left corner. Inside was an entire dossier on Ragnar Steinarsson, most of which Lauren couldn't read.

'It's in Icelandic,' she said, closing it shut.

He reached over and snatched it from her. Muttering to himself, he flipped through the printouts with one hand while driving with the other, head bobbing from road to paperwork. 'Take the wheel,' he growled.

She grabbed the steering wheel with both hands while Berg looked something up. She was crammed between Berg and the dashboard, trying to stay in the lane and not draw attention to their vehicle.

'OK,' he said and she let go, collapsing back into her seat. The seatbelt had almost strangled her. 'We're on Route 1, the Ring Road heading toward the Snæfellsnes Peninsula. Ragnar owns at least five properties he could be heading to. No use calling it in when we don't know where we're going yet.'

'Don't you think we should call for backup?' she asked, as he took the third exit of a roundabout.

'In Iceland, your backup could be hours away. You learn to make do once you get out of the city. It's no use having four police cars following us, following him. When we know where he's stopping, then we'll call it in.'

She could tell from the passing signs that they were on Route 1, like Berg said. She quickly googled that on her phone and saw that the curvy road would take them all along the coastline until they got to a place called Borgarnes. On Berg's side was nothing but ocean and sky. On her side the city began to fall away until it seemed all they were passing was a series of wooden poles laced together with barbed wire to form a seemingly endless fence.

'What's that for?' she finally asked. 'Cows? Sheep?'

He glanced out to see what she was talking about. 'Horses,' he said, looking forward again. 'Icelandic horses.'

As soon as the words popped out of his mouth Lauren spotted six or seven in the distance, lit by the slowly rising sun. They seemed to all be eating from the same hay bale. Even farther in the distance she could see a single long, low building where they must have been kept. 'Ponies,' she said, filled with wonder at seeing the stout beasts in so desolate a landscape. 'They're beautiful.'

'Not ponies,' Berg said sharply. 'Horses. Iceland is famous for its horses. Did you know once you take an Icelandic horse out of the country, it can never come back in? They are very prized and cherished here.'

'No wonder Bjarni's friend flew him north to work on his

barn,' she said, trying to cover her faux pas, although why they were arguing about horses versus ponies in the middle of a police pursuit was beyond her.

'They are a source of pride. That thick, shaggy coat they have now gets shed in the spring. Then they look more like the horses you're used to. My daughter belongs to a riding club. She goes every weekend, if she can. You should try it while you're here.'

'Maybe when I'm not on the trail of a dangerous murderer.'

Berg shook his head. 'I find it hard to believe Ragnar snapped. We may trace our lineage directly back to the Vikings but we're a peaceful people. We don't even have an army. I remember seeing your American soldiers walking around Reykjavík in their uniforms as a boy, when the Naval base was still open. I was afraid of them. Isn't that funny?'

'You might have seen Gunnar's father passing by. That's how Gunnar came to be.'

'We didn't get a lot of tourists back then, not like now. Those service men were a big deal. I also remember when they closed the base. A lot of merchants loved the servicemen spending their American dollars in the city.'

'Why did the base close?'

He shrugged. 'Money? Politics? The end of the Cold War? Who knows? But now there's talk of them reopening it.'

Lauren pictured a young, handsome John Hudson walking up to Gunnar's mother in a nightclub, looking dashing in his pressed uniform. It was easy to see how a young woman might get swept up in the romance of the moment.

'It's just hard for me to imagine Ragnar hitting Gunnar with a brick until he was dead,' Berg said, snapping Lauren out of her momentary daydream. 'We just don't have that level of violence here normally.'

'That's a lot of rage,' Lauren agreed. 'But love, or lust, is a great motivator for violence.'

'And so is money,' Berg put in.

'Combine the two,' Lauren added, 'and it can be a recipe for homicide.'

An hour ticked by. The sun rose up, casting its weak winter rays across barren snow fields. White-capped mountains rose in the distance. The road snaked and curved as they followed Ragnar's Rav4.

'I hope we don't blow our cover,' Lauren said as a tractor-trailer passed them, heading back toward Reykjavík.

'Believe me, Ragnar knows he's being followed.' Berg's eyes met her in a sideways glance. 'Wherever he's taking us to, be ready for anything.'

'I'd be a lot happier if we had a gun,' Lauren said.

'Of course, you would. That's why I brought one of my personal firearms with me today.' He tapped a bulge in his coat over his hip Lauren hadn't noticed before.

'I thought you said you didn't need a gun because we're on an island.'

The mischievous smile was back. 'I may be cocky, but I'm not stupid. He left that apartment to find Freyja. If he killed Gunnar, whatever he has planned for her is nothing good.'

'You could have brought one for me.'

'And get you in trouble with the authorities? What kind of law enforcement officer would I be? Besides, I'm an excellent shot. One gun will be more than enough.'

Lauren let out a small sharp laugh as she joked, 'And I doubted you.'

He snorted in reply and told her, 'Never doubt a Viking.'

FORTY-TWO

They headed northwest from Borgarnes along Route 54. The scenery around her was spectacular: sun, sea, quaint fishing villages, and mountains, but it was certain now Ragnar knew he was being followed. Lauren half expected him to pull over and confront them. Her whole body was tense and alert, ready for the confrontation that was surely coming. *What is Ragnar thinking?* She studied the back of his Rav4 as the paved road twisted and curved along the coast. Dried salt painted the rear hatch a grayish white. *We're right behind him. He's got nowhere to go.*

Except to Freyja.

'Maybe we should just pull him over,' Lauren said.

'And if he does pull over and refuses to talk? We have no evidence he committed a crime.'

'You can bring him in for questioning though,' she pointed out.

Berg considered this for a moment, never taking his eyes off the road in front of him. 'I would think it would be more effective if we had his wife as well. Divide them and see what they say at the police station. Isn't that what you do to suspects and witnesses in America?'

He was right. They could jump the gun and grab Ragnar on the road, but without Freyja, they had no leverage. They could at least point out her lies in the hopes that she slipped up, and use that against Ragnar.

A small sign announced they were heading toward a town called Búðir. 'Be ready,' Berg said again as Ragnar pulled off the main route onto an even narrower, more desolate road.

The wind had picked up, throwing snow across their windshield and battering the car as they made their way through the remote countryside. 'Take the wheel,' Berg told her and once again, Lauren found herself crammed between Berg and the dashboard, steering while he flipped through his files.

'Ragnar owns a farm only a few kilometers from here.' He looked up, almost smacking his head into Lauren's. Straightening himself, he tossed the file across Lauren's lap. 'We should be able to see it soon.'

The sparse patches of birch trees became thicker the farther inland they got. Lauren noticed areas on the ground roped off with bright red string, with white steam rising from them. Berg noticed Lauren noticing. 'Those are hot springs. Don't walk through them, you'll burn yourself.'

'Like the famous Blue Lagoon?'

'A little, but you don't know how hot any single one is, that's why they have to be roped off. If there's been geothermal activity, it could be scalding hot. You just don't have any idea.'

The land of fire and ice, Lauren thought. *Instead of just snow and ice, like Buffalo.*

On Lauren's right, she could see a farm complex up ahead: two houses, a collection of out buildings, and one of those long, low barns, all surrounded by trees. Ragnar's car turned into the main driveway to the complex, which looked well maintained, though didn't look to Lauren like it was a working farm anymore. There was no sign of the famous Icelandic horses or sheep that seemed to populate the countryside. Smoke rose from a stone chimney in the main house. Someone was home.

Berg pulled over, still a quarter-mile down the road, taking what cover they could from a copse of skinny, barren birch trees that looked more like overgrown scrubs. He reached across Lauren into the glove box and extracted a pair of binoculars.

'What do you see?' Lauren asked as he scanned the property.

'I see the green Rav4. I see Ragnar jumping out with a duffel bag. He just went inside that house.' He paused, turning his head with the binoculars ever so slightly. 'There's the white Skoda. Ragnar and Freyja are both here.'

He passed the binoculars to Lauren. She studied the property in front of her. The white Skoda was parked near the barn-like structure. Ragnar had pulled the Rav4 right up to the front door of the house.

Lauren's phone buzzed in her pocket. She'd set Matt to vibrate; everyone else was set to go straight to voicemail. Against her better judgment, she pulled it out as Berg inched his way cautiously up toward the main driveway. She needed to focus on the situation at hand, but it was a text from Matt. And he was typing in all caps.

WE JUST GOT THE TRANSLATIONS OF GUNNAR'S EMAILS. WE WERE WRONG!!!

Three dots glowed on the screen indicating another message was coming. Lauren looked up from her cell in confusion. 'Berg, I just got a text from Matt—'

BOOM!

'Was that a gunshot?' Lauren asked, scanning the front of the house for movement.

'It certainly sounded like one.' Berg's voice was tight as he slipped his Glock out of its holster and rested it on the seat next to him.

'We can't wait.' Lauren dropped the binoculars on the floor of the car. 'We need to grab him now. What if he just hurt Freyja?'

'Agreed.' Berg hit the gas. 'Let's do this.'

A bullet hit the front grill of the car. Berg slammed on the brakes as two more shots rang out. 'Get down!' Lauren screamed, pulling him from behind the wheel, across the seat just as a bullet pierced the windshield. He managed to yank the gear shift into park, so they didn't roll closer to the shooter.

Lying on top of each other in the front seat, Lauren reached for her door handle. 'We can't stay here like sitting ducks. Can you see something to cover us?' she asked.

He raised his head up and quickly brought it back down as another shot rang out. 'On your side, there's a small shed. I'll cover you. Then I'll come.'

Thunk.

Another round hit the car. 'On three.' Berg grabbed his Glock with both hands, rolling onto his back as best he could.

Lauren pulled up on the passenger side door handle, cracking the door ajar. 'OK.'

Berg popped up and released a barrage of bullets toward the main house where the shots seemed to be coming from.

Lauren leaped from the car and ran in a crouch toward the large, windowless wooden shed. A shot hit the shed and pinged against something metal inside. Lauren ducked low beside the door and motioned to Berg, who was sprawled across the front seat, gun in hand.

Ragnar's Rav4 was parked directly in front of the main entrance, slightly crooked, like he had made a hasty exit into the house.

Another shot rang out, followed by the sound of a bullet hitting their vehicle. The front windshield was spiderwebbed by least three gunshots. It sounded like rifle fire to her. Maybe a .22, maybe a .410 shotgun. But Lauren was no expert in long guns. She hoped whatever it was wasn't powerful enough to go through the shed, or at least there was enough heavy-duty equipment inside to shield her.

Berg held up a finger, signaling for her to get ready then hurled himself out of the truck and scuttled over, keeping his head low, as more shots rang out. 'That son of a bitch,' he breathed hard, trying to peek around the corner to see the main house. 'I think it's coming from that window there.'

'How many bullets do you have left?' she asked. The front door of the main house had another of those cheery Icelandic wreaths on it. The house itself was two stories, the wood painted a pale bluish-gray color and trimmed in a darker navy. Heavy curtains hung in every window blocking their view of the interior.

'I have these.' He slipped two extra magazines out of his coat pocket, then let them drop back in. 'I shot eight rounds. I should have ten rounds left. Who knows what kind of arsenal he has inside the house.'

'If you can distract him, I can sneak that way and go in the back,' Lauren motioned to another small building off to their right. From there she could make her way around the side of the house and try to get in the rear door. 'No one locks their doors in Iceland. You said so, right?'

'Let's hope. I can try to get back behind the Santa Fe,' he said, peeking again and getting a shot that ricocheted off the shed in response. 'I'll have a better angle on that window and the truck is better cover than this shed.'

'OK,' she agreed.

'Wait until you hear me call out to Ragnar. I want his full attention on me.'

She nodded and they both got into position. She was bent over and pointed toward the next building. He was in a runner's crouch, with fingers spread on one hand, steadying himself and the other with his gun in it. 'On three,' he said. 'One . . . two . . . three!'

Berg raced for the rear of the Hyundai, firing at the house as he went. He positioned himself as best he could, trying to put the engine block between him and the shooter. He popped his head up, let off two more rounds, then dropped back down. 'Ragnar! Stop this! Come out with your hands up!'

Lauren waited until she heard Berg getting fired on before she ran for the next building. She could hear Berg yelling in Icelandic now. He was trying to get Ragnar to waste his bullets. She peered around the corner of her new position. This shed was made of corrugated metal and a bullet would pass through it like a hot knife through butter. She had to get around to the side of the house.

Berg yelled something that sounded particularly nasty. The curtains in the front left window next to the door rustled, and a round hit the Hyundai, going straight through the front of the windshield and out the back. Lauren sprinted for the side of the house.

As she turned the corner, she tripped over a red string and landed on her stomach, knocking the wind out of her. Two inches in front of her face, a small stream bubbled and fizzed with steam, stinging her cheeks. Thankfully, her scratched glasses shielded her eyes. The smell of sulfur burned her nose. She struggled to her feet, ignoring the pain in her hands from where they'd had to break her fall. Hurriedly, she brushed the snow and rocky black pebbles from the front of her, and backtracked until she was hugging the house.

Trying to keep the crunching of snow under her feet to a minimum, she rounded the corner to the back of the house. The missing blue Toyota Land Cruiser was parked there. Its front driver side headlight was cracked and there was a nasty dent just above it across the hood, where Matt had hit and spun off. Somehow Ragnar had managed to get the damaged Land Cruiser here and get back to his high-rise in Reykjavik.

From up front, Lauren could hear Berg trying to negotiate with Ragnar, punctuated every few seconds with another shot from inside the house. As she crept up the steps to the back door, Lauren wondered if Freyja was already dead.

Berg had been right when he told her no one in Iceland bothered to lock their doors. The knob turned easily, and she eased the door open slowly so as not to alert Ragnar she was in the house.

Lauren found herself inside a very modern kitchen for a rustic-looking farmhouse. The acrid smell of gunpowder assaulted her nose as soon as she slipped in. She hadn't thought this far ahead, and she needed to find a weapon. Over by the stainless-steel stove was a wooden block with knives in it. Edging past the center island, she slipped a long-handled blade from the block.

Ragnar had shot off a lot of rounds. What she needed to do was to get a visual on him, then wait until he needed to reload his weapon. She would make her move then. Berg just had to keep Ragnar firing without getting himself killed.

She could see a dining room off of the kitchen. At the far end was an open archway. It sounded like the shots were coming from just beyond it. She had to be careful: her heavy boots weren't made to sneak around. Even the fabric of her parka wanted to give her away, with its nylon *whoosh-whoosh* every time she moved too fast.

Slowly, she made her way through the dining room, sticking close to the wall but not hugging it, trying to get past the enormous polished table fully set for a Christmas feast. *This place must be where Ragnar and Freyja come to celebrate the holidays when he's not trying to kill someone,* she thought. *How cozy of them.*

There was a commotion in the front room. Lauren froze in place. She heard Ragnar and Freyja's voices. Something smashed to the ground and a door opened, then slammed shut. Footsteps pounded up some stairs. From outside, she could hear Berg yelling commands in Icelandic and more sounds of movement.

Two things could have happened: either Ragnar gave himself up and was outside with Berg, or Freyja had escaped and Ragnar was now upstairs with a higher vantage point. Lauren had the element of surprise, but she knew if Freyja was safe they needed to retreat and call for backup. She moved as fast as she dared, peeking around the corner into the living room.

The space had been purposely decorated in rustic farm-chic charm, complete with a huge oil painting of geese in flight over the mantle. A fire was smoldering in the stone fireplace, wood shifting and snapping as it burned down. An overstuffed floral couch and its matching chairs sat poised in front of a glass and wood coffee table with a lace doily on it. Between them and her was the front door. Blood smeared the knob and was streaked onto the wood around it. The window next to the door was wide open and the thick, heavy lace curtains sucked in and out, pulled by the wind.

Propped next to the front door, across from stairs leading up to the second floor, was a .410 Mossberg pump-action shotgun with a wooden stock. A box of shells lay open on the floor and spent cartridge casings littered the polished hardwood. She needed to get the gun outside.

As she crossed the living room, a frantic scream came from up the stairs. Freyja flew down the steps like some sort of Nordic banshee, ramming into Lauren and sending them both flying into the coffee table, which smashed into a thousand splintered pieces of wood and glass. The knife went skittering across the floor.

Lauren hit her head when they crashed through the table. She blinked away stars as she grappled with Freyja.

'You couldn't just leave us alone!' Freyja was on top of Lauren, trying to pin her down. She was incredibly strong, a mad, wild look flashed in her eye. The glass had cut a deep gash in her forehead, and blood ran down the side of her face. 'Why did you have to come here? Why couldn't you just leave me be?'

Freyja's blond hair had unraveled from her fancy bun and hung in limp strings around her enraged, bloody face. She looked old and wretched, a caricature of the former beauty queen she'd presented herself as in the penthouse.

Freyja grabbed Lauren by the neck and bounced her head twice on the floor, hard. Lauren struggled against the bulk of her thick parka, while Freyja attacked, unencumbered by any heavy outwear.

Reaching out with her left hand, Lauren brought up a jagged piece of broken table, cracking Freyja on the side of the head with it. She fell off as Lauren scrambled for the front door, but Freyja whipped out her arm and caught her by the ankle, dragging her back. Lauren flipped herself over, kicking at Freyja with her heavy boots, as she scooted away.

Freyja snatched up the knife. She maneuvered herself between Lauren and the front door, broken glass crunching beneath her expensive-looking fur slippers.

'You killed Gunnar?' Lauren croaked out as she crab walked backwards toward the fireplace, barely staying out of range of the knife Freyja was brandishing, and trying not to slice herself on the remains of the shattered coffee table.

'Do you want to know what the funny part is – if there is a funny part to a man almost thirty years younger trying to steal my husband?' she asked and slashed through the air, missing Lauren's legs by inches. 'The whole time in the alley Gunnar never fought back. He just kept saying, "Please!" and "I'm sorry" as he tried to get away from me. Even when I was hitting him. Can you believe that?'

'He didn't want to hurt you,' Lauren managed. She saw decorative fireplace pokers in a wrought iron stand off to her left. All she needed to do was keep Freyja talking so she could grab one.

'*Hurt* me? He already hurt me! And you two police people show up, all the way from America to try to arrest Ragnar for killing Gunnar. It's so ridiculous! *Gunnar* was ridiculous.' Then she began to repeat over and over in a mocking sing-song voice the Icelandic words for *I'm sorry: Því miður, Því miður.*

The reality of what really happened crashed over Lauren harder than the fall through the coffee table. 'You called Bjarni and told him to leave the bar. You ran Matt over, not Ragnar.'

Freyja closed in, knife thrust out in front of her, thumping her chest with her other hand. 'Ragnar is *my* husband. *Mine.*'

Lauren scrabbled to get back on her feet, lunged toward the hearth, and wrapped her hand around the fire poker. She yanked it out of its holder and wound up, ready to knock Freyja's blond bloody head out of the park, New York Yankees style.

'Freyja.'

From the doorway, a man's voice filled the room. Freyja froze, knife stopping its downward arc in midair.

'Freyja.' The man Lauren recognized as Ragnar from his photos was standing with one hand wrapped around his belly, blood seeping through his fingers, while Berg supported him on the other side. He said something else to her in Icelandic, his handsome face twisted with pain. Somehow blood had streaked through his graying blond hair. His light blue dress shirt was soaked red across the front.

'Stop this now. It's gone too far,' Ragnar continued in English.

She spun around, knife still at the ready. 'You did this. I turned a blind eye for over thirty years. I did my best. I tried everything.'

'You did. And you were a wonderful wife. You are a wonderful mother. But I can't deny who I am any longer. I fell in love,' his voice broke. 'I still love you and our children, but I fell in love with Gunnar and you took that away from me.'

'I had to,' she snapped and motioned around with the knife. 'You forced me to do all of this.'

He nodded, grimacing in pain. He slumped forward and Berg shored him up. 'You're right. I should have told you. I should have explained. I tried to protect you. I'm still trying to protect you. Put the knife down.'

The last sentence was punctuated with a deep, gurgling cough. A thin trickle of blood ran down his chin from the corner of his mouth. Even with Berg supporting him, Ragnar sank down to his knees. 'Freyja, please,' he begged.

'He needs a hospital. I called for backup, they'll be here any minute,' Berg told her in his no bullshit Viking way. 'But we really should be putting pressure on his wound instead of trying to talk you out of killing my American partner.'

Freyja looked over her shoulder, like she had forgotten Lauren was even there. A look of clarity washed over her face, as if she was really seeing Lauren for the first time. Dragging her arm across her forehead, it came away bloody. She glanced down at it, her perfectly shaped eyebrows pulling together in concern, then at her wounded husband. She dropped the knife on the floor with a *clang* and rushed toward Ragnar.

'Put him on the couch,' Freyja said, grabbing his other side. Together, she and Berg managed to lift him up enough to get him to the sofa. Laying him down, she pressed one of the decorative throw pillows to his wound. Lauren let the poker drop to her side but didn't let go.

'This was an accident,' Freyja said to Ragnar, now oblivious to Lauren and Berg. She knelt on the floor next to him, ignoring the pieces of wood and glass that were surely digging into her knees. 'You startled me when you came in the front door. I thought the police were coming for me.'

'Better you shot me than one of them,' he said weakly, the blood loss starting to take its toll. His face was a ghastly white.

Freyja laid her beautiful, bloody head against his legs as she continued to apply pressure. 'I'm sorry. Því miður.'

Sweat beaded up on Lauren's upper lip. The bandages on her hands were bloody, either from her own wounds or from Freyja's. She resisted the urge to put the poker away or sit down. There was still a murderer in the room.

Catching her breath, Lauren surveyed the damage. A family picture of Ragnar, Freyja, and their children lay smashed at her feet. The rest of the living room was in shambles. Berg walked over to where the shotgun was propped up, grabbed it, and took the remaining shells out. He pocketed them as he stood watch from the doorway. The only sounds were Ragnar's heavy breathing, the wind rattling the windows, and Freyja's quiet sobs of 'I'm sorry.'

Því miður.

It wasn't lost on Lauren that those were Gunnar's last words as well.

FORTY-THREE

Ragnar survived.

That was the only happy ending in the story Lauren and Berg relayed to Matt back at the University Hospital, which, ironically, was where Ragnar was also being treated for a shotgun slug to the gut. Freyja went willingly with the local police after she made sure Ragnar was strapped onto a gurney in the back of the ambulance. Holding her head high, she walked from the house like she was on the pageant stage again, knowing all eyes were on her, back straight, chin up.

She was a remorseless queen covered in blood.

Lauren watched from her perch on the back of her own ambulance. She refused to ride in it to the hospital, but she let them rewrap her bleeding hands and put astringent on the little burns speckling her face like freckles from when she almost took a nosedive into the boiling stream.

Now, back in Reykjavik, they were catching each other up on the events of the last twenty-four hours. 'When you told me to double check everyone registered in the hotel, I also expanded our flight search to include every name we'd come across: Jakob, Bjarni, Stefan, and Freyja.' Matt was doing much better. Lauren thought he didn't look so sallow in his mint green hospital gown and that his color had come back. They'd detached him from all the bags and drips and he was sitting up on his own. 'Freyja popped up on a flight into New York City the day before Gunnar was murdered. Then it had her leaving the day after the murder. It never dawned on me that Icelandic women don't have the same last names as their husbands and that she might have flown in from somewhere else.'

Berg gave the rail of his bed a playful shake. 'We are a mysterious people, my friend.'

'Then we got the text message translations. Freyja was desperately texting Gunnar. He had let it slip which hotel they were in. He never expected her to show up. I guess Gunnar finding out he had a millionaire for a father really scared Freyja because she couldn't use her family's money against Ragnar anymore,' Lauren said.

'Ragnar told us he went looking for Gunnar when he didn't come back from the ATM,' Berg explained. 'He found Freyja in the alley standing over Gunnar with the brick. He told her to turn around, get back in her rental car, go back to New York City and fly out as soon as she could. Then he packed his things and left out of Toronto.'

'So they hatched this cover up when they both got back to Iceland?' Matt asked.

'Freyja was the mastermind behind it, I'm sure. She fooled us all,' Lauren said, sitting on the edge of Matt's bed, cupping her hands in front of her. 'Now comes the fun part. Extradition.'

'Is she fighting it?'

Berg let out his bellowing belly laugh. 'Of course she is!'

'Ragnar wants her committed into psychiatric care. She's looking at a murder charge in America and assault and attempted murder here, but I think she'd rather do hospital time in Iceland than jail time in Attica,' Lauren said. 'Our district attorney has already forwarded all the legal documents to the New York State Executive Office. They'll petition the Secretary of State, requesting that a President's warrant be issued for her arrest and for extradition back to the states. The US Marshals handle extradition once the warrant is issued. It's out of our hands now. We get to go home, while the lawyers fight it out from here.'

'Ragnar is cooperating,' Berg told Matt, hitching his thumbs in the waist band of his jeans. 'He says Helga called Bjarni, who in turn called Freyja and gave her the heads up we were probably coming to the bar. Freyja told Bjarni to leave; she didn't want him to tell us that he'd told her about Ragnar and Gunnar's affair. Then Freyja got in her car, sped over and waited in an alley. After she hit you with the Land Cruiser, she called Ragnar. He met up with her and they drove out to their cottage to stash the Cruiser and came back in the white Skoda. We didn't have a car sitting on their penthouse until that next morning, so they snuck back in the underground parking lot and holed up.'

'What flushed them out?' Matt asked.

'They had that big fight, where she left in the middle of the night. Apparently, he wanted her to turn herself in. He says he was heartbroken over Gunnar's death and wanted her to do the right thing.' Berg didn't look convinced. 'He still went ahead and covered up Matt's assault. For their children's sake, he said.'

Lauren shook her head. 'Ragnar was protecting her. He's still trying to protect her, although he says he's filing for divorce. That might not be enough to keep him from getting charged in this whole mess as an accessory after the fact.'

'Freyja must have been really desperate to go to those lengths to kill Gunnar and then try to stall our investigation,' Matt said.

'She's in denial. Ragnar is who he is, and she can't accept it. I guess she thought by going to trainers three days a week and being the ever-dutiful wife, Ragnar, somehow, would fall out of love with Gunnar.' Lauren picked at a loose thread on her bandage. 'It's sad really. She'd rather kill Gunnar than be embarrassed or alone.'

'At least this whole affair is not at the top of the nightly news,' Berg added cheerfully.

'Why not?' Matt asked. 'There's only one murder a year in Reykjavik, right? You two were in a shootout with a homicidal former beauty queen. There should be news crews camped outside my hospital door right now.'

'Something juicer came up,' Berg said. 'They arrested my cousin on public corruption charges last night. And he's taking down every dirty politician he knows with him. There's money missing, powerful people pointing their fingers at other powerful people, the Russian mob is involved; it's a huge scandal. The entire city is in an uproar.'

'I guess yesterday was your lucky day,' Matt said.

Lauren glanced down at her hands. When she'd stood in front of the mirror in her bathroom this morning, both of her knees and elbows were black with bruises. 'If you say so.' Somehow, catching Gunnar's killer should have made her feel better, or at least like she accomplished something, but instead there was the empty feeling that Mr Hudson wasn't going to live long enough to see Freyja go on trial. Catching the right person was a step towards healing, but it didn't bring the victim back. Gentle, handsome Gunnar was still dead and his loved ones were still left to mourn.

'Is Sam here yet?' Lauren asked, picturing Matt's boss walking around in the same stupid polished black shoes that Matt had worn. Berg had wanted to stop at a store and get him a decent pair of practical boots. Lauren talked him out of it. Matt seemed like he'd rather freeze than tarnish his polished, professional image with snow boots.

Matt nodded and put his good hand on some folders on his nightstand. 'He came by early this morning. Dropped off about a year's worth of paperwork I have to finish as soon as possible, told me he was proud of me and then left. Apparently, he has lots of important meetings with important people to discuss these important matters.'

'You sound like me now,' Lauren smiled.

'Maybe you've rubbed off on me,' Matt grinned back.

'Enough with the love fest,' Berg interrupted. 'Lauren has a date with the Blue Lagoon Spa. It's touristy, I know, but she'll regret it if she came all this way and didn't see it before she leaves.'

'Like me,' Matt groused. 'Who didn't get to see a thing.'

'Well, brother, if you have to come back for Freyja's trial or a hearing, I have a friend who runs a *Game of Thrones* tour. He takes you to all the places they filmed here. You can even dress up like a Wilding and get your picture taken.'

Matt's eyes went wide. 'I am so there.'

FORTY-FOUR

B erg and his family drove Lauren out to the Blue Lagoon, stopping on the way along one of the wood and barbed wire fences that lined the highway. They all got out of Berg's personal car – his poor work car had been blasted to pieces by Freyja and had to be flat-bedded back to the city – and stood on the side of the road. Berg produced a loaf of bread and began to give short sharp whistles.

A wide ice field stretched in front of them with mountains visible in the distance. One of those long, low buildings and a small house set back from it were the only structures she could see.

'What are you doing?' Lauren asked. If his wife and daughter hadn't been standing there, grinning, she'd have thought he had finally lost his mind.

'Just wait.'

He gave another long whistle and then she saw them. From a distance a group of small dark blobs were coming their way. It took a minute for her eyes to focus through the glare off the snow. It was a herd of horses, their long manes blowing with the wind, slowly clomping across the ice field to get to them

Berg passed slices of bread to everyone. 'Watch your fingers,' he admonished Lauren. 'Put the bread flat on your palm or hold it out by the edge so they can grab it.'

The beautiful brown and white horses came right up to the fence. Lauren reached out and touched one's velvety nose and he nuzzled her bandaged hand. He turned his watery brown eyes to her and she fed him a slice of bread, which he gently pulled from her fingertips.

'Have you decided what you are going to do about your house guest?' Anna asked, feeding a white speckled mare that had come to her.

Lauren looked out across the ice field, taking in the snow-topped mountains in the background and the bright blue sky. 'I think I'm going to stop looking for something to be there. I think I'll just wait and see how things turn out, instead of trying to wish things into reality.'

Berg handed Elin more bread. She happily began feeding it to a smaller horse that could barely get its nose over the barbed wire. He turned his face to Lauren's, his cheeks blazing ruddy red from the wind. 'Follow your heart, my friend. And if it gets broken, you can always run back here to Iceland.'

Her heart. Where was her heart?

Lauren looked at the happy family and suddenly had an ache to see her own daughters. They'd be home from college when she flew in, probably lying around her living room, arguing about politics or YouTubers or the best way to use contour makeup. They were her heart. And if there was a piece or two missing, she'd have to live with that. 'I'm done running from things,' she said. 'I think I need to be happy where I'm at.'

Berg fed the horse in front of him another slice of bread. Lauren watched the horse's jaw work from side to side, eyes locked on Berg, already anticipating more.

The wind made the plastic bag he was holding ripple and snap. He reached over and squeezed Lauren's shoulder with his free hand. 'Then be happy, sister.'

FORTY-FIVE

Lauren didn't get back to her hotel room until late that
night. She'd showered in the dressing rooms at the Blue
Lagoon, changed into the bathing suit Anna had lent her
again and then had rushed through the twenty-three-degree
weather into the blue-green waters of the enormous hot spring.
Berg was waiting for her, soaking himself along one of the
walls, with goop smeared all over his face. 'It's a mud mask,'
he told her and pointed to a stand where workers were scooping
tan and green mud from buckets into the palms of waiting
bathers. 'There's a silica mud mask or an algae mask. Both
are wonderful for your skin. Go try it.'

Elin and Anna came with her and the three of them painted
designs all over each other's faces in the creamy mud. Just
like in Berg's hot tub, the steam from the hot water warmed
the air, so it felt like they were in a tropical pool instead of
an icy island in the North Sea. There were even drink kiosks
set up serving beer, wine, and mixed drinks. A group of ladies
in their sixties lounged a few feet away from them, laughing
and sipping champagne.

Lauren could feel every muscle in her body unknot and
relax.

When they were done bathing, Berg sprung for an expensive
dinner at the restaurant inside the hotel attached to the Lagoon
complex. Lauren ate fresh baked fish with root vegetables,
while Berg ordered them all *malt og appelsín*, a traditional
Icelandic Christmas drink, with which they all toasted the
holidays. Elin giggled, feeling so grown up because the waiter
poured hers into a wine glass. For dessert, Lauren ordered the
skyr with fruit. She'd seen it on almost every menu since she
got there, but hadn't yet sampled the creamy yogurt-like dish.

'We'll make a Viking out of you yet!' Berg announced as
she took a bite of the sugar-topped treat.

Back in her room, her whole body felt like jelly, ready to

collapse into sleep. She could feel the heat she'd soaked in radiating out of her as she changed into her bed clothes. It had been a good day, but she was ready to go home. She wanted to see her daughters and her parents. Berg told her to buy gifts at the airport so she didn't have to drag things around, but she wanted to buy both the girls heavy Icelandic wool sweaters she had seen in one of the stores downtown. She'd already bought her mother a mud mask from the Blue Lagoon's Spa shop along with some lava soap. Her dad was getting a bottle of liquor that was lovingly referred to by the locals as 'black death'. She knew he'd appreciate the dark humor in that. Reese would be harder to buy for. He loved baseball hats and she wasn't sure if that was a thing over here. She'd have to ask Berg if any of their national teams had that kind of merchandise for sale.

She was just about to climb into bed when her phone on the nightstand began to buzz. She picked it up and looked at the screen.

It was Reese.

She had talked to him right before they left the Blue Lagoon, checking in and letting him know she was going to try to get a flight into Toronto the next day. It seemed odd he would call her now.

'Hello?'

'Are you sitting down, Riley?' There was a note of excitement in his voice that scared her. It was five o'clock in Buffalo. She didn't like surprises anymore. They were almost always bad news. Her gut twisted in knots as she got up from the bed and went to the window.

'Is everything OK?' she asked, pulling the cord to lift the blind. 'Are Lindsey and Erin home? Are they all right?'

'Riley, shut up. Everyone is home and fine. Just listen.' She could hear him taking a deep breath on the other end of the line. 'The woman from CODIS just phoned the office. Doug Sheehan took the call and got ahold of me. They got a hit on the DNA found on Billy Munzert's bike. A guy who molested his stepson just got convicted and processed, including giving a swab of his DNA. His name is Steven Harrott and he's never been arrested before. He lived three blocks away from Billy at the time of his abduction, then moved to Rochester three weeks later.'

For a few seconds Lauren forgot how to breathe.

'Are you there?'

'They're sure? It's a match?' she whispered.

'It's one in 575 trillion. It's a match. It's him. And he didn't want to give his DNA. He fought with the jail personnel when they came to get the court-ordered swab. I'm going to wait until you get back and then I'm coming out of injured reserve. You and I are going to take a ride to Attica to talk to his cellmate – you know the cellmate always has information, those guys love to blab – and then Steven Harrott.'

She swallowed hard, fighting the swirl of emotions that threatened to overwhelm her. Reese knew what her silence meant and knew what she needed to hear from him most at that moment. 'Congratulations. You found that evidence and had it retested and didn't give up. You got your killer. I never doubted you. Not for a minute. Ever.'

Tears ran silently down her cheeks. She tried to keep her voice even. 'Do Billy's parents know?'

'No one knows. Not yet. I figured you'd want to talk to Harrott first. If anyone can get him to tell where Billy's body is, it's you.'

'They shouldn't have to wait another minute,' she said.

'What do you always tell me? We can do it fast, or we can do it right. We're going to do this one right. And that's for you to do; tell the parents. That's all you.'

She put a bandaged hand to her forehead and stifled a sob. 'I can't believe it,' she whispered. Now his family would know for sure Billy was dead. Maybe she and Reese actually could be able to convince Harrott to tell them where the body was. Maybe Billy's family would have an ounce of closure after all these years.

'Believe it. You didn't stop working the case and you found the bad guy. If you hadn't come along, that bike would still be sitting in evidence, gathering dust, and Steven Harrott would have gotten out in three years to victimize more kids.'

'But he did victimize one more,' she choked out.

'Lauren Riley is a badass detective who doesn't quit and

is going to make sure he never lays his hand on another kid as long as he lives. Everyone forgot about Billy Munzert and his family. Everybody. Everyone but you.'

'I have to get back to Buffalo,' she said, turning her eyes to the clear, cloudless sky.

'I'll take care of all the preliminary stuff that has to be done. Just finish up over there, do everything by the book, and then get your ass back to Buffalo so we can tell the Munzert family by Christmas Day.'

'Thank you,' she breathed, putting her hand to the cold glass of her window, touching her fingertips to the stars that seemed to fill the skyline over the harbor.

'Don't thank me. Just get back home.' There was a long pause and she heard Watson bark in the background before Reese spoke again. 'And I'll be waiting here for you when you do.'

At that moment, the Northern Lights flared up and danced across the night sky.

ACKNOWLEDGMENTS

Special thanks and love to my husband, Dan. And to my daughters, Natalie and Mary Grace. Without the three of you, none of this would be possible. You are my inspiration, my hope, and my heart.

Thank you to Carl Smith, Natasha Bell, and everyone at Severn House. You gave Lauren a second chance and she really appreciates it!

Much gratitude to all my friends and family and to everyone in the entire Buffalo region. I love my book club visits, trips to the libraries, and talks at clubs. My neighbours are the best. Your support has been amazing, and you keep proving over and over why I could never live anywhere else. Thank you!